The Aphorism Club

Tracey Lee

ABOUT THE AUTHOR

Tracey Lee is a published author who has been writing since she was eight-years-old. *The Lily O'Hara Mystery Series* has been widely praised for its addictive storylines and its keen observation of family dynamics. A prolific writer, Tracey intends to continue this series and is publishing her new, independent novel, *The Aphorism Club*, in December 2025. Her book takes its title from the writing group which was founded by Tracey and a group of close friends in 1994. This group and the work they did together, including publishing an anthology in 1999, remain integral to Tracey's writing process.

Tracey holds a highly distinguished, 38-year career as an English/Behavioural Science teacher who has taught in Tasmania, Western Australia, Canberra and most recently in New South Wales.

In 2005, Tracey completed a Masters in Creative Writing at the University of Canberra. Both her teaching and writing are interested in what motivates human behaviour and what maintains equilibrium, as well as the disturbances that threaten this balance. Her fiction often follows ordinary people as they face extraordinary circumstances.

Since retiring from the classroom, Tracey has run several writing sessions at local libraries, joined the Eurobodalla Writers Group and hosted local panel discussions for International Women's Day and Crime Writers of the Eurobodalla.

Living on the far south coast of NSW, she now spends most of her time writing.

HEMBURY
—BOOKS—

First published by Hembury Books in 2025
hemburybooks.com.au
info@hemburybooks.com

Paperback ISBN 9781923517356
Ebook ISBN 9781923517349

A catalogue record for this
book is available from the
National Library of Australia

Dedication

To the women of the past, for their spirit and their fight.
To the women of today, for their continued courage.
To the women of tomorrow, may all our work bring you
a future of equality, peace and hope.

Aphorism

A short expression about a big idea.
It reflects an important truth about life,
a universal truth or just a morsel of wisdom.

THE
BEGINNING

CHAPTER 1

It was definite and certainly could not be denied. Ruby Pearl Hart killed her mother. If the absence of Alma Hart was not evidence enough, the great port wine stain on Ruby's face spoke to her extended family of the misery she had wrought upon them. Alma had died on the same day that Ruby was born. The bleeding could not be staunched. The sheets and paper packing on top of the mattress were drenched in her deep raspberry-red life sustaining blood. The midwife despite having delivered fifty or more babies could not save the young mother. She packed her uterus with washed linen rags and encouraged the barely conscious woman to drink a herbal tonic that should have helped the contractions to compress the bleeding placental site. But nothing could stop it. Ruby had been placed on her mother's bare breast in the hope she would suck some nourishment and calm her neonatal wrath after her tumultuous birth. It gave momentary hope. But hope could not be sustained.

Even when the doctor arrived, he possessed no skills to reverse the inevitable. He spent more time wringing his hands and speaking in hushed tones about the need for a priest rather than a medic. In the few hours he attended the dying woman he spent much of the time having a calming whiskey, or three, in the drawing room with her in-laws. His announcement that the baby would live but the mother would die accompanied each glass. The subsequent statements of doom became a little less sombre in tone and ever slightly more slurred. All that was left for the others who stayed with Alma, was to find milk to quell the mewling infant's screams and pack towels under the mother to prevent complete ruination of the mattress. Death came twelve hours after the birth.

Douglas Hart could not face the heinous sight of his exsanguinated bride nor the ruddy disfigured face of his new daughter. He retreated to his parents' drawing room with the doctor to wait for the inevitable silencing of both Alma and Ruby. His parents, Edwina and Lewis sat quietly, both pondering the next steps. Douglas was their only child, the bawling girl, quite likely to be their only grandchild. Now 35, neither felt Douglas would marry again. They were both surprised when their dour, socially reclusive son married Alma a respectful ten months before this catastrophe. When he met the young woman in the city, they were surprised that he had bothered to tell them about her. Their surprise grew as he made further overtures to make the relationship a more permanent thing.

Douglas had met Alma in the tearooms in the city centre where he worked with Foy and Boyle Engineering. After finishing his degree at the Melbourne School of Engineering he went to work for his father's friend Theodore Foy. Alma was a typist for Galante and McKinney Solicitors. Both companies were side by side on Spring Street. The Bloom Tearoom was always crowded with businessmen and the occasional working woman. Alma stood out from the clamour of men discussing football, weather and money. She was tall and dark featured. Olive skin, blue eyes and dark hair gave her an exotic look. Douglas was drawn to her immediately. He, in fact, could not take his eyes off her. He always sat at a table by the window, his back to the sun and his copy of The Age held in front of his face. When Alma came in for tea and a sandwich Douglas would lower the paper enough so he could peer over the top to watch her. He was mesmerised by her liveliness. On the day she sat at the table beside him he could no longer use the paper as a prop to mask his gawping. They introduced themselves, engaged in some appropriate chit-chat and shared their responses to the news of the day. Polite greetings lead to longer tea dates and eventually dinner at the Grand Sorrento Hotel. An engagement, a wedding at St. Barnaby's and a short honeymoon at the Palace Hotel in Torquay were done and dusted within the year.

1909 was a wonderful year. Alma finished work one week before the wedding and settled into Douglas's rooms in his parent's home on Southey Street in Elwood. The house almost straddled the suburban demarcation between St. Kilda and the preferred address of Elwood. It was a large Italianate design which allowed the Harts senior to have privacy and Douglas and his new bride to have a suite of rooms that would do until Douglas could build on the land he'd bought in Clifton Hill in 1901. With the tram network now moving beyond the Melbourne city precinct the suburb was a desirable place for a man and his family. But fate seemed to have other ideas.

The year was romantic but also tumultuous in many ways as Alma had a mind of her own and desires for a simpler life than the one the Harts lived. Alma's mother was estranged from her, the father dead in her childhood. At 25 she was full of life, ambition and exuberance and had spoken of her hope to have her babies early and return to work after the family had settled into the home she was happily planning for them. She imagined a small red brick house with stained glass and bay windows. She drew a picture of a house with return verandas and leafy gardens at the front and back. She had even found magazine pictures of tessellated tiled entry ways, pressed-metal ceilings, turned-timber posts and fretwork. 'A perfect place for children to play. For us to watch our family grow and for us to grow old.' She often described this idyllic life for her fiancé and then husband. At this point Douglas was willing to give her whatever she wanted.

Douglas, despite his infatuation with his new wife, remained a sour character, meticulous and methodical, unimaginative. Alma was a spark. She lit up a room, she was all movement and noise. Douglas moved to the beat of a dirge and Alma danced to jazz. But the rapid onset of pregnancy, a few weeks into the marriage by the calculations of the social doyens, slowed her down. Morning sickness, lethargy and constant biliousness did not make for a glowing mother-to-be. Alma's once glossy dark hair and skin became limp and sallow as the months passed. As her baby grew, Alma diminished. And Douglas already profoundly uncomfortable at the thought of fatherhood and alarmed at the sight of his wife simultaneously expanding and deflating fled to work for all the hours of daylight and some of night. Returning to his childhood bedroom after a few minutes of polite conversation with the woman who had become a stranger in the months that the pregnancy consumed her. Alma's pregnancy malaise robbed her of her dreams. She no longer spoke endlessly about the life to be in Clifton Hill. She spoke little of the joy a new life would bring the couple. She could barely ask Douglas how his day had been before his mere presence exhausted her.

The in-laws did not enquire after the ailing bride. Neither bothered to visit the wing in which she had been installed. They asked no questions about the impending birth. Made no comment on the possibility of a granddaughter or grandson. In fact, it was as if Alma had ceased to exist.

And thus Ruby Pearl came to a world of relatives that could barely stand her or even bother to acknowledge she was in the house. Douglas had not once lifted the infant into his arms to wonder at her existence. Her grandparents had bought the best care they could afford and relegated their infant granddaughter to the status of necessary nuisance. They did not look upon her and only occasionally asked the nanny if the child was well. 'Has that stain lessened?' Edwina Hart enquired several times during the first year of her life.

The first nanny was the cousin of the midwife who delivered Ruby. She was a sturdy woman of 30 who had never married. Alice Bond was not bothered by the death nor the apparent callousness of Ruby's family. She was all business and broached no interference in her attendance on the new baby. She had sourced a newly available infant formula and a glass bottle with a rubber nipple to ensure the baby had a chance at thriving. It was better than the soft rag that had been used to soak up boiled cow's milk and sugar that the midwife insisted would prevent starvation in the hours after her birth. Mrs. Carleena Rowlands, the Hart's housekeeper, had heated canned evaporated milk and attempted spoon feeding the tiny girl. 'It worked for my sister's babies. Ain't none of them died from waiting for a feed.' Her gentle Welsh accent lent some authority to her proclamations.

But with Alice's arrival, Mrs. Rowlands was sent back to the kitchen and the midwife back to the nursing agency from where she had been sourced. Miss Bond attended upon the newly arrived infant with both efficiency and tenderness. She fed, bathed, clothed and soothed the somewhat cross baby day and night. She worried about the disinterest shown by her father and grandparents. The birthmark was the only thing the Harts asked about. In her heart she wondered if the raspberry splodge would ever fade and what that might mean for Ruby's future.

Mrs. Rowlands showed more interest in the baby's welfare and at times had to be shooed away from the cot by Miss Bond. 'Enough of that cooing and babbling.' But over the first few months the two employees united to provide the necessary warmth and gentleness both believed essential to create a suitable environment in which a child might flourish. And despite the rocky start, disaffected family and lost mother, Ruby did blossom.

CHAPTER 2

Ruby became a jolly baby. Her wispy dark hair and startling blue eyes were the genetic legacy of her mother. Her pale skin and frightening tendency to stare at people definitely traits of her father. But the birthmark remained a mystery and in the absence of any scientific explanation the old wives' tales ran riot. At the local markets Mrs. Rowlands spoke to the other housekeepers who insisted that the mark on the baby's face was a definite sign that it was all the mother's fault. 'She had the cravings for red food. You know the beets and the berries.' Hardly a scientific analysis but one that Lena Bell, who worked for the Cladwells insisted had been stated in a very reputable ladies' magazine. Theresa McDermott had gleaned her theory from the Indian housekeeper she worked with at the Hotel Esplanade. 'Sunita says her uncle does *harry vader* medicine and cured half of St. Kilda with his herbs.'

Mrs. Rowlands had heard of *ayurveda* from her cousin who had been with the British in Calcutta during the raj. 'It ain't harry anything Theresa. It ain't spelled harry. And I can't imagine getting Alice fancy pants to take baby Ruby to a place where they get you to drink goat piss.'

The women all recoiled in horror at the thought of Ruby red-face, as they called her, being fed urine from any living creature.

'Step too far that. Even if it did cure the babe. I heard of Dr. Morse's Indian Root Pills. Maybe they would work.' Lena offered hopefully.

'Wrong kind of Indian Len. Those ones are from the American type of Indians. Can't see how they would help.'

'Well they are red-Indians.' Despite the jibe at little Ruby's face the women all had a laugh.

Even though they could not agree about a cure for the birthmark the house-keepers were all certain that it had some meaning of a supernatural leaning that no medical science would ever dissuade them of believing. Sign of the devil, angel's kiss, royal blood or from the mysterious Sunita a badge of reincarnation after she died in a fire in her first life. As they made their way to their respective employers they all sent a silent prayer that the Hart child would outgrow her disfigurement or that a cure that didn't involve urine might be discovered.

But cures were likely to be cruel things. And unbeknown to Mrs. Rowlands, Edwina Hart was seeking something to rid the baby of her stain. A granddaughter without a burnished splodge around her right eye might make the child more palatable to both her grandparents and father.

Only when the nanny was taking her day off and the baby was in the care of a somewhat inattentive teenage maid did Edwina subject Ruby to a series of ill-informed and illogical treatments. The simplest and less invasive was the use of lemon juice. It was used by women to lighten their hair and skin in the absence of a decent hairdresser or therapist. Edwina and her coterie of friends had a profound belief in their skin guru Doctor Cary Jarsdel. He was not a Doctor of Medicine, nor in fact a doctor at all but used the title to sell his facial treatments and products to a certain type of woman. One with lots of money and very few brains. The doctor had allegedly read Dr. John Woodbury's book on cosmetic surgery and facial blemish removal. While Woodbury had a medical degree his dermatology skills were self-taught and his practice ended in bankruptcy and tears. The 'self-taught' element appealed to Cary who thought Ruby was an experimental canvas for his treatments. So for three years when an opportunity presented itself the child's face was bleached, slathered in oil of cloves and phenol. All stung Ruby's eyes and burnt her skin. She was not a compliant recipient of the doctor's remedies and she had to be held down forcibly so a miracle might occur.

Ruby screamed. Edwina became more determined. The doctor pressed on.

In one session he arrived with raw meat from the butcher. Sliced wafer thin and nearly on the turn from fresh to rotten. 'The cool meat and the slight greening will draw the underlying blemish to the surface where I'll be able to lift the mark away.' Only a fool would believe that a baby's face would benefit from near-rancid beef cuts being laid upon her. For this treatment Ruby luckily slept. She was less settled for the egg, honey and oatmeal concoction that filled her eye and nose when she hollered with the outrage of being held down once again. 'This will lighten the stain. Ladies I recommend this to all of you if you would like glowing skin.'

And the doctor was right in one way. While Ruby's birthmark did not diminish she was as glowing as a newly scrubbed brass pot when the mess was finally washed from her tiny, bewildered face.

Not to be deterred Doctor Jarsdel tried one more concoction before resorting to radium laced creams, arsenic complexion wafers, freezing and some idea of scrubbing and cutting the infant's cheek. Edwina was impassive about the escalation in treatments and frustrated by the lack of progress. 'It's very costly Doctor Jarsdel and the stain if anything is worse.'

'Beauty is all about a bit of suffering my dear Mrs. Hart. And in your case the child feels the pain in her face and you feel it in your purse.' He smiled benevolently. 'I'll make an exception in your case and discount the more complicated treatments. And give you a free facial mask to keep you looking perfect.' Placated by a fawning compliment she gave her permission for Ruby to be slathered in Gentian Violet.

There was no hiding the purple pigment that adorned little Ruby's face. Where her rosy birthmark sat like a molten teardrop starting on her eyelid and flowing over her cheekbone, the purple concoction swept over the right side of her face and onto her lips. She looked like a harlequin clown with half its makeup which had been applied by a terrible amateur. When Alice Bond returned from her day off there was no disguising the therapy that Ruby had been subjected to.

Ruby was three. Her grandmother and the quack practitioner had tried twenty or thirty treatments. None had worked. Nor even partially lessened the size, shape, or colour of the mark. Jarsdel had made a hundred pounds plying his trade and was readying himself to try some minor surgery on the child.

With Ruby in her arms, Alice protested. 'Mrs. Hart I can't allow this to continue. This is a cruel and utterly unfounded medical flimflam. I will speak to both mister Harts about this.'

Which she did. Her dismissal was immediate. Both Douglas and Lewis felt the nanny had overstepped her station and that Edwina was acting simply in the child's interest. 'The treatments have been taking place for nearly three years Miss Bond and you failed to notice anything. And a little bit of Gentian Violet has sent you into hysterics.'

'He's planning on cutting that baby.' Alice was almost shouting by this stage. 'I'll get the chief constable if anything else happens to her.' With threats of their own regarding Alice's employment anywhere in the city she was sent to her room to pack her case, pick up the envelope on the scullery table which had her final wages and leave the premises. But despite Alice's brusque approach to childcare, she had actually come to adore the little one that she had seen through weaning, teething, toddling, falling and her first wonder at the world. Having the last word came in the form of a letter.

Ten blocks away from the Hart mansion, in a neat Edwardian terrace, Minerva Hart, Lewis' spinster sister, took receipt of a hastily penned letter from Alice Bond. The gardener's boy had been made to take his bike and ride like fury in an attempt to rescue little Ruby from further torture. Aunt Minnie, as she was known, took a breath, thanked the boy with a penny and another letter for Alice Bond and made her preparations.

Minnie was the formidable younger sister of Lewis. The dreaded sister-in-law of Edwina and a most terrifying aunt of Douglas. Not surprisingly in her short tenure as Mrs. Hart, Alma adored her. And that adoration was to be repaid in protecting her great-niece from her stupid relatives.

As a post-suffragette feminist, Minerva fought for a woman's right to vote, studied at university, worked with Mary Lee and Vida Goldstein as the former founded the women's trade union and the latter rattled the government's cage to abolish child labour and give women property rights. Minerva Hart was no shrinking violet. And if anyone was going to raise a knife against her great-niece they had better prepare for a fight.

As she made her plan to rescue Ruby, Alice received the note from the boy as she left the property through the front gate. As a final act of defiance she stormed out of the property ignoring the rule that insisted that staff enter and leave by the back gate. At the same time Cary Jarsdel was arriving with his scrubbing machine and scalpel.

But before the knife was wielded Minerva appeared on her own bicycle, skirt tucked up to reveal her cycling bloomers, hair escaping her bun, and pedalling at a most determined pace that would have been deemed unlady-like if it had been any other woman.

The door was breached more than it was opened. Douglas and Lewis had retreated to the den for a whiskey as they expected that the procedure would cause Ruby to scream and the noise might be distressing to them. Edwina, the charlatan doctor and the hapless teenage maid were blithely preparing the drawing room for the procedure.

'What on God's earth do you think you are doing to my great niece?' It wasn't a question that Minerva had any intention of awaiting an answer. 'You touch her and I will take that scalpel and peel your fiddle spindle back to the bone.'

Cary Jarsdel immediately grabbed his crotch as he suspected this harridan meant to remove his manhood in a most violent manner.

'Good God Minnie. How dare you use such vulgar language in my house.' Edwina was genuinely offended by any reference to the male appendage.

'Vulgar fucking language you simpleton. Offended by the word dick but you'll cut a child's face because her little birth mark is too much for you.'

The hysteria began. Firstly, Cary had a fit of the vapours and languished in a chair. Edwina was outraged and started screaming and bawling. The teenage maid fled the room with Ruby in her arms.

'What is going on?' The Hart men finally appeared fearing a murder had taken place.

Minnie turned on them. 'You idiots have allowed this quack into your home to torture Ruby. You don't deserve her.'

Douglas wrought immobile by his aunt's wrath could neither defend nor refute her accusations. Mumbling that he had no knowledge of what was happening Lewis tried to calm the situation. 'Minnie. Edwina was just trying to do what was best for the child. She's disfigured.'

'She is not disfigured Lewis. And she is your granddaughter. She has a name.'

And now Ruby Pearl had a champion.

Without a fight the Harts yielded to Minnie's suggestion that Ruby come to stay with her while the ruckus in the household was calmed. There were frayed nerves and a long list of issues to be dealt with that might more effectively be undertaken without a traumatised child in the home.

A hastily packed case, a pram and a wooden fruit box of toys accompanied the small entourage lead by Minerva Hart back to Mary Street. The gardener's boy wheeled Minnie's pushbike, and the terrified young maid was enlisted to pull a small hand cart with Ruby's things. Within a block Alice Bond had joined the little saviour parade in response to Minnie's request that she take up employment as Ruby's nanny under her roof. As a childless woman she felt she had little skill to raise an infant. Other than love and a fierce protectiveness of a little human who had an uphill battle from the start.

CHAPTER 3

What was meant to be a short respite became a new life. Douglas was relieved that his daughter became someone else's responsibility, Edwina could simply turn her attention to rejuvenating her own waning looks and Lewis had barely noticed the infant's existence, so her absence was irrelevant.

The Mary Street terrace was a substantial home. The reception and lounge rooms shared the bottom floor with the kitchen. It was decorated in deep burgundy and luxurious sage green fabrics. A treasure trove for a toddler who loved the soft drapes and voluminous couches where Minnie or one of her many friends read Ruby stories, played dolls or fed her sticky honey toast. It was a haven and an adventure particularly in comparison to the austerity of the Hart's mansion. A child's face smeared with food, on top of the great stain would have been too much for all the adults in that house.

But Minnie's home provided Ruby with everything that was absent in Elwood. Alice Bond would stay with Ruby until she was ready for school at the age of six. In the three years she lived with Minnie her father visited occasionally. Her grandparents never. On the eve of his departure for England in 1915 Douglas had a long discussion with his aunt about Ruby's care and in the advent of his death overseas as part of the First Field Company of Australian Engineers. He presented her with legal papers that outlined his paternal obligations to his daughter. The infant would have a considerable endowment including the land in Clifton Hill. She would also be the only heir of Edwina and Lewis's property. The documents stated that Minerva would be the child's legal guardian and therefore entitled to reasonable payments and everything else would be held in trust until Ruby reached the age of twenty-five unless her family lived beyond this age and then she would be eligible for inheritance upon their deaths.

It was an emotionless discussion. Pragmatic and brief. Ruby saw her father as a stranger. At four and a half years of age she looked at him as one of the curious visitors who spent time coming briefly and staying for indeterminant time frames. The five bedrooms on the upper floors were always occupied by a visitor.

'Be a good child Ruby. Aunt Minnie will look after you.' Douglas could not have orchestrated a colder farewell if he had been standing on ice. 'I will try to see you again at the end of this terrible time.' The austerity was laughable. Ruby waved goodbye as she had been asked to do. 'Ta tah Dog gas.' Not father, nor daddy or even Douglas. But *dog gas*.

It caused laughter among the current crop of residents when Minnie retold the story at dinner that night. Two actresses shared the top bedroom and a milliner who had fallen on hard times was in one of the small rooms next to Ruby's. He spent his time creating ostentatious hats for both Minnie and Ruby as a means of paying his board. 'Dog gas.' The table erupted several times.

Ruby sat at the dinner table and often fell asleep on a convenient lap after wondering at the noisy repartee of the guests. The actresses sang songs, the milliner cried, Minnie laughed and stretched over the half-eaten dishes to smooth Ruby's hair and smile at her good fortune in having rescued the little one. The war would continue on the other side of the world. Rationing and hard times would come but the Mary Street terrace had enough people, food and love to keep their spirits high which allowed them to weather the awfulness of the news that could not be kept out of the house.

Death accompanied all wars. And with Europe on fire and the march of Germany and its allies seemingly unstoppable Australians waited for the dreaded news that someone they loved had perished. Minnie and her guests lost friends and relatives. They grieved and they rose again. No news of Douglas came. Nothing from Elwood either. So Ruby's life moved forward. She never mentioned her father or asked about her mother.

Soon enough, Minnie enrolled Ruby in school. She notified both Douglas and the family in Elwood. No response came.

'Merrington Girls School will be so wonderful Ruby. You will make lots of friends and learn so much.' Minnie had already taught Ruby to read and do her numbers. She was as quick as a wink when it came to adding and subtracting. The milliner had shown her how to size heads and fabrics so she had an excellent understanding of measurement. She knew songs and had started piano lessons with another of the guests.

'What will the other girls make of Ruby's face?' One of the actresses asked. 'I have some stage paint that we could cover it a bit.'

'Ruby's birthmark is not to be covered up. It's not going anywhere. It's also not all she is.' Minnie had never entertained the notion that the child's face would be given any treatment and certainly a six-year-old was not going to school on her first day in make-up.

'She will be fine. Ruby will find her people and in no time they will stop seeing her birthmark and simply see her for who she really is.' Minnie was adamant. The actress less convinced. And the truth of the matter more complicated than the belief in the good nature of young humans.

'I hate school. I hate them girls.'

'Those girls Ruby.' Minnie regretted correcting the grammar given the flood of tears that followed. The first day at school had not been a success. The first thing, even before Ruby could hang her satchel on the hook outside her room, saw a group of older girls surround her and ask *what was wrong with her face.* 'Did you get burned?' 'Are you a clown?' 'Who did that to you?' 'Did you put your face in paint?'

According to Ruby it was relentless until Sister Regina broke up the inquisition and accompanied the somewhat rattled child to her room. Thankfully, the older girls were not a part of the early education group of 6- to 8-year-olds.

Ruby's face had flushed so dramatically that her port wine stain was indistinguishable from the rest of her skin.

Despite the disaster one small light was shone. Winifred Alice Kincade sat quietly beside Ruby most of the day. Occasionally, very shyly, taking a peek at the miserable face of the girl who would become her dearest friend. Her ally and her partner in crime. By lunch time Winnie had plucked up the courage to speak. 'Don't worry about them big girls. My cousin Lou Lou says they're big bitches.' Ruby's head snapped around to look at her fellow six-year-old. 'Big bitches.' Winnie enunciated again.

Ruby had heard plenty of swearing before. Afterall her house was full of loose talk. Bitches was the least of it. But she was terribly surprised that the tiny girl sharing the hard timber seat would so clearly and precisely state such a fact. It could not be denied. They were bitches.

'So what did happen to your face?' Winnie ventured a little further.

Ruby shrugged. 'Just born with it.' She smiled a teary smile. 'Just lucky I guess.'

Some of this was conveyed to Minnie through the sobbing. Ruby was hot and bothered. Learning that the world is not fair is a cruel lesson. 'But there was a light my love.' Minnie held Ruby on her knee. 'You're new friend. Winnie. That's a light.' Ruby had come to understand that her great-aunt would not accept defeat nor a descent into misery no matter the pain. 'Look up and find a light.' It was the unofficial motto of Mary Street. 'And if you can't find the light, bloody build a fire yourself.' Thanks to one of the actresses Ruby had, even at her tender age, learned that she might have to be strong if she was going to survive a world where the light switches were not always within reach.

The war years were simple for Ruby. School became, as predicted, her oyster. She grew into a clever and engaging child who could generally outshine her classmates in most disciplines. In particular writing and mathematics were areas in which she shone. Her reading skills were more advanced than the girls in the higher classes thanks to Minnie's extensive library and Ruby's immersion in storytelling. Her success had to be balanced with the social complexities her birthmark provoked. She, however, overcame the burden the other girls tried to heap upon her. 'You're ugly Ruby Hart.' 'Clownie get back to the circus.' 'Got a face like a slapped arse.' And so many other unkindnesses that an entire dictionary of insults could have been compiled. The only description she chose to believe was delivered by the terrifying Sister Rose-Phillipine. A large nun, with a hawkish face and at least one hundred years old in Ruby's mind, insisted on the child standing in front of her while she inspected the mark. 'It's a teardrop Miss Hart that you have there. It's an angel's kiss. It will remind you that you are a very special girl who has Heaven's protection.' Despite her dreadful fear of Sister Rose-Phillipine, Ruby decided that the nun's wisdom would be the words she'd believe, and all the other insults could run away like water off a duck's back. Or like 'piss down the gutter.' Thank you, actress number two.

With Winifred as her best friend, Minnie and the guests as her family and Sister Rose-Phillipine's intervention with the bullies, life went on. The war ended. Douglas Hart returned to Elwood and remained out of his child's life except to announce he was moderately pleased that she was doing so well. Ruby at 8 years of age had little interest in the person she now had to refer to as Father. At Christmas in 1918 Minnie and Ruby were invited to Elwood for lunch so that the child could be reacquainted with her grandparents and indeed her father. 'What do I have to say to them?' A reasonable question. 'Tell them about school and Winnie. But try not to mention all our guests. Edwina wouldn't like my friends.' Minnie rarely asked her to be quiet about issues but there was something in her tone that alerted Ruby to the need for silence.

'Well you are going to be a big woman like your mother Ruby.' A waspish greeting from Edwina. Ruby had learned that her mother was tall but the way her grandmother said *big* it sounded insulting. 'I see there's been no fading.' A disappointed reference to the birthmark.

Both her father and grandfather said nothing in the way of greeting. They merely nodded at the two strangers from Mary Street.

Lunch was lavish. How the Harts had managed to purloin so much food remained an unanswered question. Conversation was limited to Douglas's experiences overseas and his decision to take up a post as chief engineer at a strangely named power station in Launceston Tasmania. 'Duck Reach is a funny name. Why is it called that.' Ruby's natural inquisitiveness prompted her to ask the question on her mind. Not 'will I be going with you?'

'A reach is part of a stream and before it was a power station wild ducks gathered there.' Douglas had obviously done some homework. 'I'll be gone for a while.'

This elicited no response from either Minnie or Ruby. Although not communicated, obviously neither were concerned that their lives would be interrupted by his presence or absence.

'Ruby will continue to stay with you Minerva.' Edwina making sure that she would not have to take any responsibility for her granddaughter.

Dessert arrived. Mrs Rowlands placed Ruby's portion in front of her with a wink and whisper. 'Surprise in that puddin' for a gorgeous girl.' Ruby took this to mean that the threepences and sixpences that were stirred into the batter before boiling might have made their way into her slice. It was a sign of good luck and wealth. Two concepts that Ruby thought redundant in her mind because Minnie had given her both a fortunate and ample life but the little cache of coins could be given to Winifred as a Christmas gift and acknowledgement of her friendship.

Lunch ended. Farewells as stiff as the greetings saw the two wander down the driveway with some small packages, a basket with some leftovers and in Ruby's hand the lucky coins. Minnie had enjoyed a few sherries with lunch and they had buoyed her spirits. She laughed and giggled with Ruby about how much fun lunch was. Ruby looked at her aunt and laughed too but she needed to ask a serious question. 'They don't love me do they?'

Minnie stopped abruptly. Struck by the sadness of the question. She knelt down and pulled Ruby's face to hers. 'Love is so very complicated my darling girl. Some people just aren't made for it. But you are loved. And nothing will ever get in the way of that.'

The terrace on Mary Street filled the neighbourhood with noise. Music and singing spilled out the open front door to greet them. The guests had started a party to welcome them home. The food parcel joined the other dishes that had been laid on the table under muslin cloths to keep the flies off. The milliner swept Ruby up into the air. 'Merry Christmas Rubicus Rubilina.' He'd obviously had a few sherries too. The actresses had gifts for Minnie and Ruby that they had wrapped in silky scarves. *This is love*. Ruby could see the difference between the family you got and the family you made.

Good fortune and happiness are gifts. Not always sustainable. Not always long lived. As the Mary Street family celebrated Christmas and then the New Year as one full of promise and peace something else lurked. With the war behind them it meant 1919 was to be a year of wonders but it was to be a year of pain.

CHAPTER 4

It started when ships carrying soldiers home from war were stranded in harbours and there was talk about the borders closing to prevent interstate movement. The Spanish Influenza had arrived in Australia. Schools, theatres, and the Melbourne Baths shut immediately. Churches ran their services to dwindling congregations and only if everyone wore a mask. For Ruby and Winnie it was an absolute bonus. The school holidays stretched passed the Christmas and New Year break and into the long months of summer. Melbourne remained warm and sunny throughout the change of seasons. March weather could be fickle but in 1919 the days were rain free and warm enough for them to run about the beach in bare feet and cotton frocks. The disaster of the pneumonic influenza had little effect on children who remained untouched by the fast-spreading lurgy. Until they were not.

Winnie and Ruby had loved the postponement of school returning for the first term and the announcement that it would recommence on the 18th of March brought a sense of loathing. They had even enjoyed the wearing of masks as they played together and went on the occasional outing on public transport. Ruby liked the idea of a face covering which detracted from her birthmark. It would be mandatory for attendance at school. 'You won't be wearing your fancy masks when you get back to Merrington. Plain white muslin has been mandated by Sister Rose.' During the long days of the epidemic Ruby wore coloured and embroidered masks made by the milliner. He had drawn and sewed fancy images that made them more fashionable. 'You look like an Egyptian princess Ruby.' She didn't have the heart to say that Egyptians wouldn't wear masks and princesses were called an iryt. Because no-one likes a know-it-all apparently. So at home and around the neighbourhood she would wear her haute couture adornments and often look at herself in Minnie's long mirror thinking she was certainly more lovely with her face covered. Her birthmark was never a part of the conversation in Mary Street. Not like it was in Elwood. In fact at times, she forgot about her stained face until she caught the distraught glances of women in the street or at the shop. With it covered her blue eyes were a striking feature. Unusual and more remarkable when only her eyes peeped out from her dark fringe.

School curtailed freedom. Pinafores and long socks and lace-up shoes restricted body and mind. Masks made for anonymity which confused the nuns who resorted to calling all the students by a single identifier. 'You, girl.' A call which elicited several small faces to turn in the direction of the caller.

The flu had started to wane, and safeguards lessened and hope, despite being misplaced, lead to fewer precautions. The reduction in diagnoses turned out to be merely a lull. Within weeks the second surge washed through Melbourne like a tidal wave. The hospital set up beds in the Royal Exhibition Building to accommodate the ailing and the dying. The poor, the elderly and the very young often died on the same day as they became ill. At times it seemed like no-one would survive.

The virus ignored social borders and infiltrated the suburbs. And schools. At Merrington a dozen girls became ill within the second week of winter. Then a dozen more. Ten of them dead within days. The youngest girls were most affected. They fell like ten-pins. One after the other. Winnie included. She became ill at school. Looked forlornly at Ruby and brought out of her pocket a lace hanky. In the cotton square she had tied the lucky coins Ruby had given her at Christmas. Not so lucky after all. One of the sisters walked Winnie home, holding her hot little hand in hers. By the time the child had been delivered to her parents she was limp with fever, blue lipped and fighting for breath. In the household her grandfather, baby brother and her cousin Lou-Lou had already abandoned life. The brutality and speed of the disease traumatised and bewildered the living.

Ruby was heartsick and terrified. Life could not be worse.

Mary Street was not left unscathed. One of the actresses had been taken by horse and cart to the makeshift hospital in Carlton. She did not return. The milliner and the other actress, under instruction from Minnie, commenced the disinfecting of the entire house. Phenyl was used to wash every surface. The place smelled of tar and camphor. Ruby wore a camphor bag around her neck and Minnie occasionally dosed her with Hearne's Bronchitis Cure as a preventative. The guests wore masks and no-one ate a meal together. The coming and going of musicians and artists ceased. Sorrow was heavy in the house. A message came from Elwood to say that Douglas had arrived safely in Tasmania and avoided the dreaded virus but sadly Ruby's grandfather had succumbed. Minnie had no tears for her brother, Ruby had shed all her tears for her dear friend and there were none to shed for a stranger, albeit her grandfather. A funeral service would not take place. He would simply be buried in the Melbourne General Cemetery in the family plot. A service would follow once the scourge had ended. Surely nothing more could be visited upon them. Ruby had no more space in her heart for sadness nor could she bear the thought of one more goodbye.

It started with a scratchy throat in the morning. The fever set in by lunch. The wheezing, coughing and the blue lips by nightfall. The storm within Minnie's body could not be halted. 'Keep Ruby downstairs.' Her only instruction. 'Love you always my Ruby.' Her only message of hope called from behind her closed door. No prayer or lucky coin or phenyl drenched surfaces would save her. By the time the volunteers arrived in the early evening to take her to hospital Minnie was gone. Ruby sat rigid in stony silence with the actress and the milliner, aware, even in her shock and grief, that everything would change. Her light, her champion, her dearest aunt was gone. And what would become of her. Exhaustion and eventual sleep deprived her of an answer.

The weeks that followed saw more calamity and the ongoing spread of the deadly virus meant no-one had the capacity to ask, let alone answer Ruby's question about the future. The actress and the milliner continued as best they could. School was closed again. Ruby waited at home with them practising her writing and her numbers. She began to write long and elaborate stories about saving people from all manner of disasters. Herself as the main character, a saviour and a superhuman. At other times she sewed with Caleb, the milliner, and cooked with Elvie, the surviving actress. Finally, she knew their names. They all scrubbed with phenyl. They spoke in low voices and shopped covertly. When Ruby cried for want of her aunt, they held her and encouraged her to believe all would be well.

Life went on despite the awfulness and madness of so much death. The house had become a place of silence and soft shoe fall. It was unspoken but it seemed that a single loud noise might call the beast to the door. The three crept through the weeks after Minnie's death. There had been no funeral, just a burial in the same place as her brother. Elvie and Caleb had lit a candle and read a verse from Minnie's Bible to mark the day she went into the earth. Elvie read Isaiah 41:10 and although the passage started with *fear not, for I am with you*, Ruby felt little comfort. As a good Catholic girl she knew it was God who was with her, but she did not want Him. She wanted this cruelty undone. God, if he loved her at all, should give Minnie back. It remained an unanswered prayer. Life was askew. Pain, the new normal.

And eventually life did right itself. The second wave diminished, school re-opened and Elvie and Caleb recommenced work in various capacities. But according to the law a child could not inherit her aunt's house no matter what the legal documents said, and she apparently could not live with strangers. Questionable strangers as alleged by the legal person who came to explain what would happen to Mary Street and indeed to Ruby. 'The child simply must return to her father's custody and in his absence to her grandmother, Edwina Hart.' It seemed to be another blow to Ruby's ever waiving faith in a benevolent God or the goodness promised to those who did the right thing.

The legal representative droned on impervious to the hurt, disinterested in the upheaval he delivered and ignorant of the individual turmoil growing in the Mary Street residents. Being unsympathetic, offhand and direct gave him the means to make a pronouncement with no responsibility for the outcome.

Mrs. Rowlands was dispatched from Elwood to fetch Ruby and her belongings back to her grandmother's house. The terrace would be packed up and Minnie's things sold but the house would remain uninhabited. But on her arrival to fetch the child Ruby refused to go until it was made clear that her two friends would not be put out on the street. Mrs. Rowlands had no intention on insisting on anything that would upset the little girl further. 'Stay or go, not my issue. And I can tell you old Mrs. Hart won't be coming round to check.' She nodded at Ruby as if she had solved the problem. Elvie had carefully packed Ruby's clothes and favourite books and toys into Minnie's best cases. The bags stood at the door signalling the final farewell to Mary St. All the memories could not be packed into any luggage. The happy times, the lessons and the sadness would remain in Ruby's mind and on the pages of the stories she had written over the years. All the familiar sounds and smells, the softness of velvet couches, the heat of burning fires, the laughter of the cirle of friends, the safety, the love would all have to be left behind. Before her, the life with her grandmother seemed bleak.

Be the light Ruby. Minnie's words were in her head. *Make the world a better place*.

'We will stay for a while Ruby. We will get it all sorted. The bailiffs will have to come before we leave.' The milliner hugged Ruby and carried her bags out to the waiting cart.

'Don't let that old bitch touch your face little girl. You are beautiful just the way you are.' Elvie sobbed at the thought of sending her little friend back into a world of potential pain. 'You take her on if she comes near you. A good punch to the kazoo.'

And Ruby thought she could punch Edwina Hart, but she'd have to work out where the kazoo was exactly located before such an undertaking.

CHAPTER 5

As lives had come and gone the chaos of the flu went too. The papers were filled with news of the lives lost. Fifteen thousand Australians and fifty million world-wide had been taken. The country had been spared the worst of it. Isolation from Europe most likely the reason. The statistics heartened the government, and life went back to normal for those who had not lost loved ones. The Exhibition Centre divested itself of all the hospital beds, the city cleaned and scrubbed the shops and businesses for a return to work, the trams and buses roared back to life and things resumed their rhythm.

But for Ruby it all meant a lonely return to a near silent house in Elwood. Mrs. Rowlands provided the only connection to the comings and goings. Ruby's grandmother barely spoke a word to her and only occasionally did a letter arrive from her father in Tasmania. Letters in which he spoke only of the marvels of the new power station and the wonders of electric street lighting. For an eleven-year-old the news could not have been any duller. She could barely recall her father's features nor any of his interests, other than power stations. He remained a mystery. Her grandmother bewildered her too. Ruby could have imagined that just herself, Mrs. Rowlands and a few other staff lived in the house. Rarely did anything good come from being summoned to the front room where Edwina Hart sat like a fat spider in the midst of her web.

If Mrs. Rowlands announced Ruby's attendance was required it could only be bad news. Ruby had been too noisy, too slow coming home from school, too rough on her clothes, too big, too alarming or too disfigured. On one auspicious occasion she was summoned to the front room where Edwina Hart would announce the next chapter in Ruby's life.

'Merrington has an opening at its boarding house. I think it will be better than being a day girl.' Edwina stopped for a moment almost surprised that the child was in the room with her. 'More fun to be with children your own age than here with us.' Her attempt at softening the decision with a smile more frightening than the announcement.

'Well you are old.' Ruby's parting insult providing a near fatal blow to her grandmother's ego. Perhaps the fragile sense of self was where the kazoo resided. All those pounds spent on Dr. Jarsdel's magic potions had done nothing for her. Edwina's face remained ravaged by the passing years and if anything, the concoctions and treatments applied left the woman looking a strange shade of ash. She must have been at least seventy. Maybe more. Ruby had little interest in doing the maths to work out her age.

Merrington College was in the neighbourhood. 'Just round the corner little Ruby. I can be there in a flash if you need me.' Mrs. Rowlands had taken on the role of parent, carer and grandmother in the absence of any love from anyone else. She knew the pain Ruby felt in losing her Aunt Minnie. The gap could not be filled adequately but any kindness shown made a small difference in the life of the marked waif. The housekeeper walked with Ruby to the front gates of the school, the gardener's lad wheeled a barrow with her belongings and they left her in the care of the nuns in what seemed an act of abandonment. But eventually became the greatest thing her grandmother ever did for her.

Sister Regina ran the boarding school and while she had equally terrifying facial features, she bore none of Sister Rose-Phillipine's gruffness. Reggie, as the girls called her, was tender and nurturing. 'We are a family girls. While you are here with us, you belong.' Often said as she patted someone's head or wrapped an arm around the nearest student, or the saddest one.

The dormitory was not Dickensian. The actresses in Mary Street had taken turns reading Oliver Twist to Ruby. Her initial fears that her new situation might resemble the workhouse that Oliver found himself consigned to did not come to fruition. The meals provided were a thing greater than sustenance, the dishes were full of fresh vegetables and fruit grown predominantly by the order of nuns. Fresh fish, lamb and the occasional chicken the main protein, milk and tea, sugared almonds and petite cakes not just for celebrations but offered as pick-me-ups after tedious days in the classroom. Kindness, games and lolling about under leafy trees when the sun shone and curling up in front of fires when the winters blew in icy southern barbs were the stuff of dreams. Lessons were challenging but Ruby's intellect was a match for any problems thrown her way. The nuns and teachers adored her. 'Pequena maravilla.' Senora Morelo congratulated Ruby on her excellent musical ability and growing vocabulary of Spanish. *Little marvel* was quite the compliment.

The final years of junior school were very pleasant. Friends made, success attained, minimal interference from her family and only awfully long weeks of the holidays had to be endured in her grandmother's presence. Or non-presence. Edwina had taken to having spa treatments at the weekends. Submerging her withering skin and brittle old bones in salted pools allegedly promoted good health. 'Hope she doesn't sink, or boil or desiccate.' Ruby did hope that one of those possibilities might be realised. She had even researched osteogenesis imperfecta in an old medical book in the school library imagining that Edwina could be encouraged to snap in two if caught in something slightly stronger than a breeze.

Little of that mattered in the greater scheme of things. Time passed. Edwina lived. Her father never appeared and school was marvellous.

Ruby qualified easily for high school. Her grades were so high that two of the academic sisters went to see Edwina Hart as there were some rumblings from the Elwood house that Ruby should finish school and find work. Edwina had friends everywhere who were apparently keen to do the Harts an enormous favour by employing the poor granddaughter. *She has a disfigurement, and Edwina has tried everything to cure the child.* So respective wives of the business owning husbands sought a placement for the Hart child. Something in a back room, a factory floor, a kitchen or a seamstress somewhere in the Collingwood textile mills. The rumours had reached Sister Rose-Philippine via other parents at the school. She acted immediately. Sisters Consolata and Dolorosa were dispatched to the Hart mansion.

'I don't want to tell you what to do with your granddaughter Mrs. Hart but Ruby is simply academically exceptional. We feel she is a likely candidate for university when she has finished her studies.' Edwina appeared bored with the conversation. 'Ruby is an excellent student. She excels in languages, mathematics and all the sciences. And reads as well as any learned adult. Her level of interest in learning is a gift.' Sister Consolata persisted when Edwina responded only with an exaggerated sigh. 'Perhaps we should be speaking to her father. Afterall he is a learned academic and would surely want to know his child is extraordinary.'

Edwina sat up, ruffled by the suggestion that she was not smart enough to make the decision. 'Well she will have to board. I'm not well you know and trying to raise the child by myself is really out of the question.' Sister Dolorosa sighed almost as exaggeratedly as Edwina had.

'Of course. Ruby has a place with us as long as needed. We can also accommodate her during the holidays.' The news that her granddaughter would finally be someone else's responsibility seem to be a relief to the woman who barely acknowledged her guests until the offer of a permanent solution. 'I assume we will discuss the financial arrangements with Mr. Hart.'

Edwina nodded. 'Money of course is no issue Sister Consolata. It's just that Ruby is unsuited to this kind of life. She is at times sullen and disinterested in the finer things of life. Perhaps it's her face that has caused such discontent in the child.'

The visit ended abruptly as the two sisters rose as one, gave a contemptuous look at the wittering woman and begrudgingly wished her all of God's blessings.

But the greatest blessing was the sisters' generous offer of a haven, a home and an enormous opportunity. A life with purpose, expectation and self-determination.

CHAPTER 6

Latin, music, European languages and history, geography and mathematics filled Ruby's high school days. The nuns and teachers who had mainly escaped the ravages of war and influenza were a fine substitute for family. Occasionally she even saw Elvie and Caleb who were allowed to meet her in the city for afternoon tea. They always had a lavish gift that had been made for her. Caleb's skills extended from hats to gorgeous silk shirts and embroidered skirt sashes. Elvie brought her sheet music from some of the shows she had worked in. Once Elvie arrived with a swollen tummy and a man with dark skin who she introduced as her husband. The baby sadly was born too early and did not survive and the 'husband' disappeared on a ship departing for the United States of America. Caleb brought a special friend once too. A young man with soft eyes and a flat cap made of gold and green velvet who draped his arm around the milliner's shoulders and spoke to Ruby about socialism.

The visits from Mrs. Rowlands happened every Sunday at 4pm. She came to have tea with the borders and nuns and always brought a cake she had made. She spoke about Edwina in an almost derisive manner. 'Her ladyship has been enjoying sometime in the Salon de Jarsdell. He calls it a beauty salon.' Mrs Rowlands laughed and raised her eyebrows.

'So she is ageing backwards is she?' Ruby spoke with equal sarcasm.

Mrs. Rowlands hesitated to add that Douglas Hart had briefly visited but hadn't had the time nor inclination to see his only child. But she did. 'Your father was here last week. Had an important meeting in the city.' Ruby just nodded. 'I wouldn't recognise him. I can't really remember his face at all.'

'He ain't changed. Still a mute as far as I could tell.' Mrs. Rowlands felt she had overstepped. 'My apologies Ruby. That was a rude thing to say.'

'Just the truth. And that's okay.'

More importantly Mrs. Rowlands had brought Ruby a gift. She passed it to her almost covertly, as if she knew the present was tantamount to theft. Inside a cardboard sleeve made from an old flour box were ten photos of Ruby's mother. Alma had so little presence in Ruby's life. The images were of a stranger who just happened to look a little like her, except for the angel's kiss. Both Alma and Ruby had been cut from the same cloth. There was so little of the Harts in her makeup. 'A precious gift Mrs. Rowlands. Thank you. I'll never tell them that you gave these to me.' Ruby hadn't hugged the Elwood housekeeper for years, but the photographs of Alma warranted heart-felt affection. A memory of her kindness would stay with Ruby every time she looked at her mother.

The girls in Ruby's dormitory were also enamoured by the photos. 'You look just like her Rubes. Just like her.' Anne-Louise Beaufort was always effusive in her praise. And always called Ruby, Rubes. Al, as Ruby called Anne-Louise, played the violin and loved Home Arts. She worked in the kitchen with the sisters as a form of recreation not as a series of chores. Rubes and Al played songs together at the end of the school day making good use of Elvie's showtunes sheet music. Other girls joined in by singing or tapping tambourines. Senora Morelo even lent the little group of musicians her collection of maracas and castanets to provide more rhythm and noise. It couldn't be described as particularly good music but the girls had so much fun. *Toot Toot Tootsie, Some Sunny Day* and *I'm Just Wild About Harry* formed part of the Friday night show the girls put on in the dormitory lounge. Sister Reggie had concerns about some of the lyrics, but the naivety of the performers negated her fears. If some of the older sisters had their hearing, then perhaps there'd be a problem.

And there was sport. Or more specifically swimming. The Merrington girls made heroes of the champion Australian swimmers Fanny Durack and Mina Wylie. Both women had won medals in the Stockholm Olympics and were known as gifted athletes. Which was possibly enough, but for Ruby and Al and the dozen other girls who swam weekly at the Melbourne Baths, it was the epic battle for training opportunities in a male dominated field that really inflamed the worship. Fanny and Mina were Sydney girls who not only won Olympic medals but had to pay their own way to Stockholm. They faced a battle with finding a place to train when mixed bathing was not allowed and further trouble when their swimming tunics were deemed unseemly. With the rise of women seeking self-determination and Ruby's memories of her Aunt Minnie, the Merrington girls became more committed to pushing the boundaries that previous generations set.

'Pool day.' Al was up early on Saturdays to rouse the girls into action. The twelve girls committed to training happily packed their bags with tunic swimmers, towels and warm clothes. The ladies' pool was open from 9 am to 11 and to make the most of it they caught the 8 am tram into the city. 'What's your best time Rubes? For the breaststroke.'

'One second.' Marjory Fipps interjected before Ruby could answer. Smirking she salaciously ran both hands over her breasts. 'Two seconds if I want a bit more fun.' She was a good swimmer, but she was a bit wild. It was rumoured she had a boyfriend. 'What do you think of that Miss Ruby or don't you know what your duckies are for?'

'I suspect you might know more about it than us Marj. We just think they fill our shirts.' Al made the veiled comment regarding the gossip. Anne-Louise had six older brothers. She could hold her own in a verbal stoush and given her build possibly in a physical one as well if she needed to.

'Why duckies?' Ruby was less interested in the fight than the etymology. The brewing tension went from the carriage as the girls all grappled with the images. 'Kittens would surely be a better image if they had to be named after animals.' Ruby persisted.

'Grapefruits.' Offered Lucy Helms.

'Golf balls.' A miserable observation from the rather flat chested Dottie Parker.

'My gran always called them her girls. Got to get the girls under control.' Mary Cord was a fairly lumpy girl who might need help with containing her *girls*.

'Why don't we just call them breasts? Duckies. It is just so weird. I mean they are unlikely to quack.' Ruby hadn't meant to be funny but the thought of quacking breasts united the girls in explosive laughter.

'It's men who call them all sorts of names.' Marj added.

'Well that's enough reason for us not to call them anything but what they are.' Al concluded the breast discussion.

The pool added further distraction as the girls all shimmied or hauled themselves into their woollen tunics. The one-piece togs were made more comfortable by the narrow straps that gripped their pale strong shoulders. The fabric was baggy and the longer legs covered them with a degree of modesty. As Ruby submerged into the blue water of the ladies' pool she wondered at her body. At 14 she was already a woman. Her monthly period had arrived with her curves and pubic hair. Under the water she surreptitiously ran her hands over her breasts and waist. She was a strong young woman. She was no waif of a thing. Big like her mother as Edwina had described her. But she was lean and tall in the body. Good shoulders, more grapefruit that golf ball, toned thighs and long legs that bore her gracefully on land and allowed her to move through water like she was born to it. She could feel her long hair splay out around her before she pushed away from the edge of the pool. Here she was a goddess. Her stain concealed and distorted by the movement of the water. No-one could see her face.

The birthmark had not been much of a feature of her life since living at Merrington fulltime. It wasn't the subject of conversation and the bullying had long stopped. The talk of men and the thought of Marj and her boyfriend made her face suddenly an issue once more. All the girls talked of marriage one day. Of romance and fluttering hearts and the places they'd call home. Ruby believed that being a wife was an unlikely scenario for her. The face after all would be something of a deterrent.

Tears accompanied her first lap of the pool. Self-recrimination for being so soft in the second. And steely determination in the rest of them. She thrashed the life out of the water as she repeated her mantra. *Life is what you make it Ruby.* Then she lost herself in the long list of careers she intended having. *Maths teacher, doctor, scientist, Olympic swimmer, engineer, musician, tram driver, magician, watch maker, baker, writer.* Over and over she repeated her list. The hour of swimming passed in a moment and on exiting the pool she stood taller, more confident, more hopeful for a life of wonder.

As always it was lunchtime by the time they all rinsed off the pool water and changed into their clothes, got on the tram and made it back to Merrington. Saturday lunch was always sandwiches and soup. Followed by a cup of tea and a hearty bun full of fruit and peel. The afternoon would be for reading, writing, study or daydreaming. But an interruption to proceedings waited in the dining room of the boarding house. The interruption took the form of a new student. Sitting at the main table beside Sister Regina an extraordinary young woman cut a profound contrast to poor old Reggie's heavy face. Della de Guise was gorgeous. Chiselled features stared out from a face framed by glorious blonde hair. Pale blue eyes took in the ragtag unfinished girls, who in comparison looked like gorgons. Still wet haired and flushed from their exertions Della must have imagined that she had been transported to a farm and her new companions were not employees but the farm animals themselves.

'Hello ladies. So nice to meet you all.' Spoken in perfect English with the most enticing accent.

'You're French.' Al identifying the obvious.

'Non. No not French.' The delightful roll of the r and the stretched vowel seem to prove otherwise. 'I'm from Belgium.'

Ruby knew that Belgium had been occupied by the Germans for four years during the war. The death toll had been horrific. Most of the Belgium army had been wiped out in three months and thousands of civilians were casualties of the invading forces.

'I'm sure you will all have questions for Della but let's have some lunch. I'm sure you are famished girls.'

Reggie had shaken the girls out of their stupor in the glare of the newcomer's glamour by appealing to the base drive of their appetites. Ruby found herself seated beside Della. Her hair shone as if it had been polished. And her skin…lustrous, reflective, perfect…like glass. All the confidence that she had pumped into herself vanished in the glow of this model of flawlessness. The doubt crept into Ruby like poison. She began to shrink.

'You are the clever girl Sister Reggie had told me all about.' Ruby could barely lift her head to meet Della's gaze. With her perfect hand she touched Ruby's shoulder. 'We will be great friends Ruby Hart. I simply know it.' The guttural rrrr sound Della used to say her name was like a magic spell being cast. Ruby had friends. She was kind to everyone but there had not been a best friend in her life since Winnie. Della was so utterly convincing that Ruby simply did not hesitate to believe that a new force for good had entered her world.

CHAPTER 7

Beauty and deportment were not Della's only gifts. She was well read, sang and had a deep interest in science. Not many of Ruby's peers were as academically driven as her. Not that they weren't smart because they were. Even Marjory had skills, but she was more intent on using them to snag a husband. Even Al thought she'd be married by twenty and therefore her career ambition didn't extend beyond working in her aunt's haberdashery shop in Seymour.

Della also brought from England, where her family migrated to in 1919, some very interesting reading. The girls of Merrington rarely saw a magazine. Occasionally Dottie returned from her parents' home in Bairnsdale with a slew of *Women's Mirror* and a *Woman's Home Journal* for Australia. And Ruby had a small stash of *Melbourne Punch* and *Science of Man* that she had found in a box of Minnie's things. They were all out of date but she still liked the articles. But Della had introduced something quite amazing.

Ruby, Al and the other swimming girls had never seen an unclothed body. Not even their own given the bathrooms had no mirrors and one would never consider prancing about *sans vetements*.

'What is sans vetements?' Dottie had never mastered French or any of the other European languages.

'Without your clothes on Dottie you idiot.'

Le Vie Parisienne and *Le Petit Echo de la mode* were eye openers for the girls. Scantily clad and bare-chested drawings of women languishing about in the company of men had remained unimagined, let alone seen by the bumpkins of Merrington College.

'It's 1926 ladies. Time you had your eyes opened.' Della was as frank as ever. 'They are just drawings darlings. Just bodies. You all have one.'

'I don't have one like that.' Dottie was both mesmerised and miserable as she flipped through the pages.

'Don't let Reggie see these. She'll have a heart attack. No she'll have two heart attacks and then she will have to get big Rosie P involved and we will all have heart attacks.' Marj always referred to Sister Rose-Philippine as big Rosie P.

'Relax girlies. We are only interested in the articles. And they are just about fashion and beauty products.'

'So we are going to say we only have them to improve our French by reading the articles.' Ruby's eyebrows were so raised they almost disappeared into her hairline. 'Because Reggie will never see those…' Ruby hesitated for a moment. 'Duckies.' It almost came out as a scream.

'You want to be a doctor Rubes. Think of it as biology.' Al laughed. Ruby blushed as red as her birthmark.

The magazines were well read. Even the girls like Dottie who couldn't read French found the articles endlessly fascinating.

Della became a fascination. She spoke quietly and thoughtfully and after the initial concern about her European sophistication the girls embraced her as one of their own. Particularly Ruby. She was drawn to the Belgian girl's stories of her country. The matter of fact telling of her family's plight during the war became more embellished when Ruby wrote stories about her female saviour character rescuing women and children from the clutches of unrestrained brutality.

The de Guise family were educated people who worked for generations at the Catholic University of Leuven. Della had lived on the university precinct and had spent many happy hours in the library with her father who was a curator of the extraordinary medieval manuscripts held in the vaults. But as the *rape of Belgium* commenced in August 1915 the lives of the citizens changed. With the burning of the university library the 750 precious and meticulously preserved ancient manuscripts were lost. Along with the 230,000 books that were destroyed, 248 people were killed.

'I don't remember much of it. Just the noise and the chaos. The fear.' Della spoke without grief. It was as if she had read about the events in a book rather than lived through it. 'We had to hide for a while, in a wine cellar. Just the children as the adults had to find a way out for us.'

Ruby often just sat still and listened to Della speak. Occasionally she asked a question or two. 'What about your family Del? What happened to them?'

'We got out. Eventually to England. And now to the great land down under.'

Ruby always felt there was more to Della's story but as the sequence of events were unpicked she would shut down the discussion and talk about the more mundane subjects of maths and Latin. Or the more salacious topic of boys.

The brother college of Merrington was St. Julians. And once in a blue moon a dance was held where all the students aged sixteen and above were invited to attend. The Palais de Danse on the lower Esplanade had been booked for a spring ball prior to the final entrance exams. The excitement among the girls became an uncontainable force. Every conversation started with what one might wear, or which boy might ask which girl to dance. 'Bring on the fancy footsteps and the kissing.' Marj could think of nothing else, and she made the statement ten times a day in the lead up to the big night.

The country girls had been home for the holidays prior to the spring dance. Their mothers had sent them back with money to shop for appropriate ballgowns in Melbourne city. And a list of instructions about how low the neckline could be, how much skin could be shown and the appropriate colour for a young girl. '*No red.*' Every mother's instruction.

Della had a gown that had been bought in London for her mother. It was altered to show her pearl like skin and gorgeous figure. The back of the frock scooped low to show her shoulder blades and thin bands of gold beads held the low bodice in place. The gold and black threads skimmed her waist and hips and cascaded in shimmering fringes all the way to the floor. When she moved the dress seemed to be alive. The other girls, although envious, could only marvel at the glorious sight of Della when she tried the frock on.

Ruby had asked her grandmother for money to buy a dress for the ball. She walked the five blocks to the Elwood house rehearsing her request all the way. Mrs Rowlands greeted Ruby with a hug. 'You just keep getting more beautiful everyday Miss Ruby.' She held her back and smiled up into the dark blue eyes of the child who had become a young woman before her eyes. 'And tall like your mama was. She was a beauty too.' Ruby had hardly heard about her mother and apart from the photos that the housekeeper had squirrelled away she barely knew whether her mother had been anything other than *big*. Edwina Hart and never said anything about Alma other than that one comment.

Edwina sat in the drawing room, in a kind light that filtered through the fine net curtains. Her hair had been bleached and the startling white cropped style framed her over made-up face. 'This is a surprise Ruby dear. Why on earth would you come around in the middle of the week?'

Because you're my grandmother! Ruby left the thought unsaid. Instead, she asked about her father. 'Have you heard from Father lately? I haven't received a letter since Christmas.' Douglas wrote to his only child twice a year, her birthday and Christmas. He had been back in Melbourne on the odd occasion since his move to Tasmania, but he had never made time to see Ruby.

'Yes he was here last month. Very busy. His work is very important.' Edwina seemed reluctant to share even the smallest snippet of her son's life.

'Well it was a shame I missed him because I would have been able to ask him instead of you for some money to buy a dress.' Edwina's eyebrows, or what was left of the over plucked hairs, rose considerably.

'I'm not a bank Ruby.' She flustered at the mere thought of parting with cash. 'What sort of dress? The last time I saw you, and now, you were perfectly well turned out.'

Ruby inhaled deeply trying to stuff her resentment and loathing down. 'Merrington and St. Julians are having a ball in the spring, and I'd like to go and have something appropriate to wear.' Speaking quickly she worked to keep the sarcasm out of her tone. 'I can hardly go in my uniform or weekend dresses.' She eyed her grandmother directly. 'Or my sports tunic.'

Edwina gave a half smile. 'I've heard about the girls getting around playing sports in sleeveless frocks that barely skim the knee. You'd certainly attract attention if you appeared at the dance like that.' A pause in which she caught her eye in the mantle mirror. After adjusting a strand of hair she gave a melodramatic sigh. 'We are not made of money you know Ruby. Money for ball gowns is out of the question. Besides you are just a girl and I hope you haven't had thoughts about luring a husband just yet.' Her grandmother turned and walked towards her taking Ruby's chin in her hand. 'It's a hope too far I think my dear. That face has not improved.'

Ruby reddened. Not from shame but from fury. Edwina never let her granddaughter have a moment without referring to her birthmark. The tut-tutting intended to soften the insult.

'You could look at your mother's wardrobe. I don't think Douglas ever got around to throwing anything out. You're almost as big as she was when she died so there might be something appropriate there. Feel free to rifle through and take whatever you need.' She turned and muttered to herself. 'I'll get Rowlands to pitch the rest one of these days.'

Without thanking Edwina, or even acknowledging that the conversation had ended, Ruby left and sought Mrs Rowlands. She needed sympathy and some guidance on where her mother's dresses might have been stored.

'What you want with those old things? You're a young girl and the fashions are very different.' Ruby's face revealed her disappointment at the refusal of funds. Mrs Rowlands led the way to the room in which Ruby had been born, and Alma had died. 'No money. What a load of horse shite. The old biddy's got pounds coming out her arse.' None of that diatribe was intended for Ruby's ears but the housekeeper's muttering made her laugh. Images of shillings and pound notes flowing out of her grandmother's nether regions struck her as both hilarious and hideous.

'They will be a bit dusty dear girl. But a good seamstress might be able to do something with them. Your pals Caleb and the lovely girl might be able to help.'

It felt like an intrusion to be in her mother's room. Not sacred but almost. Afterall Ruby did bring about Alma's demise. Her difficult birth brought on the bleeding which ultimately took her life. Aunt Minnie had made it clear that Ruby should never bear the burden of her mother's death. Mothers died; babies lived. Sometimes both were lost in the ferocity of childbirth. None the less being in the room for the first time in nearly seventeen years made Ruby shiver and for the first time feel the liability of her existence.

The wardrobe had hardly been disturbed. One side held her day wear and the other several gowns, including her wedding dress. The cream chiffon over lace had not discoloured through the years it had remained entombed in the oak cupboard. Her satin gloves and veil were wrapped in a muslin shroud to protect them from the moths. The dress, while dated, was beautifully made and helped Ruby visualise her tall, willowy mother as she placed her hands on the narrow waist band.

'She was a beautiful woman your mother.' Mrs Rowlands spoke almost in a whisper. 'Just like her daughter.' Her voice caught in her throat with the terrible sadness of it all.

'These dresses have some potential.' She changed the subject. 'These two are silk and chiffon. Your father let her have whatever she wanted in the early days.'

Ruby held the two somewhat old-fashioned floor-length gowns in her arms. The salmon pink one had an interesting, gathered band of seed pearls and glass beads that encircled the waist and divided the bodice with a V-shaped panel of the same decorative border. It had potential but the colour would not necessarily be a good match for Ruby's complexion. Pink and red did not match in her mind. But the turquoise silk had more going for it. 'Maybe if the chiffon could be removed and the hem taken up…' Ruby's ideas petered out. She could write a great story and create a world with words but her ability to visualise fashion alluded her.

'Maybe Caleb could do something with this. Do you think he could?'

'Of course he could. I saw the lovely blouses he made for you last year. He has a good eye that boy. And the girl…what's her name…she would help him.'

'Elvie.'

'Them two should be married I think. Make a lovely couple.' Mrs Rowlands obviously had little idea about Caleb, or Elvie. She had not seen the young man draped around Caleb's shoulders during the afternoon tea visits.

All that aside Ruby would have to contact her two friends from the years she spent with her Aunt Minnie. They weren't hard to find and always loved to see Ruby.

With the three dresses boxed carefully Ruby headed back to school. She didn't bother going in to say goodbye to her grandmother. The door to the drawing room was firmly closed against further intrusion. Ruby could have walked out with half the household without Edwina noticing. One conversation, albeit brief, was more than enough for her.

The boxes were awkward and the one containing the wedding dress was heavy. Ruby had to rest the load several times as she made her way back to Merrington. When she got to the back gate of the boarding house several of her friends ran up to help her.

'Rubes have you been shopping without us?' Al sounded almost offended. Ruby's downcast face indicated the contrary.

'No to the cash for shopping I'm afraid. But I was allowed to take some of my mother's dresses. They might be able to be adjusted.' Al could see Ruby putting a brave face on the situation. Typical of Rubes, always trying to find the light.

'Well let's have a look and see if we can't imagine how to make them look like 1927.' Al had a country girl frugality and talent for making a silk purse out of a sow's ear.

CHAPTER 8

Ruby's mother's dresses, although beautiful in their own right couldn't hold a candle to the new frocks her friends had all been able to buy on a Saturday morning excursion to the city. But it wasn't jealousy Ruby felt when the new wardrobes were modelled. It was an emotion she hadn't felt for many years. Unloved. In all its ugliness that word best summed up the dark feelings that ruined the whole idea of the spring ball. The Harts were rich enough to buy her ten dresses, but they just didn't want to. Someone, anyone in that family just had to give her a moment where she felt she existed, and that would have been enough. Someone like Minnie who allowed her to be the centre of the universe in their eyes. A person who saw her, not her face. Not that birthmark. Self-pity was not a trait Minnie Hart would have tolerated, no matter how deep the hurt. 'Pick yourself up Ruby, no one's going to do it for you. Or lay there and see how that works.' Minnie's words were never cruel, but they were blunt and influential. Sulking about a dowdy dress was tantamount to a tantrum. Pulling herself together was the only way forward.

No boy would want to dance with her anyway, but she thought if perhaps she could look like the other girls maybe her face would not be the only feature that would be remembered.

Even Al's best ideas about remodelling the three dresses still made Ruby look like an old lady. 'Maybe Caleb and Elvie could help?' Desperation preceded another trip to the city with both Al and Ruby carrying the re-boxed dresses. Caleb was thrilled to see them. 'Rubes you've grown another five inches. You're a goddess my darling.' His flattery met with smiles. While exaggerated and flamboyant it always came from a place of genuine affection.

He listened to the dress dilemma. A couple of his co-workers joined them at the fabric cutting table. Alma's dresses were laid out. 'Great textiles. And the turquoise is gorgeous. But the cut is staggeringly old, old, old.' One of the most ostentatious men Ruby had ever seen stated the obvious. 'So we are making a star of this little flapper with a new dress.' He was excited.

'Hold it together Bernie. She's a baby being raised by nuns.' Caleb tried to curtail the enthusiasm for high hems and low necklines. She was measured and re-measured to ensure whatever they could do would fit like a glove.

'Well we are making the most of that waist and bohunkus. She's a right doll.' Bernie went off to start drawing. And presumably cutting.

'I'll bring the dress out to you for a fitting Rubes. You are not to worry about anything. And I'll get Elvie to look for some shoes. Trust me you will be perfect.' Caleb hugged her close and kissed the top of her head. Ruby's replacement family knew exactly how to chase away the dark clouds Edwina Hart always managed to create.

'What's a bohunkus?' Caleb laughed at Ruby's innocence and swung around and slapped his own backside.

On the tram back to St. Kilda Ruby wondered if her bohunkus landed on the positive or negative scale of good things to have. 'You've got a great bum and gorgeous duckies kiddo.' Caleb will make sure you make the most of both of them.' The two girls laughed and an older woman tut-tutted them and made a face like a cat's bohunkus. 'Well she does.' Al said to the woman's back as she moved away to seats further down the car.

Great bohunkuses and the rest of the body had to be forgotten as the week of school had a number of challenges. The final weeks of the term were all about preparing for the exams that would follow the dance and two weeks of study leave. The upcoming holidays might start with the spring fling, but the rest of the time would be filled with writing essays and endless mathematics problems to be solved. Sister Reggie was adamant that the girls would not be further distracted by the much hoped for dance and forbade them practising the Charleston and tango. Despite her ban on the noisy, and far too frisky dances, the girls paired up and danced in the dormitory rooms without music every night. Dinner, study, prayers, baths and mad dancing filled the month of September. Ruby, although totally focused on being dux of the college joined in the frantic jazz moves with the others. The place was hot.

Even more so when Caleb and Elvie arrived with the dress. It had been transformed. The dowdy Edwardian bell skirt and lace panel that extended down the bodice were gone and had been replaced with a drop waist encircled by a silk sash in gold. Crystal beads and gold metal embroidery finished a calf length fringe that moved like water when they pulled the dress out of the box. It was sleeveless and plunged dangerously low at the decolletage and even more spectacularly so at the back. When she put the dress on over her dowdy cotton chemise both her chest and shoulder blades were covered. 'Get that wretched thing off Rubes and put on this silk petticoat.' Della had joined the dressing extravaganza. Without the frumpy and lumpy vest the dress draped over Ruby's young body as if she were indeed a goddess.

'Holy bohunkus Rubes. You look like…' Al was stumped for words.

'A woman.' Della finished the sentence.

In another box brought by Elvie two gold embossed pumps sat in a nest of crumpled white wrapping paper. They were new. And accompanied by a note. *Just a small gift to our girl. Minnie would be so proud. E & C.*

Ruby felt proud. While she didn't have a mirror to review the head-to-toe look, she could tell from the admiration in her friends' eyes, she looked better than average.

Soon enough the night arrived for the ball. The girls of Merrington College senior year stepped out of the confines of their dormitories as young women. The girls they once were left behind in the cupboards and drawers that held the trappings of their childhoods. Della had wielded the lipstick, rouge and kohl pencils with the expertise of a Max Factor model. Sister Reggie had been instructed to stand by with a flannel and cold cream to remove anything that appeared excessive or deemed far too provocative. Red lipstick had to go. Della kept the palette pale but the transformation made Reggie nervous. She had a small stack of white lace hankies to pin over the most revealing cleavages. Marj's needed four pins to restrain the bulging flesh. Reggie was totally out of her depth.

Buses had been arranged to take the girls to the Esplanade dance hall. Staff acted as chaperones but were less anxious about the bloom to womanhood than the sisters were. Once on the road Marj removed the pins that held the linen square in place and rearranged herself to make the most of her assets. The other similarly pinned girls did the same. The boys from St. Julians had already arrived at the venue when the girls deboarded and flowed into the ballroom. The lights and band music transported them all to another world. The dowdy uniforms shed, the flattering sparkle of light and the promise of being held in a man's arms and the possibility of a kiss stunned the girls. For all their womanly curves and made up faces they were for the most part unworldly. 'Close your mouths girls and follow me.' Della shook the posse of want to be femme fatales back into coherence.

As they proceeded to the chairs set out on the right-hand side of the dance floor to shed their bags and wraps the boys let out an audible sigh of appreciation. If truth be told they were as gormless and unformed as their sister students but in their suits and ties they were passable as men. The girls looked them over. Most of them looked tall and lean, some were yet to hit the change from teen to adult, several had the coarseness of hearty country lads and a couple, it appeared, may have been more at home in an abattoir.

The band played. The two groups that had initially clung to the left and right of the hall moved closer together. The smoothest of the boys made bee lines towards Della, Al and Marj. Others flustered and jostled around the rest. Abattoir one and two refused to move off the wall and just scowled at the awkward milling around. They eyed the gathering with the disregard and contempt one might view cattle to the slaughter. Ruby positioned herself at the back of the group of girls in an attempt to avoid the clumsy requests for partnership on the floor. Despite her dress and initial confidence the reality of her proximity to scrutiny by the opposite sex waned very quickly when she noticed several sets of eyes roam appreciatively over her curves and the recoil when she perceived they noticed her face.

Edwina's criticism of Ruby's face refused to be contained. All the gold shoes and beaded gowns in the world didn't have enough weight to stuff down self-doubt.

'What are you doing Ruby?' Della had one whirl around the floor with a particularly handsome boy. She stopped when she saw the panic rising in Ruby's eyes. 'It's okay you know. You look beautiful.' Della reached out her hand and took Ruby by the arm. 'We are going to Charleston.'

Momentarily the joy of dancing with Della and some of the other unpartnered girls reduced Ruby's anxiety. The pulse and the bounce of the dance step freed her from the constriction of the terror. Ruby loosened up and found the contra movement of arms and legs, twisting forward and backwards took her to the hopeful anticipation she felt as she boarded the bus. In the pumping noise of the hot jazz played by the band it seemed the whole group had been secretly practising the step, tap and swing of the new dance craze.

In the wave of movement everyone forgot what anchors weighed them down. The lean, the stout, the plain and the perfect all pounded the floorboards with a unifying twist and stamp of gilded feet. Noise, movement and freedom rolled into one happy moment.

More dancing, some as groups, and then partnered filled the night. The supper at 9.30 was a less civilised affair. Some boys had obviously been schooled in how to ask their partners if they would like a drink or sandwich, others rushed the table like starving children. The cool and detached stood back and the two boys who refused to join in the earlier frivolity had other antics on their minds. Ruby's face had not gone unnoticed by the two flushed and fleshy boys. They moved off the wall where they had skulked all night and took two glasses of the fruit punch, iridescent with red sugar syrup and dotted with fruit.

Their intention was not to imbibe the syrupy drink. They sidled up to Ruby and Della who were choosing finger sandwiches and canapes at the trestle table. Ruby sensed the closeness of the two boys and stepped back assuming they were trying to fill their plates. She gave a shy smile as one of the boys acknowledged her politeness.

The smile left her face as quickly as it arrived. The glass of punch splattered the front of her dress and she gasped at the shock and icy cold of it. 'Oh jeez love so sorry. God clumsy or what.' He held a paper napkin up as if he was about to touch her and blot the soaked front of her dress. Ruby instinctively stepped back.

'It's not just on her dress.' Boy two entered the game. 'It's on her face. Look mate you've splodged her eye with it.' He leant forward with a second tissue. Their grins were lascivious and mocking. 'That's not punch that's her face.' Boy one laughed.

'What the hell is it?' He laughed and looked horrified at the same time. 'Syphilis?'

By this stage they were double up with laughter. Others had turned to watch the humiliating antics and Ruby's deep shock. Her beautiful dress stained, her face flushed with agonising mortification and tears welling up. Some of the St. Julian's students shuffled with embarrassment at the poor behaviour of the two boys. A chaperone stepped forward to mop up the spilled drink. And in the chaos Della moved in.

'That's not punch on her face. But this is on yours.' Her delicate little hand clenched into a fist and connected with the laughing hyena's nose with a delicious cracking sound. 'That's a punch.' The guffawing ceased immediately. The intake of collective breath was audible. The intervention of the adults followed. Della grabbed Ruby's hand and led her to the bathrooms, followed by Al and Marj. The latter standing guard at the door in case the lad with the bloodied nose and his foul friend attempted retribution.

In the mirror Ruby could see the raspberry mark on her dress. It did match the pink tear drop around her eye. Her eyes watered and the thick kohl pencil lines under her bottom lids started to melt down her cheek as well.

'Stop crying Ruby. It's just cordial. The dress will clean.' Della used her white hanky to attend to the black drops around her eyes and removed a diamante broach from her own dress to cover the mark. 'All fixed. No one will know there's been a problem.' Della's matter-of-fact attitude eased some of Ruby's tension. 'Some boys are pigs. They don't know how to be anything else.' Della looked at her own face in the mirror beside Ruby's. 'But some of them are wonderful. And they will be the ones who love us.' Her smile didn't reach her eyes but it offered enough encouragement for the band of girls to re-enter the ballroom.

'Trouble's brewing.' Marj made an intuitive observation of the situation. In the few minutes they retreated to the bathroom for repairs the headmaster from St. Julian's had been gathering statements regarding the ruckus at the supper table. He had been told that a drink had been accidently spilled on one of the Merrington girls and a wild foreigner had assaulted the hapless young man who had simply been clumsy.

One thing a career priest and educator did not counter on when gathering his evidence was the formidable power of the female collective. Within minutes of him informing the Merrington staff of the uncivilised behaviour of their female charges, Al informed him otherwise. With dissecting accuracy she explained the plot concocted by the two boys. 'A nefarious plot to attack and insult a female student cannot be explained away by clumsiness.' The priest looked bewildered at the eloquence of Al's opening statement. 'We are not going to take the blame for your students' uncivilised attack.'

'Just stop…'. The headmaster attempted to interrupt.

'Don't speak over the top of me please Father Hewer. We know what happened and perhaps those boys should make an apology.'

'Listen here young lady one of your friends hit a boy in the face.' Before he continued Al interrupted again.

'What proof of that do you have? Does the boy wish to make it known that a frail girl took him out with a single punch?' She raised one eyebrow. 'I doubt it.'

She turned her back on the flustering priest.

The night ended with polarised opinions. The St. Julian's students shamed by the act of two stupid boys and the Merrington girls championing the single blow for their rights not to be victims of that stupidity.

But of course, victories can be short lived. For Ruby the night did not end with a sense of her power over unkindness. The reference to her facial mark simply reinforced her belief that her life would be one buried in books, studying and writing, isolating herself so no-one else could make her feel so terrible. She knew that she was more than a birthmark, but the world seemed to conspire to reduce her to that.

CHAPTER 9

Father Hewer wanted to pursue the events of the night and in Sister Rose-Phillipine's office he made it clear that the Merrington girls who were at the heart of the upset at the spring dance should be made to explain themselves.

Sister Reggie called their names at breakfast on the Monday morning of the first week of the study period. The girls were not in uniform, their hair not drawn back into severe neatness and their spirits not dampened by conformity. Al, Marj, Della and Ruby stood outside the headmistress's office until Reggie reappeared, flustered and a face full of concern for her girls.

When they entered the office the priest sat behind Rosie-P's desk, and she sat in the visitor's chair. The four girls stood in front of the desk, lined up in front of the firing squad.

'Father Hewer tells me that not only were Merrington girls involved in a clumsy act of spillage at supper but that one of you behaved raucously and violently and another spoke with insolence to him.' Big Rosie had a way of pausing at the end of major statements that left everyone wondering if they were meant to fill the gap with a response. In this case silence seemed the best choice.

'It seems the young ladies are speechless Sister. Perhaps this is an admission of guilt.'

Pompous and wrong. 'We didn't do anything wrong. Those boys....' Father Hewer raised his hand to stop Al in her tracks. Her initial confidence waning with his intimidatory stare. Marj tried to take up the defence.

'That boy was having a go at Ruby. He threw a drink on her to make fun of her...' Marj couldn't finish either. Not because of the priest's imperiousness but because she didn't want to embarrass Ruby by mentioning her birthmark.

Both Sister Rose-Philippine and Father Hewer leaned forward as if they expected more from Marj. But for all her usual careless big talking she too was stumped as to how to proceed.

Della stepped in. 'I think Father that you have been misled by the tales that your boys have been telling you. And you have been too quick to believe their lies.' Hewer's face flushed bright red and he made to disrupt Della but she put her hand up to stop him. 'You have come here to listen to our explanation so you should at least show us the courtesy of doing just that.' She pressed on. 'The two young men who I refuse to call gentlemen made a poor pantomime of spilling punch on Ruby's dress as part of an ill-conceived and quite frankly imbecilic plan to humiliate her and make fun of her face.' Della raised an eyebrow. Directly staring into the eyes of the man whose indignation grew with the rising colour in his face.

'I defended my friend when one of those *le voyou* went to touch her breast. And I would punch him in the nose again if the same situation arose.'

'Stop speaking.' His voice shrill and loud. 'How dare you suggest that any St. Julian's boy would act so inappropriately.' Spit formed at the side of his mouth. He stood and pointed at Ruby. 'You seem to be the silent subject of this indiscretion. What did you do?'

If she could just disappear, fade into the beige background of the office walls or sink into an endless hole in the floor Ruby would have been content. But something bigger than her own skin was on the line. Her three friends had spoken in defence of her, they had acted to protect her, being silent now would be a betrayal of that loyalty.

'Those boys...' Ruby started tentatively. 'Deliberately set out to mock me because of my birthmark. They threw a drink on me and then pretended that the mark on my face was part of the spilled drink.' She drew a breath. 'And then he went to touch me while he was laughing like a jackass.'

Sister Rose-Philippine touched Ruby's arm gently. A sign of her approval.

'Well that is hardly a reason for what ensued.' Father Hewer lent back in his chair. 'Such a silly thing and such a poor excuse for unladylike behaviour.'

'Well you would be wrong old man.' Della spoke with deliberate slowness. 'It was disgusting and low class. The sort of thing the scum down at the docks might try on. What kind of men are you growing over there at St. Julian's?'

Al and Marj joined the condemnation with much nodding and sounds of assent. 'Bunch of shit kickers.' Al must have used that phrase to describe her farm family a hundred times but in the sanctity of the sister's office it landed heavily.

The priest lost all comportment and turned on the headmistress. 'What kind of girls are you raising here Sister? Ones that would speak with such vulgarity. No wonder Mr. Cordell had a broken nose at the end of it.'

'Lucky it was just his nose.' Della finalised the conversation.

He turned on big Rosie-P. 'The four of them should be expelled and refused entry to their final exams.'

Ruby thought she would die. All she had worked for. And her friends bearing the punishment for her weakness.

With the threat of the priest's wrath becoming uncontainable, Sister Rose-Philippine stood up. Her height and heavy features made her appear formidable. The four girls expected the worst. They waited while she straightened her scapular and adjusted her cincture.

'Father Hewer. Thank you for your attendance here today at Merrington. I'm aware that a ruckus broke out and that things may have become heated. Young people can over-react but I won't be expelling my girls. I won't deny them entry into the exams they have worked so hard to excel in. We will discuss how they might have better channelled their energies into problem solving at a later date.'

Nearly apoplectic the priest moved to the door. He turned as if to make a parting shot but the nun got in first. 'And by the way here at Merrington we are raising the right kind of women. Those who will stand with their friends in the face of poor male behaviour. Women who know their strengths and use their intellect to refuse to succumb to anything less than gold standard behaviour from others.' She drew breath and pressed on. 'I can't condone physical violence but sometimes it's all a woman has left when men insist on behaving like…' She didn't get to finish her sentence before Hewer slammed her office door.

'Swine.' She turned her eyes to the four bewildered young women. 'Hmmm that was interesting. Don't you have study to do? Get going.'

The four girls turned to leave the office. Ruby turned back to the sister who had so frequently over her many years at Merrington both inspired and frightened her. In an act of impulse Ruby hugged Sister Rose-Phillipine. 'Thank you for everything Sister.'

'I told you years ago Ruby Hart. You have greatness within you. God bless.'

Waiting in the study room Reggie and the other boarders paced fretfully at what might be the fate of their four friends. Their reappearance was accompanied by cheers and clapping. Sister Reggie collapsed in a chair with the absolute relief that no punishment would derail her students in the final days of their lives under her care. Al and Marj lead an impromptu version of the Charleston to the girls singing 'If You Knew Susie.' It had been a win, but it wasn't without its price.

Ruby slipped away to her dormitory room. While the impromptu celebration reflected the victory over the spring dance fiasco something else seemed lost. She couldn't put her finger on it but it felt like a dangerous thing. Like putting your head above the trench, like drawing a target on your chest and calling to the enemy to show the exact spot they could hurt you. So much safer to withdraw into the bland landscape of a colourless world where she could hang her head down and become unseen. There were tears. They did not go unnoticed.

'Petite larme.' Della had followed her. 'Little teardrop is my name for you Ruby Hart.' Della sat with Ruby. 'That is the shape of your mark Rubes. A little perfect drop.'

'Not perfect Della. It's a stain. The scarlet *tache* you might say. Or *mancha* in Spanish. Or just plain old tarnish. No matter what language you use it's a big old blot that is the only thing people see when they look at me.'

'La foutaise Ruby.' Della frowned. 'The shit of the bull is what all this self-pity is.' She leaned in and hugged Ruby. 'You make this little mark a great burden. Like a wound that won't heal. One that you just keep hiding behind.' Della shifted her position. 'You use it as an excuse to hide from the truth that you are destined to fly.'

'But what if I can't fly Della? What if it's all a myth?'

Della stood and walked to the window. She was quiet for a moment and without looking at Ruby said. 'It's the wrong question that you keep asking. The question really is what if you can. And the answer to that question terrifies you.'

She came back to Ruby's bed and put her hand on the mark. 'This is not a wound Ruby. It is skin deep. It is not the essence of you. Other pain, other wounds that can't always be seen sink into the core, into the soul and maim the spirit.'

Silence for a moment. 'I saw things in Louvain. Even as a little girl I knew that I'd never be able to unsee them. Men digging their own graves before they were shot. Women and girls raped and mutilated. People so terrified that they betrayed their own people.' She looked into Ruby's eyes. 'Even my own family were not exempt. My grandfather shot, my older sister violated and killed.' She breathed deeply. 'We escaped because my father betrayed his people. We had to come to this far away island to forget who we had been.' She raised her head, refusing to shrink from her revelations. 'These are wounds.' Her hand touched Ruby's face again. 'This is nothing petite larme. Nothing.' Ruby had always suspected that Della had borne horrors of her family's experiences in Belgium. Like a goddess she rose above the memories, determined and fierce. She could have been crippled by what she witnessed but she had a greater strength, the wounds were there, buried deep, shaping her but not defeating her humanity.

The two young women embraced. Their sadness and their resolve intermingled. Life would be what they made it. Fly or fall. It was a choice. The thought of which gave them courage. But people often placed things in the way of the hopeful few. Sometimes there was a meaner spirit, a cruel intent that aimed to curtail the optimism of young women.

CHAPTER 10

The tripping point came in the form of Father Hewer. He was not to be bested by a nun and chorus of young girls. *Bright young things* the newspaper called the generation of women who felt emancipated and yearned for self-determination and freedom. But in Hewer's mind the flapper era simply encouraged girls to be vulgar, frivolous and disrespectful. They would be brought to heel as far as he was concerned. It was his duty, and in his eyes, a proper punishment would be to put them in their place. Snip away at trivial and vain dreams, clip their wings before they elevated themselves to giddy heights. He prepared several letters, embellishing each one with dire warnings.

He sent them to the girls' parents explaining most explicitly that the girls' behaviour had generally been incited by the two perpetrators who he described as *the disfigured one and the foreigner*. Della's parents' letter stated that St. Julian's had in fact sought a legal opinion and that the police had been informed. He demanded that they remove her from Merrington immediately. The letter to Douglas Hart had been sent to the Elwood house and had been promptly opened by Edwina. In it the priest explained that a girl with her physical disadvantages had probably been led astray by the low European standards of her friend. It intimated that Ruby had limited capacity to determine right from wrong despite having had a lifetime at Merrington. He advised, most strongly, that the family take some control over the direction Ruby's life was taking. *Particularly as she had shown some ill-conceived notion of attending university after the leaving exams.* This foolish intent could only lead to further disintegration of her moral compass.

The uproar exploded in all directions. The families arrived and the shouting from Sister Rose-Phillipine's office could be heard all over the campus. Al and Marj bunkered down in the dormitory while their respective parents shouted about the school's lack of supervision over what the girls had been doing. How could their daughters have been drawn into such a scandal. Violence no less. One voice boomed above the others. He said, 'What the hell have you been teaching our daughter? Boxing?' It was Al's father who under any other circumstance might have been proud of his girl throwing a big right hander. She had settled more arguments with her brothers that way than Mr. Beaufort was likely to admit in these circumstances. The other parents joined the chorus of complaints.

'I am asking you to calm down.' Big Rosie P's voice drowned out the Beaufort and Fipps parents in an instant. 'This is a storm in a teacup. Your girls did not behave as monstrously as Father Hewer outlined in his letter. Yes, there was a ruckus and a boy was hit.' She paused for dramatic effect. 'Deservedly so because his behaviour towards your daughters and their friends was loathsome as far as I'm concerned.'

Al and Marj's parents did calm down. They had little love for the church, and the men who ran it. Despite being Catholic they were hard working country people who happily attended Sunday mass, but they weren't having their lives directed by the local parish or the big city priest from St. Julians. They blustered and kept a stern tone but they acquiesced to the nun's request for peace. 'No decisions can be made in anyone's interest if we discuss this with such agitation. Let's have a more composed discussion about how to proceed.'

After a few minutes, and a pot of tea, the parents were placated. Angry about the situation, furious with Father Hewer, the adults came to a suitable conclusion. Both girls were allowed to stay and complete their exams on the proviso that on the moment they completed the last sentence, they would both be on the train to their respective homes. Life in the city ended with a full stop. No celebratory shenanigans would be tolerated.

Della's fate an even worse outcome. Her mother and aunt arrived the next day to remove Della from the school. She would not complete the exams. There would be no time for a farewell. The family would move to Sydney and forget the whole terrible situation. Not even Rosie-P could dissuade them from this unfortunate decision. The two women, as composed and as elegant as Della would not be persuaded. 'It's not as bad as you might think Madame de Guise. Della is a wonderful young woman who was rightly defending her friend.' But she simply shook her head. 'We take her away today. It is best for Della.'

Ruby and Della barely had time for a final conversation. 'I don't understand why they are taking you away. Can't we get them to change their minds.' Ruby's hopeless tone revealed the unlikeliness of such a thing. The two girls held each other, a fierce embrace of shared pain.

'When you have learned to hide Rubes, you have to keep hiding and lying. We are meant to be shadows. To stay low so no-one will find out who we really are was not well served by me snotting that nasty little boy.' Her smile belied the agony of the defeat. 'I will write to you. Sydney is not so far away and when we are free of our families we will meet again.' She touched Ruby's face. 'I'll find you petite larme.'

Then she was gone. Trunks packed. A wisp of her blonde hair caught in the cover of her bed, the fragrance of her perfume, the space she inhabited and the hopefulness she brought disappeared in the time it took to lift a hand to wave.

And then Edwina arrived. She had a telegram from Douglas with instructions regarding Ruby. Douglas, if not much of a father, was a man who appreciated that Father Hewer's description of his daughter's inadequacies was all wrong. He knew Ruby had a great intellectual capacity; her birthmark did not diminish her ability to learn. She would complete her exams. Return to her grandmother's home directly after and as 1928 began she would take the passenger ship, The Loongana, from Melbourne to Launceston where she would find work and live with him at Duck Reach. There would be no more talk of university. 'These girls have their heads filled with flighty notions of grandeur. They need to manage their sense of self-importance.' Edwina's tone was scathing.

'Ruby is an innocent victim in all of this Mrs. Hart. She really is not deserving of punishment.' Sister Rose-Philippine spoke with a coolness that reflected her dislike of the ageing doyen. 'She is a gifted…'. Edwina cut the nun's extoling of Ruby's skills with a blunt interruption.

'She is arrogant. Like her mother was.'

And that was that. All that had been worked for. Everything that mattered had been buried by one letter. As Della had evaporated so had Ruby's hope to soar.

The time evaporated as well. The exams came and went. Ruby found them easy and despite her broken heart and shattered ambition she couldn't help but do her best. Al and Marj had limited success, barely completing the physical science paper and making a half-hearted attempt on the French and English ones. The goodbyes strained them all. Tears, clinging hugs, promises of letters and better days featured in every farewell. Not even Ruby's achievement as Dux of the College brought a smile. Not even the fact that she had outscored the boys at St. Julians on every subject brought the girls out of their misery to celebrate such an extraordinary achievement. The teachers, the nuns and Rosie-P spoke of their pride in their wonderful young student's accomplishments. But the grim reality of Ruby's dreams being shattered could not be bested by congratulatory rhetoric.

Ruby had to take the short, yet eternally long, walk back to Elwood. The cart had collected her things. Her typewriter, her ball gown, her mother's wedding dress, dozens of books, all her writing and a small address book in which she had recorded everyone's residence so that the letter writing could begin. The farewell with Reggie was wordless. The nun who had raised the so called wild young things felt she had let her little girls down somehow. She had sent them off with a card wishing them the best for the futures that lay ahead. And in Ruby's card she wrote:

I am no bird; and no net ensnares me: I am a free human being with an independent will. Charlotte Bronte 1847

Sister Reggie knew how much Ruby loved this book, how the central character resonated with the life she had lived thus far. From Reggie's point of view, it meant that all the girls would eventually find happiness. But Ruby felt it meant that women might feel that their paths were pre-ordained, but it was not so. The world of men seemed to think life should include a little school, a little work and then becoming a wife and, God willing, motherhood would round out a woman's life. But *Jane Eyre* spoke of a woman's capacity to strike out on her own, to make decisions that stemmed from her own character, to live a life that may or may not include a career or love. An adulthood in which one could outrun a childhood of loss and find strength in that suffering.

Ruby tucked the beautiful message into her folder of treasures. She repeated the line from the novel with every step and by the time she reached her grandmother's house she stood taller, had made her plans to weather the storm that lay ahead and believed that there would be a life of her own making. Not today, maybe not tomorrow. But one day.

ANOTHER BEGINNING

CHAPTER 11

Christmas and the long warm days of the new year were a sombre affair. Her grandmother barely spoke to her and Mrs. Rowlands attempted to fill the void with busyness and fussing over what her beloved Ruby would need in the wilds of Tasmania. 'I'm not a convict Nanny. I'll survive.' She tried her best to smile and reassure the old housekeeper that she would hold her chin up and face whatever the island state would offer. 'It can't be colder than Melbourne at its worst nor as hot or wet or wild.'

'True darling girl but you will be down there alone.' Mrs. Rowlands teared up at the thought of Ruby struggling to navigate a new life without her Sunday cakes and sneaky gifts of things she found in the Elwood house. Alone, without her friends from school. Without Caleb and Elvie and Sister Reggie. Alone, except for Douglas. Her father was just a stranger whose parenting skills had never been put to the test. Ruby wondered what she would call him. In the last 18 years she referred to him as her father or as Douglas. Ruby couldn't remember a single time when she actually addressed him as Father. *What if she tried papa, daddy or da. Pater or tata.* None fitted. All terms of affection spoke of an intimacy that Ruby did not share with Douglas Hart. Perhaps she would never address him, maybe she would simply answer his questions and nod her assent should it be required. In public she might gain his attention by calling him sir or Mr. Hart.

Ruby packed and repacked her cases and trunk for her journey to Launceston. Her typewriter and journals were part of her hand luggage. Caleb and Elvie had insisted on one final teary afternoon tea where they gave her more gifts of exquisitely sewn muslin shirts and a delicate scarf hand knitted in lapis cashmere. Its softness would give both warmth and comfort in the long months of winter but also reflect the extraordinary blue of Ruby's eyes. The Christmas cards from Della, Al and Marj were squeezed in with all the other important keepsakes. The cards were full of hope and the determination for reunions and rescue attempts. They fitted in a tightly filled cloth bag of papers, photographs and small items from Aunt Minnie's writing box. Her little diaries full of secrets, small notelets and gift cards were just as precious to Ruby as the real treasures that had been left her. The house in Mary Street would be hers on her 21st birthday. In three years she would be a property owner and inherit the money left to her by Minnie. Three years of exile and of waiting, isolation and loneliness. The self-pity rose like bile in her throat and could only be stuffed back down with a small attempt at optimism. It would be time for reading, studying and writing. Three years to prepare for the life she intended having. A place in university, a career and a home of her own. 'Flight delayed but not denied.' Ruby spoke the words aloud. She could feel Minnie's presence, perhaps her mother's too as she stood tall, pulled her shoulders back and buttoned her long jacket and tucked her new scarf under the wide lapels. She had turned 18 as the summer began but there had been no celebration. Legally she remained the property of her family, hence she had none of the freedom that comes with adulthood. Her statuesque image reflected that of a woman. Inside she felt like a child impersonating a grown-up. But it was what it was, and it would have to do.

A yellow cab had been organised to take Ruby and her luggage the five miles to Station Pier in Port Melbourne. Edwina had summoned her to the sitting room ten minutes before the driver arrived. She remained seated looking out the window. 'I hope you make the most of this time Ruby. Even you should be able to get a job doing something useful down there.' She turned her head briefly to sneer in the general direction of her only grandchild. 'You brought this on yourself really. If you'd been less arrogant maybe you could have found a nice job in one of the department stores here, lived in the city and maybe even you could have found a husband.'

Edwina obviously thought Ruby had been tried, convicted and sentenced to transportation. Ruby wanted to say cruel things to the painted, bloated carcass perched so primly on her fat arse, but she knew a greater revenge awaited her. 'I will be fine Grandmother. I'm smart and strong, well-educated and as you have pointed out and several occasions, I'm big like my mother.' She could sense Edwina's comprehension of the words tinged with sarcasm. 'I will become all the things I've dreamed of. A doctor or a teacher or a scientist.' Ruby paused for effect. 'But firstly, a writer. And you know what they say about writers.' Another pause and no response. 'They put their enemies in a book and kill them.'

Becoming everything her family thought she was incapable of would be her revenge. But first, survive her banishment.

The vessel in which she was to travel over Bass Strait had been refurbished after the war to be a comfortable passenger ship moving people and cargo between the mainland and the ports in Devonport and Launceston. The first-class berth at the front of the boat had enough creature comforts for her to survive the 15-hour crossing of Bass Strait. It was a notoriously rough journey with unpredictable southerly winds whipping the sea into a rollercoaster of salt and spray. Her father and a life she could not even begin to imagine waited for her in Tasmania. All her reading had Ruby wondering if the island would be as wild and isolated as it had been described. She had two books in her hand luggage to read should the weather permit and although both harkened back to the convict days Ruby imagined she would find something akin to her own sense of exile in Marcus Clarke's *For the Term of his Natural Life* and Carolyn Woolmer Leakey's *The Broad Arrow*. If nothing else she might identify with the convicts who for so little a sin were ripped from their homes and hurled across the globe to unknown worlds.

A bit melodramatic but it suited Ruby's mindset. Fear, anger, distress and perhaps a little excitement. Afterall, a certain sense of freedom and adventure were part of every journey.

The driver helped Ruby with her trunk and case, walking her to the embarkation point. She carried with her a handbag, overnight case and her portable typewriter. She simply refused to have it stacked up with the other baggage and stock making its way to the island.

She stood among the other passengers. While the Loongana could take up to 200 travellers, she was well under capacity. Ruby estimated that there were fewer than 100 people milling about the pier in preparation for her evening sailing. Mainly men, dressed for business stood by the entrance to the gangway. A small number of families with over-excited and fidgety children stood further back farewelling non-travelling relatives and friends. A couple of young men in naval uniforms smoked by the embarkation point, possibly returning home after deployment and one older woman stood under the covered walkway. She held a walking stick and a large carpet bag. She looked steely and unfriendly but after surveying her fellow passengers she made a beeline for Ruby.

'Are you travelling on your own?' And before Ruby could answer, she continued. 'I am Miss Jessie Burke and I think you had better stick with me. A young woman on her own at sea may just attract the attention of dragons.'

'Dragons.' Ruby raised her eyebrows. 'The fire breathing reptile versions?' she questioned.

'No. The single male ones who blow a lot of hot air and occasionally singe the innocent.' Miss. Burke's matter of fact, no nonsense attitude convinced Ruby that it might be good to have an ally on the trip. At least she might be someone to talk to.

'Call me Burky. Everyone else does. What do I call you?'

'Ruby. Ruby Hart.' The older woman put her hand out to take Ruby's in hers. Her firm grasp and decisive handshake spoke more about Burky's capacity to handle any dragons, should they dare come near.

The passengers were shown to their cabins. As luck would have it, Ruby and Burky were opposite each other.

'Get settled Ruby Hart and meet me in the lounge for some tea. You seem to have a story, and I'd like to know it.' Jessie Burke open and closed her cabin door with the same forthright physicality as her handshake. It wasn't an invitation, more a command.

The lounge had begun to fill as Ruby arrived. Burky was not there so she chose a table by the windows, away from the noisy families who had also decided on afternoon tea before departure. The waiter arrived at the same time as Ruby's new friend. Even before she sat down she ordered tea and sandwiches for both of them.

'Proper sandwiches I hope. And a variety please. My companion here looks like she could make her way through quite a few.' The waiter glanced at Ruby and silently determined that she might just be able to consume a loaf of sandwiches.

'Now what's going on in your life that your off to Launceston?' Ruby described in the briefest of details that her father worked at Duck Reach, that he was an engineer, and having finished her leaving certificate she should join him there.

'Did you pass your exams?' Burky was nothing if not direct. Ruby confirmed that she had been very successful.

'Dux of Merrington. Very impressive Miss Hart. So why are you being buried in the southern outpost instead of going to university?'

It wasn't easily answered. Ruby provided sketchy information about her grandmother not being supportive and a sanitised version of Father Hewer's machinations in bringing the girls' dreams tumbling down.

'But I sense you haven't given up hope Miss Hart.'

'I will eventually get to university. However, I'm taking the circuitous route. A small delay while I find my feet. I'm going to write a novel while I'm in exile.' Ruby's childlike hopefulness brought a smile to Burky's lips.

'Good for you. We writers need to stick together.'

Ruby's interest drove her to be more inquisitive that social politeness would dictate.

'What do you write Burky? Tell me about you.' A pause while her manners overrode her enthusiasm. 'Please.'

The day ended, and dinner service had commenced in the dining room before Jessie Burke had finished her story. The woman had led an extraordinary life, an exemplary life that shone a bright light into the darkness of the world Ruby thought was lost to her. Burky had been born in 1870 into a farming family in South Gippsland. When her father died the bank took the land and her mother, Burky and three younger sisters were made homeless. The little family made its way to Melbourne and they eventually, due to poverty, were split up with all the girls going into care. But the fire of injustice ignited something in the young Jessie. 'I heard Henrietta Dugdale and Annie Lowe speak about the possibility of suffrage for women. They talked about not only getting the vote for women but the growing opportunities for us to go to university and be on an equal footing with men in professions like law, medicine and journalism.' Burky barely drew breath. 'Eventually graduated from Melbourne university with a degree in Classics. I wrote articles and textbooks for years on the changing roles of women. And lectured there myself until I was asked to join the National Council of Women.' Ruby's eyes widened at the life Burky had fought for.

'Became a researcher for Margaret Dale who headed the Traffic of Women and Children Commission and went to the international League of Nations as a humanitarian advisor.' Her list of accomplishments was astounding. It seemed a most serendipitous meeting.

In her mind Ruby thought that Burky had paved the way for girls like her. Had fought foes bigger than block head boys and intractable priests and disaffected fathers. She was everything Minnie had been and so much more. But Burky didn't have a face like Ruby's and the mere thought of it started to drain the confidence and hope.

'And your birthmark Miss Hart. Where do you stand on that?' It was as if the older woman had a psychic ability.

'I've been told it's an angel's kiss or a devil's mark. I think sometimes it's all people see.'

By this time the two women had finished dinner and the ship had left its berth.

'Well, that's some pretty heavy bullshit isn't it. Why do you think it's all people see?'

Ruby filled in the gaps of her grandmother's treatment. The stares and taunts of her early school mates and of course further detail about the night of the spring dance.

Burky didn't miss a beat. 'Your choice then I guess. Be your face or be yourself.'

'Is it a choice when other people only see this?' Ruby touched the long teardrop that ran around her eye and down her cheek.'

'You know what I learned long ago Ruby. What other people think of me is none of my business. It's what I think of me that is the most important opinion. If I see myself as strong, smart and a leader, then I am. Likewise if I see myself as small and unimportant then I guess that's all I'll ever be.'

The evening ended with an exchange of addresses. Jessie Burke was destined for Hobart after a brief stay in Launceston. She would take up a position at the beginning of the academic year at the university.

'I hope to see you there one day Ruby. Soon.'

Bass Strait behaved itself on the night crossing. The Loongana rocked gently over the waves and the wind hardly ruffled the crew who, at dawn, steered her across the northern coast to have a short stopover at Devonport to unload goods for local markets, fabrics and seed stock. Several of the families disembarked at the tiny port. Employment in mining and farming had boomed in the post war years and the appeal of work and cheap land had become a drawcard for many who couldn't find work in the cities on the mainland.

Within the hour the Loongana left to seek the mouth of the Tamar River. The heads of the western and eastern banks were quite narrow, but the sleek ship navigated the slightly rougher waters with ease. Ruby stood on the bow deck to watch the farms and tiny hamlets that populated the 43-mile winding estuary. By the time they had passed the Low Head lighthouse it was 9 am. Breakfast had been a noisy event but the food plentiful and quite delicious. Burky had not appeared, so Ruby ate alone. After her second cup of tea, she pocketed two apples and went on deck to see her temporary home appear. The calm waters of the river offered no impediment to the captain who slowed the engines to negotiate the ever-narrowing channel.

'She's very shallow here.' Ruby took her fellow passenger's commentary as a reference to the river. 'Tends to be a silty waterway from here on.'

Ruby turned to see who had joined her on the forward deck. A casually dressed young man introduced himself. 'Wally Pascoe.'

Ruby didn't know if she should give the man her name given Burky's earlier warning. But before she could even offer it he went on. 'So going to Launceston are you. It's a great little town. Grew up here but I've been in Melbourne for a year. Love the city. Think it will be a bit boring here now.' He didn't draw breath. 'Why are you coming to the island? Are you on your own?'

'To see my father. He's been working here.'

Wally stepped closer to Ruby and stared briefly at her face. 'Well maybe we will bump into each other. What did you say your name was?

'Rub…' It went unfinished.

'On your way lad. Her name is none of your business.' Burky had finally arrived. Wally somewhat taken aback muttered as he wandered off but not before he'd given Ruby a wink. The older woman watched him go and then said to her young acquaintance, 'Dragon.'

The two women laughed and continued watching the wide tidal flats spread out to the wooded hills. Within two hours the ship passed Beauty Point, Egg Island and Deviot. 'It's greener than Melbourne. More hills. Strange.' Ruby almost said this to herself.

'It is still got a sense of its earliest self. You can imagine what those first white settlers must have thought when they got here. Not to mention what the local indigenous people thought.' Burky and Ruby became lost in their own thoughts as the Loongana made her final turn into the confluence of the three rivers where Launceston had been founded. The Tamar ended and the North and South Esk Rivers began. The town had settled itself into a deep valley between steep ridges that had been gouged out millions of years before. One wondered how or why the town had come into existence given its distance from the bustling lives of the mainland cities. Yet here it was.

CHAPTER 12

Douglas Hart paced nervously by his new car. It had not long before arrived on a boat not dissimilar to the Loongana. The Citroen Estate Wagon was one of a handful of European cars tackling the poorly formed roads of the northern towns of Tasmania. But Douglas had been used to driving and loved the freedom of long exploratory trips to the northwest and east coasts. He never stopped marvelling at the diversity of the island state which seemed to divide itself neatly into four parts. The east coast defined by the long white sandy beaches, the west - wild and rugged, impenetrable in parts and the north and southern districts delineated by the towns in the midlands. He smiled at the thought of the tiny population separating itself so emphatically that maps may very well have had a black line stretching from one side to the other.

His thoughts interrupted only by the Loongana making her final turn into the Queens Wharf. Her long sleek body creeping forward into the berth set aside for her. The stevedores readying to secure the mooring ropes, at the bow and stern, chatted among themselves, dislodging butt ends of their cigarettes into the water. They wore a semblance of a uniform, *a grubby lot* Douglas thought. But he couldn't keep his mind on the milling workers and welcoming crowds. His thoughts ultimately went to his daughter. Ruby was a complete mystery to him, a stranger really. He had seen so little of her after she went to live with

Minnie and even less when he returned from the war. His visits to Melbourne during the last few years did not include making the effort to contact her. And now this. A ruckus at the school dance, his mother hysterical over the burdensome responsibility of a recalcitrant young woman and Ruby's flights of fancy about furthering her education. At university no less.

While Douglas tut-tutted about the encumbrance now foisted upon him, Ruby made her way from the boat to wharf. She carried her carpet bag and typewriter case, as she had done when she embarked in Melbourne. She too wondered at the complications to be faced when attempting to live with her father, in a place unknown to her. Without the support of her friends and Sister Reggie.

It took some time for the luggage and goods to make their way to the collection point at the mustering station located at the beginning of the timber walkway. Ruby identified her trunks and a small, somewhat ancient, porter hoisted her belongings onto a wooden barrow with surprising dexterity. 'Where 'm I taking your boxes miss?'

'I think my father has come to collect me. He might be waiting in the parking area.' Ruby of course had no idea if her father would be there or not. His last communication indicated that he would bring his car to meet her but gave no details about what the vehicle would be.

'Where y' headed miss.' The old man asked as he started to wheel his barrow towards the open area above the wharf.

'Duck Reach.'

'What 'cha gonna do up there? It's the power station. Nothing to do but watch the water come down the gorge.'

Ruby had no idea what she'd really be facing. 'I'm going to write a book.'

The old man looked at her with a degree of scepticism. He trudged on.

'Ruby.' The voice lacked any warmth. 'Unload that lot here old man.' Douglas readied some coins to press into the porter's hand when he had piled the luggage beside the car.

'Hello Father.' The words were awkward to say. Her mouth felt like it was filled with sand. 'Thank you for coming to get me.'

Awkward. Unfamiliar. Odd. Anyone witnessing the reunion of father and child would never have guessed the relationship. Ruby stood tall, statuesque, her long dark hair twisted back into a loose plait. An obviously athletic woman of a unique beauty marred only by her birthmark stood begrudgingly greeting a doughy, po-faced and cheerless man who seemed unable to unhunch his shoulders. He seemed to have developed a stoop, a potbelly and a grimace so well practised it seemed he had no other facial expression.

The two stood momentarily uncertain of how to proceed. Ruby broke the ice.

'Shall I get my luggage into the car.' Her voice spurred Douglas into action. With Ruby's help the steamer trunk and other items were stowed in the back of the wagon.

Ruby sat beside her father once they had everything sorted. 'This is a nice car. I don't think I've seen anything like it before.'

Douglas was suddenly on safer ground. He knew cars. 'It's a 1452 cc four-cylinder, French built beauty. Ten hp and all steel bodywork. The timber panels are connected to the frame. My friend in France organised to have it shipped out.' He didn't pause. 'HP is horsepower. It was conceptualized by James Watt. He was a Scottish engineer. Do you know what it means.'

Ruby didn't get a chance to answer despite knowing exactly what it was. Douglas continued.

'One horsepower is defined as the ability to move 550 pounds one foot in one second, or equivalently, 33,000 foot-pounds per minute.'

'The town looks bigger than I expected.' Ruby interrupted the diatribe on horsepower and engines.

'Wait till we get up the hill. You can look down and see how it's growing.'

True to his word, as the car rumbled up Cataract Hill, Douglas stopped so Ruby could look back over her shoulder to see the town as it filled the valley between the two ridges. Church spires and the post office clock were clearly evident on the eastern side of the town. Tram lines stretched in a t-shape taking residents to the south, north and west of the city centre.

'The tram will take you from the city centre to the top of Hillside Crescent and then it's quite a walk to the Reach, but the hill is the hard slog. It takes about thirty minutes. It's okay unless it's raining.' Douglas didn't seem to be able to stop himself from talking. Ruby thought it best just to let him ramble on. In fact, she found it preferable to having to talk about herself or the future. 'The house is set up for your arrival. I'm often not there, never during the day. The other women will be company until you get a job. They will show you the ropes.' Douglas stole a glance at his daughter who sat statue still, her hands folded in her lap, eyes turned away watching the dense bush grow around the dirt road. 'It can be lonely but I'm sure you will make do.' His voice hardened a little. 'It won't be forever.'

Ruby heartened a little at the thought of a short tenure. 'No it won't be for long because I'll be moving back to Melbourne on the day I turn 21.' She hadn't meant to sound coldly dispassionate, but it left Douglas in little doubt about her plans. It bought them both some sense of relief that neither would be burdening the other for longer than necessary.

The road dipped slightly at the end. On the right, the deep chasm of the gorge burbled over enormous dolerite rocks, the power station perched just above the water on the far side. The three residences stood at the end of the road. Austere bluestone buildings on the left hardly bid welcome. Small windows and shaded verandas reflected little of the lives going on within. 'The Lumleys and Birds live in the first two. You will get to know the ladies as they have been talking about your visit since I first told them you were coming. Their husbands are engineers and the other men live in the last one there on the left. Our house is right here.' Douglas brought the Citroen to a stop in front of house reserved for him. It was detached from the other accommodations and seemed somewhat grander in proportions. Beyond it the bush extended westward. A small garden had been started but the summer heat had dried up all attempts of flourishing. Dahlias hung their heads in defeat; the delphiniums and columbines shrivelled for lack of water. 'I thought it rained a lot here in Launceston. The plants are certainly thirsty.' Ruby had loved the gardens at Merrington and this sad impersonation of greenery added to her sense of melancholy.

'It's generally quite wet in winter but it has been a very dry summer and while there's plenty of water in the rivers there's been very little time for tending gardens. Maybe you can turn your hand to resurrecting it.' Douglas led the way into the house. The inside matched the outside for austerity. In the reception room a coat stand and small table were unadorned. The floors were polished but a dullness had settled upon them. But the house appeared to be clean. It had an orderliness that obviously suited her father's demeanour.

'My room is here at the front. Yours is at the back. It has a view up the hill and you can see some of the river that still flows from Deadman's Hollow.' Douglas went back to the car to retrieve Ruby's belongings. From the front door he said, 'Have a look around. Put your bags in the room. Maybe you could make us some tea.'

Maybe I could. Ruby's first thoughts were that her father might see her as his live-in maid. Tea making, cooking and cleaning for a grumpy old man who saw little value in her as anything else. A flash of frustration, a flood of fury and a deluge of disappointment boiled in her. The feelings had a short life. Behind her she heard the sound of heels clipping on the hall floor. Turning around she saw two women, both possibly thirty or a little more, possibly less.

'So Ruby Hart you do exist. When your father first said his daughter was coming to stay, we thought he was stringing us along. But here you are.' Bonnie Lumley moved forward with her hand outstretched to take Ruby's. 'I'm Bonnie and this is Stella Bird. Our husbands work with your father. And we help out here with a bit of cooking and cleaning. Douglas is a bit hopeless in the domestic field.' Bonnie seemed to be the spokeswoman for the two. 'Take your hat and coat off. I'll put the kettle on the fire.'

Stella then took her turn as she put her hands out for Ruby's outer garments and lay them over the arm of a leather couch. 'You're a tall girl. Must take after your mother.' Stella stopped as she realised that neither woman knew anything about Douglas' wife, other than she had died.

'I didn't really know her. In fact I didn't know her at all. She died in childbirth.' Ruby spoke unemotionally and hesitantly. She also felt uncertain about how much Douglas had revealed to his neighbours and perhaps spilling all the family secrets would not do anything to develop the relationship with him in a positive way.

'Douglas tells us that you lived with your grandmother and went to boarding school. He says you're terribly clever.' Stella seemed genuinely impressed. Ruby felt bewildered that her father would comment on her scholastic achievements seeing he was so keen to tear her away from any further educational opportunities.

Douglas joined the women after depositing Ruby's cases in the room he'd set aside for her. He was grateful that Bonnie and Stella had done all the setting up. Bedlinen had been newly purchased and a small, framed mirror had been installed on the oak dresser. He had assumed that young women might like to look at themselves. Although perhaps not Ruby. He wondered about her birthmark and whether it was as disfiguring as his mother made it out to be. On meeting her at the wharf he didn't see what the fuss was about. Ruby bore no resemblance to him; she was all Alma. Same intense blue eyes, dark hair and tall. The raspberry mark dipped and arced around her eye and completed a tear shape on the underside of her high cheekbones. He wondered if she had any idea of how lovely she was.

'I see you have all made each other's acquaintance. I didn't think it would take you two long to come and meet my daughter.' Douglas turned to Ruby. 'I think they imagined I'd made you up.' Ruby nodded politely at her father, smiled coyly at the two women.

'I'm real. And I'm here.' Ruby found it hard to keep her tone light.

The talk turned to the next phase of Ruby's life. Both women drove and were determined that their new young friend should learn to do so. In the meantime, a new bicycle had been bought and it would make the journey from Basin Road to the Reach much easier. 'The walk is lovely but it does take time. But nowhere near as long now the tram comes all the way to Denison Road. You can leave your cycle at Miss Hangton's place. She is happy for you to just prop it on her veranda and pick it up when you get back from town. We've already talked to her.'

It seemed the Duck Reach welcoming committee had Ruby's life planned for her.

'And of course you will need a job.' Before Bonnie and Stella could offer further proposals, they were interrupted by a sharp knock at the door. The husbands, Alf Lumley and Harry Bird had finished their shift at the power station and were looking for their lunch. They also wanted to catch a glimpse of the boss's girl. They were as amazed as their wives that the boss had a child. They politely nodded at the newcomer. Noted the face, admired the unspoiled youth despite her birthmark and shook their heads wondering why Ruby Hart would want to be here.

The question consumed the two couples as they walked back to the neighbouring houses. 'What on earth is there for a girl of her age to do here?'

CHAPTER 13

And Ruby wondered that too.

While the area had a wild beauty and an exquisite silence it could not replace Melbourne. Ruby had grown up in the city and knew the noises of traffic, trams and people. She walked on footpaths and dodged cars and carts on her Saturday morning visits to the swimming baths. There were people everywhere, even at school; particularly at school, silence was a rare thing. Her grandmother's house resembled a mausoleum, hence Ruby's restlessness when she had to live there but she made her own noise. Minnie's home was part circus, theatre and dance hall all rolled into one. Of course, there were quiet times when she studied or wrote or dreamed but the quiet of the bush had a disconcerting element. Bird song, rustling trees, movement of water and the slight hum and reverberation of the turbines filled the first nights and days.

Ruby's first task after the unpacking and familiarising herself with the household was to write to those left behind. Sister Reggie, Al, Della, Mrs. Rowlands and Elvie and Caleb were all told the same story. The trip across the strait, the company of Jessie Burke, the reunion with her father, meeting Bonnie and Stella, and a description of the strange little town that would become her home, filled the pages of appropriate news. For Della the letter included her great pain at the loss of their friendship, Ruby's fears of finding herself bereft of purpose and the interminable months and years of her exile. In Al's letter she talked about the novel she would write, identifying the villains as her grandmother and Father Hewer. *They will hardly be disguised* she wrote. Ruby made sure that she wrote positively of her successful arrival and possible opportunities in both missives to Reggie and Mrs. Rowlands. To Elvie and Caleb, she bemoaned the lack of suitable footwear for traversing the wilds of the Cataract Gorge. *Trousers and lace up brogues are on the list of things to buy.* Her embroidered shirts and fitted skirts would be an impediment to her wild cycling and bush walks. All in all, she kept the tone light, the hopes high and her general misery under wraps.

Plus, the novel would not write itself so that task would fill the time sitting alone in her room. Bonnie and Stella called on her most mornings after Douglas went to work. They showed her the bicycle, the gorge path that would lead to the First Basin and the Reserve Gardens, also adding detailed information about the tram stop and where to store her bike. 'There are lots of places looking for workers.' Stella spoke keenly about the opportunities that had come to her. 'Kelsall and Kemp are always looking for women to work the factory floor. It might be fairly challenging but there will be lots of young ones about your age there. Chance to meet some friends.'

'The Tea House needs servers. Can you cook?' Bonnie threw in some of her own suggestions. 'Or Gourlay's Sweet Shop. I'd love to work there.'

'Why don't you?' Ruby's question hadn't meant to sound critical but Bonnie looked a little taken aback by the abruptness of it. 'Sorry Bonnie I didn't mean to sound rude. I'm very grateful for your suggestions.'

'We are just busy with the family, we have little ones and that keeps us both on our feet. Plus, we do some work for the station. Cleaning and some typing.' Stella explained.

Ruby hadn't seen the children despite seeing their swings and toys in the small front gardens. She imagined that they went to school or were too little for outdoor play. 'How old are they?'

'We only have the one. Allie. He's 8 and goes to school. You'll see him on the weekends no doubt. And Stella has two girls.'

'They are 10 and 11. Also at school.' Stella wound up the conversation about work and children by offering to teach Ruby to drive. 'We can both help you with lessons. If we could learn I'm sure a smart young thing like you will pick it up in a flash.'

The thought of driving thrilled Ruby. It would mean a little more freedom than her bicycle or walking would offer. But in the interim, before the lessons commenced, she decided to explore on foot.

The walk from Duck Reach to the Alexandra Suspension Bridge was not long but it did have its challenges. The path had been hewn into rocks and the uneven cuttings that formed most of the steps took the walker up and down the face of the gorge cliff. In parts it was steep, the steps taking two strides in places. The flatter surfaces were hardly smooth and Ruby was pleased that she had packed an old pair of canvas tennis shoes. Anything with a heel would have been disastrous as much of the path had no barrier between the steps and the plunge into the dark green water. Ruby peered over the edge of the lowest cliff. In places it moved, rippling towards the Tamar River, in other sections the water collected in deep emerald pools that were both inviting and yet frightening. She could only wonder at what lay on the bottom, or indeed where the bottom might be. It made her shudder to think of the creatures that might lurk in the dark. Slimy eels, fish with globule eyes and monsters. Perhaps her imagination might help her write a fantasy story like H.G. Wells. Places full of leviathans and fears or maybe something more tepid in its fantastical nature like Beatrix Potter. *But first a novel of revenge.* Ruby smiled to herself as she stepped away from the edge and walked towards the suspension bridge that would take her from the wild world of the cliff walk to the newly established gardens on the northern side of the First Basin.

The Alexandra Suspension Bridge surprised Ruby. It really was a swinging bridge. The timber batons formed a solid deck upon which to walk the 150 feet across the Gorge. Steel towers and wide cables were anchored through turnbuckles into the solid rock on each side. Her first steps upon the walkway seemed steady and the bridge offered little movement, perhaps a tiny vibration could be felt. But by the time she reached the centre of the bridge the movement became more of a sway to the left and right, small but perceptible. The up and down motion more disconcerting. Each step increased the sensation of instability. Her logical mind reinforced the actual safety of the crossing but the feeling in her body told a different story. Ruby increased the pace at which she traversed the bridge, but haste made the movement more dramatic. None-the-less her emotions overrode her commonsense and she ran the last 30 feet to end the discomfort.

On the other side she stood flush faced, panting and feeling ridiculous. 'For goodness sake Ruby Hart, get a grip on yourself.'

'You're not the first to have a bit of a panic at the halfway mark. I've seen less dignified exits than yours.' A young man stood five feet below the platform on which Ruby stood. He looked up at her, gently laughing. 'It can't fall down you know. It would take magic to extract those cables from the anchor points.'

Ruby was sweaty and a little beside herself. 'I didn't really think it was falling. I just wasn't sure I like the sensation of bouncing up and down over a gorge.' A reasonable defence she thought. The man, dressed in gardener's wear bounded up the steps that separated them. He stretched out his hand to take Ruby's.

'Lawton Timblett. Horticulturalist, gardener and artist.' His hand felt warm and rough in Ruby's, his smile disarming.

'Ruby Hart. Writer, seeker of work and transportee.' She smiled at her own joke.

'Oh an émigré from the great island to our north I take it. How are you finding the southern climes?'

'It's fine. I'm adjusting.' She paused and looked beyond the young man over his shoulder. 'The gardens look wonderful. Have you worked here long?'

'Long enough. Are you walking into the town?' Ruby nodded although she wasn't sure this was her intention.

'Maybe just exploring a bit.'

'I'll walk you to the main path.'

The gardener led the way to the Gorge Walk through the winding lower gardens. In the distance Ruby caught her first glimpse of the band rotunda. To her further surprise she saw several peacocks and their dowdy female mates scratching in the dirt. Occasionally raising their heads to *kee-ow* to each other.

'Noisy buggers but they are beautiful.' The iridescent jade and indigo feathers fanned out behind them or lay tucked into a long tail. The mesmerising eyespots glinting in both positions.

'They're not native to Australia. Why are they here?' Ruby always had a question about everything.

'These ones came from India. The Victorians loved them, so much of this garden is based on the exotic landscaped parks in London. Exotic plants and birds. And just to make it completely mad the locals turn up.' The gardener pointed to the wallabies that had hopped through the rhododendrons that formed a hedge around the rotunda.

The gardens were reminiscent of the Botanical and Flagstaff parks in Melbourne. Only these ones were surrounded by native bush and not traffic. It was as if the beauty had been carved out of the forest of blackwood trees and swamp paperbarks. Just beyond the neatly mowed lawns lay something impenetrable.

Lawton had a little more to say on the matter. 'You know this was just a muddy swamp thirty years ago. The locals who wanted to access the gorge spent three years dynamiting the rocks out of the main path and clearing out the lateral gullies to dry out this area. Not so long ago instead of peacocks the place was full of snakes and frogs.'

Ruby shuddered a little at the thought. 'Thanks for the information. I appreciate it.' She gave her informant a small wave. 'I'll probably see you again. I'll no doubt walk this way quite a bit.'

'Where are you staying?' Ruby stopped walking, wondering if it was right to tell him her address.

But then cast caution to the wind. 'Duck Reach. My father is an engineer there.'

'You know if you are really interested in writing and art I have a group who meets here at the rotunda on Sundays until the weather turns. You would be very welcome to join us.'

Ruby just nodded. Not an assent but more acknowledging the possibility of joining a group of writers. Not to mention the possibility of seeing Lawton Timblett again. She had so little experience of men, other than Caleb and other friends of Minnie. The disastrous encounter with the meathead boys at the spring dance didn't count nor did the bullying of Father Hewer or the disinterest of her male relatives. But a young man, full of life and interest, handsome and a little rugged…well that was altogether different. Ruby wished for Della or Al to suddenly appear. They would know how to handle an invitation. They would also know if such an experience had risk or not. Self-doubt began to move through her.

Just walk Ruby. Stop over thinking everything.

Self-recrimination wore away with the brisk walk. The path was sealed and much easier to get up to pace. The track again clung to the gorge walls, this time on the northern side. The river had picked up a little as it flowed towards the town. The Kings Bridge spanned the narrowest point between the two cliff faces. Its cream and burgundy wrought iron linked the road to the north where new townhouses clung to the Trevallyn cliffs and the small orchards lined the foreshore of the Tamar all the way to Bass Strait. It seemed that the town was growing, burgeoning in all directions. Just before the bridge and overhanging the path the gatekeeper's cottage had been propped improbably on the cliff wall. The tiny weatherboard house appeared to be in command of who came and went. The front veranda held up by wooden trusses looked unsafe at best. Ruby wondered who might now live in the house given the gardens no longer had a porter.

Ruby began to feel quite exhausted after her long walk, particularly given she wore entirely the wrong shoes for this level of exploration. She crossed the bridge stopping to look west up the river. It wound through the cliffs that rose on either side and disappeared around the bend. *A great setting for a story to unfold. Something gothic perhaps*, she thought as she walked on into the town centre. She passed a flour mill, a quarry, the Launceston State High School, the Victorian Swimming Baths and finally the main street. Brisbane Street was a hive of activity. Trams and cars and bikes fought for space on the wide road.

It certainly wasn't Melbourne, but it had that same feeling. People were going somewhere. It had a sense of purpose and Ruby felt that it might not be the worst place to live. Just maybe it would be an adventure worth having.

The Kar-Pi Tearooms in the Quadrant Arcade gave Ruby's feet some respite from the considerable distance they had travelled. She had luckily tucked her small coin purse into the pocket of her skirt which contained enough money to cover the cost of a pot of tea and a slice of lemon teacake. She realised that she barely met the dress standards of taking tea given her flushed face, untidy hair and tennis shoes. The ladies who had gathered for morning tea were somewhat po-faced when snatching glances at the dishevelled young person who arrived without a hat, or gloves. *And that face*. Ruby had momentarily forgotten that along with her general untidiness her birthmark still encouraged intrusion.

Tea consumed, cake eaten, Ruby made a surreptitious exit from the café and found the tram stop that would take her to the top of Cataract Hill. Her legs simply didn't have the strength to climb a hill of that incline. She'd still have to walk along Corin Drive to get to the Reach.

The day ended with Ruby recovering on the couch in the front room of her father's house. Feet released from those terrible shoes, legs up on a cushion she vowed to buy some sensible walking boots and clothes next time she went to town. With her notepad and pencil, and in her reclined position, she started writing. She wanted something to share with the Sunday meeting at the rotunda.

She held her under the murky green water until the bubbles ceased. In her mind she had done herself a favour, maybe the whole world. The old woman had been punished at last.

CHAPTER 14

The week had been a busy one. Her father happily parted with money so Ruby could buy shoes and a few outfits suitable for walking, and for work when it came. Bonnie and Stella drove her in their car and helped her select boots, some trousers and a few sensible dresses for the job they were sure would come. They had suggested the textiles factory and other smaller, perhaps more refined places for her to seek employment. On the way back Ruby had her first driving lesson.

She felt uncoordinated and awkward in the driver's seat. Everything felt unfamiliar but the thrill of taking the wheel soon replaced doubt. The clutch and gears required real concentration and initially she found it impossible to move the gear stick and steer the cumbersome vehicle in a straight direction. Bonnie virtually sat on her knee to ensure the car stayed on the road, somewhere in the vicinity of the lane she was meant to be in. Her husband had bought the Chevrolet Superior Tourer with money he'd been left after his father died. 'It's his pride and joy but he works so much he never gets to drive much. So it pretty much became mine.' Bonnie seemed a little breathless with the effort of helping Ruby steer from the left had side of the car. Stella offered some back seat suggestions to help the learner with gear changes.

'Is the grinding sound normal?' The older women laughed at the question. 'Well we all did it when we started. You'll get the hang of it.'

The three of them went out every day when the men were working. Alf and Harry worked shifts as supervisors at the power station. Douglas mainly worked the day shift but he seemed to spend many hours in the office attached to the turbine room. Often he would be home for a meal at 6 pm and then return to work until midnight. He never had breakfast with Ruby. He was a ghost who left a vague impression that he lived in the house. He had passed the message via Alf or Harry that the driving lessons could be conducted in his Citroen. 'Might as well wear the gears out in all the cars eh Ruby?' Bonnie laughed as the three set off.

Ruby improved rapidly. Her serious approach to learning made her a very focused and committed driving student. On the weekend, the daily driving had to be suspended as her new friends had responsibilities with their children and relatives. Douglas did not offer any outing to Ruby so with the neighbours away it made sense that she would walk down to the gardens and meet with Lawton and the other writers. While she felt uncomfortable about meeting strangers, who were most likely more experienced writers than her, she did want to see the handsome gardener again.

On Sunday Douglas had no expectation that the Harts would attend Mass. So, Ruby attired in her new boots and travelling breeches headed off to the rotunda. In her satchel she took typed pages of her novel and some examples of the short stories she wrote while at school. The walk, now familiar, became easier without the encumbrance of a long skirt and poor shoes. She had also packed the freshly baked cookies that had been left for Douglas and some cheese and bread. Ruby wanted every eventuality covered. Including hunger. Particularly hunger. Or perhaps sharing something might help her fit in with the group she had been loosely invited to meet.

The rotunda was empty when she arrived. But it gave her time to take in her surroundings. Autumn seemed to have started early. *Maybe it did in Tasmania,* she thought. The leaves on some of the non-native species were beginning to turn, a slight crimson noticeable on their edges. The peacocks were sounding far off, their calls coming from the lawn that made its way down to the northern side of the basin. To her right an echidna appeared, burrowing its long nose in the fallen leaves, searching for grubs proliferating in the dampness.

While she took in the wonders of nature she didn't see a small group of people appearing from the Gorge path. They were chatting quietly and hadn't noticed Ruby until they were at the steps. A curious group. Full of colour and what might have been described as having a bohemian flavour. As she had expected they were definitely older than her. A man, the oldest possibly, spoke first. 'Are you the delightful ingénue Lawton said might join us.' His voice sounded smooth, practiced and slightly theatrical. The look completed by his white linen suit and fingers adorned with gold rings.

Ruby gathered herself, not wanting to look like a gormless chit staring with her mouth open.

'Yes. Lawton did say you might meet here today. I hope you don't mind me coming along.' She took a breath. 'I'm Ruby Hart.'

'Hollis Bright. You are a dear young thing.' The older man stretched out his hand to take Ruby's. And very gallantly kissed the top of her hand. 'These scraggy few are some of the other members of our little club. Not everyone could make it today.' Hollis smiled mischievously, raising his eyebrows. 'A terrible collective headache has come over some of them.'

'You're a club?' Ruby's eyebrows rose almost as high as Hollis's.

'Well loosely. A kind of club. It's just so we know who we are talking about.' Lawton had appeared from behind the rotunda. 'The Aphorism Club at your service.'

'Aphorism?'

'Truth or wisdom.' The woman answered Ruby.

'Let's call it a kind of truth. An observation about life that is often true,' Hollis laughed. 'In most lives or just particularly our lives.'

The others were introduced. Jules Warner, Maxine Whitlock and Florian Smith had arrived with Hollis. They were all equally as interesting as each other.

'Unfortunately Capricorn and Pooky couldn't make it today. Still in bed I think.'

The group arranged themselves around a small picnic table that Lawton had brought and each one took a turn at introducing themselves to the newcomer.

Maxine Whitlock spoke with a no-nonsense attitude. 'I write for the local paper, The Examiner. And I'm a playwright too. Working with the Launceston Players Society at the moment getting some of our work on stage.' With barely a pause she asked, 'Do you act? You look like someone we could find a part for.'

'Florian. I write plays with Maxy sometimes, but my real work is as an illustrator. Cartoons mainly.' He shook Ruby's hand with some vigour. 'And if I want to eat and pay the rent I tend the bar at the Cornwall Hotel.'

'We all have to suffer for our art Flo.' Jules leant over the table, interrupting Florian. 'God you are a gorgeous thing. I'm writing a novel.' His face came very close to Ruby's. 'I like the fact that you don't cover this up.' His hand waved over her cheek with a flourish. Up close Ruby could see that Jules wore a smudge of eyeliner and some pale lipstick which highlighted his soft features. Perhaps he seemed a little feminine, his high cheekbones and small chin gave him something of a girlish look. 'I also teach dancing if you're interested.'

Ruby smiled and nodded at the assembled group. Lawton sat beside her. 'We are all a bit over the top on the first meeting. And we get worse on the second.' His smile, wide and genuine made her heart jump. She felt colour rising from her neck. 'I don't write. I draw and paint. And I referee this lot.'

The group laughed and then the talk moved on to the work they brought with them. While they talked and shared ideas, Lawton made sketches and added his calming directions when the group got too rowdy. There was sincere interest in Ruby's work and thoughtful commentary on the worlds she had created in the stories she read aloud.

The time went by quickly. Food and drink punctuated the readings, the editorial suggestions and the fighting. Ruby offered her biscuits and cheese to the eclectic picnic that seemed to appear out of nowhere. Wine and a flask of whiskey made their way around the table. Ruby refused both.

'You look more like a Bees Knees kind of girl.' Hollis gently mocked Ruby.

'What's that?'

'A cocktail. Made with gin and honey. But maybe you're more a Mary Pickford girl. All that pineapple juice masks the taste of the rum.'

'I'm not an anything girl. I've never had an alcoholic drink.'

Hollis almost choked when feigning shock and gave a dramatic inhale of breath. 'Never ever had a drink. Well, we will have to work on that my dear.'

Lawton gently put his hand on Ruby's arm. That smile again…calming, yet unsettling. 'You're probably not old enough to drink Ruby.'

'I'm 18. That's old enough according to the law in Victoria.'

Ruby's birthday had been and gone in the week after the exams. No fuss, no cake, no celebration. A small gift from friends. Money from her father. And a year closer to emancipation.

'Tassie doesn't have a drinking age so it's a knees up for everyone.' Hollis had another long swig from his silver flask. Fed and lubricated the discussion went on for a few hours.

The temperature dropped around 3 pm. The autumn shadows lengthened. The writing party collectively shivered, and scarves were wound more tightly around shoulders and necks. As everyone packed their respective bags Maxine stood beside Ruby.

'Are you looking for work?' Ruby nodded. 'Because I have an idea for you.'

Ruby liked Maxine's confidence. She wasn't particularly tall, in fact she was quite short, but her confident demeanour took up space. 'I'm looking for a junior to help me with the paper's supplement, *The Weekly Courier*. We also get a few stories in the *Ways of a Woman's World* in the weekend edition. And it looks like you can write. The editor said I could take on a junior and you seem to fit the bill. Interested?'

Ruby couldn't believe the stroke of luck. *Interested.* That was an understatement.

'Our editor is Stanley Dryden and while he's a bit of an old fart he is looking to encourage a wider readership. And that means women.'

Ruby could barely get the words out. 'Yes. I want to. Yes. I mean thank you Maxine.' She tripped over her words in her enthusiasm. 'How? Where?'

'Paterson Street office. 9.30 tomorrow. We will see if it's a fit.'

As the group wandered away Ruby couldn't move for her overwhelming sense of good fortune. She didn't want to break the spell.

'Been a good day then.' Lawton's voice surprised her.

Ruby could only nod. And return his smile.

'I think I'll be seeing more of you Ruby Hart.' Lawton started to walk away with his table and sketch books under his arms. 'And that will be a very good thing. I've left something for you on your bag.'

On top of her leather satchel he'd left a page. A pencil sketch of Ruby, her head down over her notebook, her hair escaping the ribbon, came to life on the page. In the hours the group chatted and talked, Lawton had captured an image of Ruby that she never seen of herself. Or even imagined. A woman, intense, amused, coy and whimsical appeared. It was her, but not her. A version that she aspired to be, lived in those pencil lines. Faintly he had drawn her birthmark as a shadow. He had made it a thing of beauty and wonder.

Her walk back over the bridge and across the cliff path was accompanied by imaginings and thoughts about how Lawton had seen her, her new writing friends and the possibilities that might come with a job at the local paper. In an instant, in an afternoon at least, the world had turned on a penny. For Ruby Hart, for once...maybe, the coin had turned up heads.

CHAPTER 15

Bonnie Lumley happily drove Ruby down the hill to the newspaper offices. She had an appointment with her doctor. *Women's business* she almost whispered it out of the side of her mouth.

'Don't worry about waiting for me Bonnie. I'll catch the tram and walk home after the interview.' Ruby could barely contain her excitement. She wanted to skip like a schoolchild but thought the editor, nor Maxine would appreciate such giddiness. Instead, she smoothed the pleats of her new skirt and pulled at the hem of the matching grey jumper. One of Caleb's shimmery scarves set off the drab professional look of the sensible ensemble and brightened the blue of her eyes. Bonnie had insisted that she at least put on some lipstick and borrow a hat. A little blue beret picked up the aquatic tones in the scarf and kept her hair in check. Other than holding it back in an elasticised band, Ruby's hair usually had a mind of its own, tending to curl and ripple out in all directions. *Like a rat's nest* Edwina Hart often described it.

Inside The Examiner office a receptionist, with a stern face, spoke over the noise of busy typewriters and journalists talking in loud voices. In the distance the sound of printing presses clanking into life added to the general sense of activity.

'I'm to meet Maxine Whitlock. She said to come in at 9.30.'

The receptionist, Mrs. Bounds, according to her name plaque, waved Ruby over to a waiting area beyond the noisy front office. Before getting to a chair, Maxine appeared on the stairs that led up to the next floor. 'Don't bother getting your bum settled on the that chair Miss Hart. Get those long legs moving and follow me.'

The stairs took them up two flights. It was much quieter on the second floor although Ruby could hear voices coming from several of the small offices. At the end of the corridor, the door marked Chief Editor opened. Stanley Dryden looked impatient and quite fed up with the world. 'Is this your girl?' Brusque and to the point. It looked like he had no intention of letting the two women into his space. 'Think she can do the job?' He looked at Ruby with a scrutinising glare.

'She's smart. She writes. She wants to learn. What else do you want?' Maxine was as sharp as her boss.

'I've never won an argument with you yet Maxy and I'm sure I'm not going to win this one.' He stopped to put his unlit pipe in his mouth. 'I've been doing this job for nearly forty years and I've not won an argument with a woman yet. Today is not the day to give it another try.'

He turned to go back in. 'What's your name?'

'Ruby Hart sir.' Ruby felt like she was back at school.

'Welcome on-board Miss Hart. Maxy's a great teacher but she'll run you ragged. If it's what you want I'm happy to put you on staff.' In the process of shutting his door he looked at Maxine. 'Don't break this one Max.' Door slammed.

The two women made their way back downstairs. 'We don't get a desk in the general journalists' room. We get a little cubby out the back. But one day I'm having that office we almost got into today. You want to start now?'

Ruby couldn't think of a reason not to begin her new career. By lunchtime Maxine had given Ruby the lay of the land. Starting and finishing times. The scope of the work, the pay, the perks, the downside, the need to finishing learning to drive and which men to avoid in *the pit*. 'That's what we call the men's club in that front room. Most of them are great reporters and can write a story that takes the reader right to the scene. But some of them are also lecherous pigs who despite having wives and kids think a woman's bum is theirs for the feeling.' Maxine sensed Ruby's shock. 'Sorry kid. Just out of Catholic school and you're suddenly in the real world. But best to know it now. Don't want any surprises.'

Ruby didn't want surprises, and she would certainly be staying out of *the pit*. She couldn't wait to write to the girls about her new job, the writers' group and Lawton. Even thinking about him was a distraction. And she didn't need a distraction as she had been given the task of sorting out the diary for the next fortnight. The women's world section reported on fund-raising parties, weddings, fashion and the importance of major world events and how they might affect a woman's home. Maxine had given Ruby several examples of each type of story and a list of times and places that such things would be occurring. 'We turn up, we take some pictures and some notes. We chat politely with the main players, and we come back here and write it up.'

Maxine seemed to be doing her best to make the days sound mundane, but Ruby found the prospect of attending community events and asking questions quite exciting. The next few days were to be filled with visits to the Albert Hall to meet with the organisers planning to upgrade the banquet room, the Queen Victoria Museum and Art Gallery to speak to the curator about the zoological display and then The Royal Society of Tasmania to attend their presentation on meteorology.

Even more important they were to do a story on the Launceston Players and the play that Maxine and Florian had written.

While Ruby made some notes and wrote what she thought might be pertinent questions for each story Maxine sat at her typewriter putting the final details on a story about Reginald and Andrea Hooper's daughter's lavish wedding. The custom-made silk dress was rumoured to have cost over £45. 'Bloody ridiculous.' Maxine muttered. 'Could feed half the women in Launceston for that.'

She went back to typing. Ruby continued filling the pages of her new notebooks with more questions than would ever be needed for the pieces she and Maxine would write.

'I've got too many questions Maxine but I just couldn't stop thinking about all the things we might want to know.'

'Calm your farm kid. Your enthusiasm is killing me.' Maxine laughed. 'Time for home. How are you getting up the hill?'

'Tram and then a walk.'

'It'll be dark by the time you get off the tram. You'll break an ankle walking home on that dirt road. Come back to our place and Lawton can drive you home.'

They left the office at 5.15 and the daylight faded quickly. By the time winter came the last light would come just after 5 pm. It would mean a dark walk in the cold if Ruby didn't learn to drive soon. It would also mean Douglas would have to let her have the car on weekdays. *Maybe she could get her own car.* Big thoughts, mad thoughts. *Hope springs eternal.*

Maxine lived in a terrace house on Margaret Street. A short walk from the office. By the time they got there the streetlights had turned on and offered pools of yellow illumination to show the way. The windows of the terrace showed someone had beaten Maxine home. The lights shone through the uncovered windows.

'I share with Hollis, Jules, and Capricorn. Hollis owns the place and we all pay a little bit of rent. Florian and Pooky live around the corner above the Blanche Café.'

'Does Lawton live here too?'

'No he lives in the gatekeeper's cottage near Kings Bridge. You would have seen it if you walked the Gorge path. He might as well live here he's here so often. And he leaves his bike on the front garden. We are like a communal carpark and flop house.'

The door was unlocked and from inside came music, voices and the smell of something cooking.

'I'm home. And I've bought the child.' Maxine laughed as she dragged Ruby through the hall to the back of the house where the action boiled. For Ruby the place reminded her of Minnie's home. The noise, the food and the shared commotion. Lawton sat on a stool resting his elbows on a long shelf that jutted out into the room. Hollis and Jules squeezed themselves together on a chaise lounge that had seen better days. Both wore matching robes. Florian appeared to be cooking.

'Ruby you haven't met Capricorn or Pooky. They be these two.' Pooky sat in an upright dining chair dressed in workman's clothes. His feet were bare, startlingly white which contrasted with the deep grime of his overalls.

'My sorrow at my dishevelment, neiti. Or should I say missy. This is right no.'

'Pooky's from Finland. His English is all over the place.' Hollis explained politely.

'All over the place with his English is so much better than my Finnish. I don't have any at all.' Ruby smiled at the man who stood and bowed at her.

'Cleaning of myself before the better meeting I think.'

The final member of the kitchen stared darkly from the doorway. 'Foreigners. Can't understand a word they say, eh?' Her own strong accent making the point more amusing than critical. 'I am Capricorn.'

She certainly had a flair for the dramatic. Capricorn's thick dark hair had been cut into a blunt bob, the fringe ending at her severely arched eyebrows. Her theatrical look continued to her long velvet jacket button on the hip, under which she wore nothing. Verdant green satin pants flared from the thigh and ended with bell-bottomed cuffs.

'Hello.' Ruby could say little more to the extraordinary woman who had not moved from the doorway. She could not have been taller than a child but still somehow looked threatening.

'She's Portuguese and her name is Beatriz. Call her that at your peril.' Lawton offered this as a way of explanation.

Capricorn moved into the room. Somewhat stiff legged and Ruby wondered if she was injured. The tiny Portuguese child-woman came right up to Ruby and stared at her. 'You are in the right place girl. Welcome to the demimonde.'

The reason for the stiff walking became apparent as the mad-eyed woman drew a sword from the deep folds of her trousers and held it in front of Ruby's face. 'By my Carracks black sword I now baptise you to the half-world.' She tapped Ruby's forehead with the flat of the sword and laughed. 'You should see your face.'

Ruby was sure she had blushed crimson at the bizarre ceremony Capricorn performed. The others completely impervious to the oddity.

'Well you belong now Miss Hart. Demimonde, half world, Aphorism Club. You're now in.' Hollis had extracted himself from the lounge and put his hands on her shoulders. 'We are all a bit on the fringe dear one, but you'll get use to us.'

The strange group gathered around the table. Mismatched bowls and plates were filled with soup and long rolls; butter and strange cheeses Ruby had never tried. The conversation covered the events of the day, their writing, the other business of money and work. Each spoke, everyone listened, they mocked and joked and complimented one another. This strange conglomerate had formed a family of sorts. Much like the one Ruby had so loved when she lived with Minnie. The unique, the intensely odd and the misfits all had a place at this table, as they had at her aunt's when she was a child.

So odd, but so familiar and comfortable. Ruby, although a real stranger, did not feel like an interloper. Did not feel outside the group. Perhaps Capricorn's little ceremony really made her part of this family. Sometimes you find your people.

But she had to return to her home. Ruby felt certain that her father would think she had been murdered or fallen into the gorge on her way from work. Lawton and Maxine drove her home in Hollis' car. Douglas had been home, eaten and had returned to the power station. He'd not really even noticed that she had missed dinner and had arrived home with strangers.

But Stella noticed. She appeared at the door just as Ruby kicked off her shoes and put the kettle on the fire.

'Long day for the first day on the job.' Stella called out as she walked in. 'Your colleagues dropped you off?'

Ruby gestured for Stella to come in and have tea. She wanted to tell someone about her day as a junior reporter. Well, that was the fancy title she gave herself.

Stella listened to Ruby's bubbly excitement about the work she imagined that was a head for her but the joy of it diminished when the real reason for the evening visit revealed itself.

'I'm so sorry to rain on your parade Ruby but I've got bad news about Bonnie. She went to the doctor this morning after she dropped you off.' Stella paused to gain control of her sadness. 'It's a tumour. She thought she might finally be having another baby but it's not. It's a terrible cancer that can't be treated.' Stella's face contorted with the awfulness of the news.

Ruby put her hand on Stella's shoulder as the older woman allowed the floodgates of misery to open. Words were useless here. All one could really do was offer comforting sounds and a place for the agony to be expressed.

Poor Bonnie. The repeated thought in Ruby's head. *Poor Stella*. So hard to lose a friend. Ruby's thoughts immediately went to Winnie and her aunt. So hard to bear the outrageous cruelty of fate. *What is God thinking in allowing all this misery?*

CHAPTER 16

The winter arrived for real. The days were short, and the night and morning temperatures were truly freezing. Duck Reach was frosty and ice dry. The sun failed to appear before 7 and condensation dripped on the inside of the windows and frost marbled the outside. Ruby had bought an overcoat from Ludbrooks. The brown woollen velour fabric felt soft and neatly cinched at the waist with a buttoned belt. Fashionable, grown-up and more importantly warm.

Particularly necessary for the drive in Douglas's heater-less car. Ruby had quickly mastered the necessary skills for driving. The gears occasionally still grated but the handling became efficient. Douglas was more than happy for her to have the car during the week, but he wanted access on the weekends to further his exploration of the area. This excluded the time he would occasionally go to Melbourne or take the train to Hobart. The car afforded Ruby a greater freedom than she ever expected.

It also allowed her to provide some support for Stella who had taken on the role of caring for Bonnie. While the doctor had given the worst prognosis and had ruled out surgery, he did think a course of radiation treatment might give her more time, perhaps less pain. 'He's just guessing at this point.' Bonnie's grim humour kept her going. 'Finally thin enough to fit into my wedding dress again.' She had certainly lost weight and her colour mutated from pale to grey. The worst of the disease was yet to come.

Work became the great distraction. Life there provided a degree of amusement and a flurry of activity. There were parties and fundraisers, social gatherings and fashion shows to write puff pieces about. The real reports about accidents, financial crises and criminality were not stories for the women. *According to the men.*

But Maxine had ideas about the stories they could write. Things happening in the shadows, things no-one was reporting on but needed the light that journalism could shine on them. 'There's stories out there in the community that no-one wants to know about.' Maxine said most days. 'We need to have the moxie to get out there and investigate.'

'What stories?' Ruby, despite having quite the education with her new social group, remained somewhat naïve.

'The shit women are enduring Ruby. The plain and simple fact that being a woman in 1928 is not all about a pretty dress and snagging a rich husband.' She barely drew breath. 'You can put lipstick on the pig, kiddo, but it's still a pig.'

Ruby wasn't exactly sure what Maxine meant by this. But it sounded like a story.

In the interim Maxine gave Ruby her first solo story. The Launceston Players were well into rehearsal for the play that she and Florian had written. '*The Happy Club*' more or less emulated the creative gathering of the Aphorism Club. The characters may, or may not, have been based on the household in Margaret Street.

'The first dress rehearsal is tonight and you, dear girl, are writing the review. Warts and all.' Maxine paused and winked at Ruby. 'But you'd better write something that gets those uptight Launceston bums onto the seats.'

The rehearsal started at 7. The two women joined the others in the group for a meal at the Dandy Café. Chicken and bacon club sandwiches with a creamy potato soup filled every belly and warmed them up for the walk to the theatre. Only Florian and Lawton were staying to watch the unfolding action on stage. Florian as the second playwright and Lawton was invited to make some sketches for promotional material. Jules, Hollis and Capricorn decided to press on to have a drink *or two* with Pooky who had what seemed to be an endless supply of gin. Rumour had it he was quite the bootlegger.

The National Theatre had a newness about it but kept the traditional style of the London West End small playhouses. It seated just under one-thousand patrons. 'We won't get that many customers for a local play. Lucky if we get two hundred.' Florian seemed resigned to the small turn out.

'You know more than two hundred people Flo. She'll be the cat's meow.' Lawton squeezed Florian's shoulder as an encouragement. 'And Ruby will give it a great plug I'm sure. You might end up having to take it to the Princess.'

'I'd better see it before making too many promises.' Ruby hoped it would be good enough to write something positive.

The first act turned out to be hilarious. The six characters were all writers who met in a rather bohemian setting to write a play about publishing a magazine. One character, named Dee-Dee used her psychic powers to analyse all the others. She uncovered some salacious details about the lives of those on stage. The readings all referred to barely disguised romantic connotations and innuendos, many of which went over Ruby's head. But the antics and physical comedy made the whole thing a great romp. The relationship between the two male leads, Hamnet and Otto surprisingly reflected Hollis and Jules and when the two accidently kiss in the final scene, Ruby had a lightbulb moment of understanding. She had always understood Caleb's relationships, romantically speaking, were with men so she didn't feel shocked or upset. She simply wondered if the audience would accept the inference.

'Not too shocked Miss Ruby?' Florian asked.

'What would I be shocked about Florian. Surely it was just a bit of stage craft with Dee-Dee moving forward and the two fellows simply missed their mark and kissed each other.' She stared at him in the dim lighting of the stalls. 'It's what you want the audience to almost believe isn't it.'

Florian laughed. 'You have a very mature head on those shoulders. At some point you must tell me your story.'

Lawton leaned forward in his seat. 'Are you colluding with the critic Flo? That's a bit corrupt you know.' He leaned over Florian and placed a folded page onto the top of Ruby's notepad. It was another drawing of her. This time with her face turned up towards the stage. The side of her face with the birthmark consumed by the shadows of the theatre.

She smiled at him. Her heart raced a little like it did the first time she met him. The moment interrupted by Florian jumping up and clapping madly as the cast took a faux bow to acknowledge the end of the play.

'They are kind of ready I think. Write something a bit positive won't you Rubes.'

Ruby had already planned out her review. It would hopefully get the bums on the seats and people might find the whole thing hilarious and not too scandalous.

Lawton walked Ruby back to her car at The Examiner offices. As they walked slowly he reached for her hand, ungloved it felt frozen. 'You should have your gloves on. This little paw is like an icicle.' He took her hand in his and placed it in his jacket pocket. 'You are a bit of an enigma Ruby Hart.' He stopped. 'And I like that.' Very gently he pulled her to face him. 'And I might just kiss you if that's okay.'

Ruby felt ridiculously childish, giddy even. She could only nod her head to assent to Lawton lowering his mouth to hers. The kiss barely brushed her lips but it sent a firecracker explosion through her body. The second contact of his mouth firmer, but not insistent. She dropped her head. For a moment they stood, chest to chest, Ruby's forehead rested under Lawton's chin. His right hand still held hers, his left arm encircled her back. 'You are so beautiful Ruby.'

Ruby's first instinct was always to deny the premise that she could be beautiful, or worthy of a man's attention but everything in Lawton's actions forced her doubts away. A man, a wonderful man, had kissed her. A real kiss. It chased away the past and any thought of what might come next. Time stopped, she lived only in that moment, for what seemed to be an age. 'You'd better get home. Your father will be sending out the troops to look for you.'

Somehow in her stupor Ruby managed to get home. The fog had fallen into the Tamar Valley, the smoke from the household fires hung low under the vapour, both reducing visibility to a few feet. Not perturbed by the darkness Ruby merely floated home. Up the steep incline of Hillside Crescent, along the muddy gravel of Corin Road and eventually to her own home. Smoke visible from the two fires lit inside billowed into the mist, lights had been left on so she could make her way inside without tripping. Her father most likely asleep or still working over at the power station which had been completely obscured by the miasma did not notice Ruby's arrival. Flushed, overwhelmed and interminably happy Ruby removed her shoes and coat, swung the kettle back onto the hob and made tea. Sugary and milky, comforting and warming, she took her cup to her room. In the mirror over her dresser she caught sight of her face. Perhaps she was beautiful, the right light, a flattering angle and with her hair loosened from its bindings her face glowed. The heat from the tea, the excitement of the kiss, the expectation of a new day brought out the best of her features. Life became full of promise.

But all that burgeoning hope was short lived given the news Stella brought the following morning. Bonnie had taken a turn for the worst. She had been admitted to the hospital and the doctor had started her on morphine. 'It's mainly for the pain. She's in a bad way.' Stella could barely say the words above a whisper. It seemed she thought saying the words allowed the worst of the truth to come to life. Time was short. For Bonnie it had all but run out.

'I'll go and see her during my lunch break. And again tonight if you'd like me to go with you.' It was a meagre offering, but it was all that could be given.

Ruby's workday started with her review of *The Happy Club*. The words came easily, and she hoped that the work captured the fun of the interplay between the characters and the hilarious stage craft. Many of the more slightly risqué moments in the play were only briefly alluded to.

'Nothing like a few euphemisms to cover the truth, young Ruby.' Maxine changed little in the piece. 'Maybe you could have ramped up the heat where you've written about the outrageous surprises. I do like the word spicy or even scandalous. It's sure to get the punters along. Some of our fellow citizens just love to have something to be offended about.'

Maxine could not have nailed the moral majority's love of the sensational any better. Ruby thought about the behaviour of Father Hewer and the punch Della delivered at the spring dance. His outrage and blistering condemnation of the Merrington girls reflected that very sentiment. Perhaps people needed a bit of a shake-up.

With her first solo effort off to the print room Ruby took herself up to the hospital. The entrance had that strange smell that wafted between sanitisation and something unclean. Illness, germs and death couldn't always be eradicated with phenol and bleach, at least not the smell of them.

Bonnie lay propped up on a metal bed, the white sheet tucked up to her chin. Her eyes were closed when Ruby stood beside her. Bonnie's hands lay on top of the starched fabric; they were mottled and blue at the fingertips. She had lost weight, even more in the last week. Her hair had been pulled back into a snood, and the starkness of her pale skin and sharpened facial bones were accentuated by the severity of the hairstyle. As Ruby touched her cold hands Bonnie's eyes opened. She smiled and looked almost happy to have a visitor. 'Well Ruby Hart. Don't you look like a professional young thing. Stella told me you were writing for the paper.' The brief sentences wore her out and Bonnie shut her eyes again.

'She'll be in and out like that.' A nurse had joined Ruby at the bedside. 'It's the morphine. It takes the patient up like they have had too many champagnes and then drops them to sleep almost immediately.'

'Will she…' Ruby didn't even know what the end of the question was. *Will she live? Will she die? When will it be over?*

The nurse seemed to sense the young visitor's bewilderment. 'Mrs. Lumley has a few more weeks, maybe a month. But depending on how the medication goes it can even be days.' She patted Ruby's back. 'It's very hard but it's better this way.' She stepped back, indicating that Ruby should leave. 'I'll tell her you were here when she wakes up again. Who shall I say visited?'

'Ruby Hart. I'm her neighbour.' Her eyes suddenly filled with tears. 'I'm her friend.'

Bonnie had been very kind to Ruby in the months she had been living at Duck Reach. Stella too. They both seemed to understand how Ruby felt about being dragged away from her life in Melbourne and they tried to fill the void with driving lessons, shopping and banter. Neither woman really knew the magnitude of Ruby's loss, but they provided good-spirited company and more importantly genuine kindness. Death was ghastly. It knew no boundaries. It took young mothers like Bonnie, little girls like Winnie, parents and aunties, those who worked and sacrificed and those who didn't. The thoughts of its indiscriminate cruelty made the afternoon's work difficult.

Maxine gave enough sympathy but also knew Ruby would benefit from immersion in work. She had planned a visit to the women's refuge. 'It's a place where we are going to find one of those stories that won't get printed in this paper.' She put her hand on Ruby's pale face. 'Doesn't mean we shouldn't write it anyway.'

Craigie House in South Launceston ostensibly ran as a rescue home for women. It had been operating for nearly thirty years. It continued to be managed by a charity who received funds through donations, a little government funding and some significant patronage from unknown sources.

'Why do women need rescuing and from whom?' Further naivety on Ruby's part.

'Mostly men. But generally from society.' Maxine wondered if this was really a bit too early to introduce Ruby to the complexities of life for the poor. 'Isn't there any poverty in Melbourne?'

Ruby knew there was. She had seen the men, and sometimes women who set up camps in the back alleys and vacant blocks when she ventured into the city. But she had been utterly protected by her life in Elwood, and at Merrington. Intellectually she knew what poverty did to people but it was a very different thing to see it.

'These women are often put on the scrap heap. They might have been abused by their husbands or others. Sometimes they fall to crime to find a way to feed themselves and their kids. Sometimes they are not married and they have babies and there's no-one to care for them. Craigie House takes them in.'

Ruby thought Maxine had sanitised the overview given. She obviously thought there was a story that wasn't just a celebration of a charity giving a few women a place to live.

It didn't take long to unpick the threads of Maxine's purpose in the visit. The door opened on a scene reminiscent of stories about Bedlam. The noise of women fighting, screaming and tussling gave the first impression that not all was well.

'Just wait here.' A bustling matronly woman instructed Ruby and Maxine. But Maxine had no intention of staying in the portico. She boldly wandered into the affray and watched it unfold. Within seconds the two women locked in what seemed mortal combat were separated. Literally pulled apart by two older ladies. 'For fuck's sake Thora you been told that Kate didn't take your blanket a hundred times. It got chucked 'cos of the lice.'

Thora, who looked like the most dilapidated human Ruby had ever seen, crumpled to the floor. 'Got to ha' me blanket.' Then the tears started.

A voice beside Ruby said. 'She got the madness that one. Her old man beat her with a pot and her head has never been right since.' A girl, maybe fourteen, or younger went on. 'She's off to the asylum when they can get her there. The old man's in gaol as he killed Thora's bubby too.' Ruby's eyes left the informant's face and rested on her swollen belly. This child was soon to be a mother. It became almost impossible to keep the shock from her face.

'Shae, this is Ruby.'

'Ruby this is who we've come to talk to.' Shae linked her arm through Ruby's and dragged her towards the back of the building.

'Outside's better. Fewer crazy old ladies.'

Maxine and Ruby sat on a timber and cast-iron bench. It was not made for comfort. Shae and her swollen belly settled into a wicker chair that had seen better days.

'When's the baby due?'

'About two weeks the quack thinks. But I can't remember the time so I couldn't count the weeks.'

The conversation appeared to be the most normal thing in the world. Shae at just thirteen would become a mother in a few weeks. She looked simultaneously forlorn and buoyant. She had quite the story which she told without shame or perhaps even any understanding of the enormity of what she actually said.

Before her thirteenth birthday Shae had been raped by a drunken uncle at her family home. When it became apparent that she was with child her parents, possibly drunks and scoundrels themselves, threw her onto the street. She was arrested as a vagrant and incorrigible child who had incurable delinquency. 'That's what the judge said. Didn't know what it meant but it's bad.' Shae paused. 'I'm bad.'

'The police arrested you for having no home.' Ruby sounded incredulous. Even younger than Shae.

'And the fact that I stole some fruit from the Chinese grocer. I was hungry. The coppers caught me at my favourite place.'

'And Craigie House took her in rather than sending her to Hobart to the Girls' Training School.' Maxine explained more. 'Once Shae had been cleared by the Mental Deficiency Board she was meant to be sent to the reformatory but because it soon became apparent that there was a baby on the way she ended up here.'

'The Mental Deficiency Board?'

Maxine smiled at Ruby's incredulity at such a thing. 'Yep. Moral turpitude is apparently an intellectual deficit.' She rolled her eyes. 'But the man who rapes a child is evidently not the problem.'

Ruby could now see the intention of Maxine's story.

'I hope things go well Shae. Where's your favourite place by the way?'

'The sea nymphs. I love them.'

Once the two women left Shae resting in the barely tepid sunshine Ruby had more questions. 'What will happen to the baby? And Shae?'

'Well now there's another part of the puzzle. Craigie House has appointed itself as a sort of adoption agency. Whether the young mother wants to or not she has to give up her baby for adoption. The charity is paid for the transfer of the infant to a new family.

'And the mother. Shae?' Ruby felt genuinely concerned for the girl.

Maxine paused. 'Apparently she goes back on the street or because of this alleged depravity she might find herself sent off to Hobart or worse than that. The same asylum that poor old Thora is bound for. It's pretty much the norm I hate to say.'

There weren't many choices here for a girl like Shae, or even poor Thora. Who was hardly old but simply worn down by life.

Choice obviously was a privilege reserved for the few women who were born into the middle class or had the strength of mind to pull themselves up by the bootstraps. Ruby immediately thought of Jessie Burke. She had to fight her way out of poverty. *Why must it be so hard for women?* The thought stayed with Ruby for days.

The past twenty-four hours had been a whirlwind for Ruby. Her first kiss, the reality of Bonnie's life ending and now the discovery that beneath the veneer of civility, human beings are capable of terrible things.

CHAPTER 17

Bonnie died days after Ruby's visit. Stella was inconsolable and Mr. Lumley and Allie were both as silent as stones. The funeral took place in the same village in which she had been born. Evandale lay eleven miles south of Launceston. St. Andrew's Church sat at the heart of her local community. The service was tender; the eulogy a true celebration of Bonnie's short life and the Country Women's Association supplied a morning tea fit for a queen. Douglas drove himself and Ruby to Evandale, they travelled in silence for the most part. But on the way back, after Ruby gained control of her sorrow she decided to ask her father some questions.

'You know you have never spoken to me about my mother. It must have been terrible for you to lose her so early.' Douglas stared ahead almost as if he hadn't heard her. Ruby waited.

'Alma was so lovely.' Clipped words, perhaps tinged with some genuine sadness. 'We could have had a very happy life.' He drove for a few more minutes before adding. 'You're very like her Ruby.' More minutes passed. 'Tall.'

A man of few words. And all of them wrong. In her heart Ruby had hoped he meant lovely, like her mother. Not just tall. She wondered why she bothered but spurred on by the priest's lovely words about the privilege of love she asked the simplest question of all. 'Did you love her?'

A humble *yes* or *no* would have sufficed but Douglas eventually found some words. 'Not in the romantic way you might mean. Young people have these notions about love that just don't stand up to real life. But I loved who she was and how she made me a better person. I'm sorry you didn't get to know her.'

'You know I never went to her grave. I don't even know where she was buried.' Ruby let a tear run down her face. 'I would have liked to have taken flowers. To just know where she is.'

The conversation ended. Douglas said nothing more until he dropped Ruby off at the newspaper office. 'I should have taken you. It was wrong of me not to.'

Yes it was. No point in confirming it Ruby thought. As Douglas drove away it struck her as strange that this was the deepest conversation they had ever had. There had been no talk about any of the things that mattered to Ruby. He didn't ask about her academic achievements, or the reasons she came to Launceston, how she felt about her mother or her opinion on the world and all the changes and challenges that were coming. He barely spoke about the meals she made, the work he did or the life she was carving out for herself. And she certainly wasn't going to tell him about Lawton.

Her father had a strangeness about him that Ruby could not fully comprehend. Surely there had to be something deeper beneath the surface. A heart that sang to some kind of music, one that loved a woman once, an inner man who had hopes and dreams. One that might just think of his daughter in a way that brought him pride. But he could only find one word to describe his only child. Tall. Like her mother. She'd never understand him.

Maxine waited in their tiny office for Ruby's return from the funeral. After a brief hug of condolence, she went on with her news. 'Great response to your preview of *The Happy Club*. Tickets are going like hotcakes.'

Great on two levels. The play would get the patronage it deserved, and Ruby's writing managed to persuade the town to turn out to see it. And somewhat sarcastically added, 'Now we can do some real writing as well as covering the latest botanical triumph that has grown in City Park.' Maxine rested her chin in her hands. 'Thoughts about Shae and Craigie House.'

Ruby had many thoughts about both. 'Who can help Shae? How do we get people involved and what would the police do if we spoke to them?'

Maxine had done her homework. 'You need to get a good look at this. *The Children of the State Act* of 1918. It's not light reading but it will give some sense of how Shae ended up where she is.' Maxine had procured a copy of the legislation from a source. She had placed markers in the sections she wanted Ruby to read. 'This is the research for our story. If it's not rooted in fact, it won't be going anywhere. As it is a story about women and their welfare it's unlikely to get a sniff but we might just be able to get a bit of support to circulate it.'

'Will it help Shae?'

Maxine looked at the hopeful face of her young protégé. 'Probably not. But it might just help other girls in the same situation.' She squeezed Ruby's shoulder. 'Now get reading. It's your only job this afternoon.'

While Maxine typed like a jazz pianist banging out her story about the giant bird of paradise that just flowered in the glass conservatory in the heart of the park, Ruby read and made notes. Little of the legislation made for uplifting reading. She read for hours. The bottom line of the legislation simply stated that children in dire need, those abandoned, or growing up in poverty were no longer seen as a criminal, just a misguided child worthy of redemption. It seemed hard to believe that a new century could be into its third decade, and the law had only just decided that a young person could not be held responsible for their own misfortune. A law that should have protected young Shae from the monster in her own family. 'A baby having a baby.' Ruby muttered to herself.

'It's not new. A girl as young as Shae being pregnant. It's happened for centuries. And it's taken us that long to realise that it isn't the girl's fault if she is raped or preyed upon by those who should have protected her.' Maxine sounded weary. 'She's not the only one and not even the youngest who has ended up on the scrap heap. Too many people turn a blind eye or blame the girl herself. We've got a long way to go if we are ever going to protect our girls. And ourselves.'

Ruby felt a great weight of sorrow. For Bonnie and her son Allie. For Shae and the other women at Craigie House. For the women and girls who were living in between the old decaying life of the past that disregarded them, and the bright future that lay ahead for those courageous enough to leap forward. 'How will Shae ever make something of her life? How does she come back from this?' Ruby's questions were naïve. Maxine began to realise what a gentle and inexperienced soul her new apprentice was.

'Well dear heart, she won't.' Ruby looked shocked at Maxine's pessimism. 'She will not be saved because there's no one to fight for her. She is likely to be sent to Hobart, released at some point and will fall into the clutches of someone who will use her and ensure her life is miserable and short.'

'We can change that can't we?' Ruby felt riled by Maxine's devastating prophecy.

'Not Shae's destiny I'm afraid. But possibly the girls who come after her. What we say now, how we say it may mean the next generation of girls and the ones after that will have the life Shae couldn't ever imagine for herself.' Maxine saw the long game. Change for women would not come from one sad story but from one or two hopeful ones. 'Change only comes from optimism and courage lovie, it doesn't move for despair and defeat.'

Wise words, hard to hear and painful for the optimist. But Ruby couldn't get Shae out of her head. The thought of someone as young as the pregnant girl not having prospects, not even a glimmer of hope felt wounding. Ruby and her school friends built their life on hope; it had been hard-wired into them. 'Sister Reggie used to say shadows are as important as the light.'

'Was she right?'

'Well Charlotte Bronte believed it when she wrote it. And I guess I believe it too. All the things I've learned have generally come from tough lessons.' She paused. 'Finding my voice, believing in myself and realising that I can make choices. It came from losing everything.'

Maxine stared at the rather amazing young woman hunched over her tiny desk, her hair escaping its band. *She really doesn't know how lovely she is.*

'You're on a winner here kiddo.' The light outside had already faded. The night came early in winter. Along with the starry night came a bone-crunching frost.

'How are you getting home tonight?' Ruby had forgotten that her father had taken the car after the funeral.

'I'd better get the last tram up the hill and then I'll walk. It's cold and dark but it's not wet.' Ruby shivered with the thought of being rained on when the temperatures were so low. 'I don't mind the walk.'

Maxine shook her head. 'Don't be ridiculous. Come for tea and then Lawton can drive you home.' She took a moment to smile. 'I'm sure you won't mind being in his company.'

Ruby blushed. Ruby red in fact. 'Ah young love. I remember that.' Maxine pulled Ruby to her feet and threw her coat and hat at her flustered young friend. 'Hollis is making something exotic for dinner. Pooky will imbue it with some life defying concoction, and we will all have a merry old time.'

And she was right. Margaret Street had a blazing fire, lights on and music blaring as the two women walked in. More exotic aromas emanated from the kitchen. Hollis and Capricorn stirred a bubbling pot with an enormous wooden spoon and flipped roasting vegetables in a blackened pan. 'Cocido for the crianca.' Ruby had no idea if Capricorn was asking a question or making a statement. 'Portuguese stew for the child. All good things in this pot will bring you much health.' She beckoned Ruby to the pot to take both a look and to inhale the spicy steam.

The heat and chilli made Ruby cough. 'É o chouriço e...'. Capricorn's explanation didn't help.

'It's spicy sausage she gets from someone in Invermay. The family are always cooking up smoked meats and this hot dog which will burn your throat out.'

'Pe de porco and orehla de porco.'

Ruby nodded enthusiastically as if she knew what delights they were.

'Trotters and ears lovie. Hooves and lug holes.' Hollis helped with the translation.

And despite the spicy sausage and the strange pig parts in the stew, it tasted wonderful. Hot and sweet, with the vegetables and meat tender and moreish.

Everyone squeezed into the table, with more mis-matched crockery and chairs of different heights. The joy in the food, the warmth in the room and the wild conversation put the events of the day into perspective. Life went on and enjoyment could be found in the simplest things.

Lawton sat on a stool beside Ruby. His thigh pressed against hers. She found it hard to distinguish between the fire, food and touch as to where the greatest heat came from. At the end of the meal he took her hand in his and raised it to his lips. The tenderness of the action might once have made Ruby feel uncomfortable but in this wonderous conglomeration of humans it hardly raised an eyebrow.

'You are making a two I see.' Pooky's only comment.

'A couple Pooks. Not making a two, making a couple.' Jules felt it important to correct all the poor expression in the house.

'Maybe Pooky. Just maybe.' Lawton smiled.

He kissed Ruby's forehead and the little gathering clapped madly. Pooky poured Ruby a small gin and squeezed a lemon into it. Gingerly she sipped the potion; it tasted bitter and strange but added further warmth to her already full belly.

After the meal the party moved to the sitting room, eclectic in its furnishings. But the chairs were big and bloated cushions created real comfort. Ruby worried about the time but didn't want to ask Lawton or Maxine to drive her home.

As if he read her mind Lawton leaned over the pillow between them. 'Home time at ten.' A statement rather than a question. It meant she could have a few more happy hours in the noise.

'I give readings now.' Capricorn apparently believed she had shamanistic powers which had her reading palms and getting in touch with the spirits. 'I start with Ruby when she has finished her tea.'

'Tasseography and oneiromancy are her specialties.' Maxine offered further explanation. 'Tea leaves and dream interpretation. She is really big on the demimonde.'

'Tell me your dreams. We find the message your mind is trying to tell you.'

'Like Sigmund Freud?' Ruby brightened up. She had read *The Interpretation of Dreams* during one of the holidays she had to endure at her grandmother's house. It was one of Minnie's books, one of the many she had kept. 'I dream of the moon, all the time.'

Capricorn's eyes lit up. 'Big moon or like this?' She made a semi-circle with her finger.

'A crescent moon, bright and close to earth.' Ruby wondered if these details gave insight into the meaning.

The group fell silent as Capricorn shut her eyes. She raised her hands up and knelt before Ruby. 'The beginning and the end of what is inside you. Inner life change. Not bad, but hard. You have to find your way alone.' Not exactly hopeful and not really what Ruby hoped for. 'You just got to leave the old behind. No more past. Just go forward no matter how hard.'

She sat back on her cushion. Crossed her legs and gave something of a half-smile. 'Now the tea and then I talk to the spirits.' Ruby drank the last sips of tea. Capricorn grabbed the cup and up ended it onto the saucer. With her eyes closed again she righted the cup, took a breath and then looked at the spread of leaves.

'Three things here.' She paused. 'Three lines means you have more change. A key too. Means you have to be careful. Something dangerous might be there. And you got a boat here too. Someone is coming. A friend.' Capricorn looked worried.

'What is it?' Ruby didn't believe in divination. She barely believed in God despite her long tenure in the care of nuns. 'I want to know.'

Hollis interrupted. 'Don't frighten the kid. You do get carried away Cap.'

'Prepare. Get ready. Know what you are up against. It's better to know that the storm is coming. You get your coat on ready for it.' She frowned. 'You are going to need a big coat.'

'Lucky she has one already eh Ruby.' Maxine wanted to shut Capricorn's foretelling session down. She worried that it might unsettle her young friend. 'Everyone gets a storm now and then.'

With her eyes closed and her head bowed the fortune teller said one more startling thing. 'A mother walks with you. Two mothers walk with you.'

At this Ruby became uncomfortable. *Two mothers?* She shivered. 'My mother or my aunt. Both are gone.' Capricorn nodded.

Hollis had another go at distracting Capricorn by speaking to Ruby. 'Tell us your story Miss Hart. You have one to tell I think.'

Somewhat rattled by the odd woman's performance Ruby hesitated to tell much of her history. It couldn't be of much interest to these people but to shake off the weirdness of the prophecies she told them as much as she could. Her mother's death, the grandmother's cruelty and Minnie's love for her. The flu that stole her aunt and best friend and all that came after. The joy of Merrington, and the girls she met. All hoping to be Olympic swimmers. 'We were pretty good but never going to get a shot at Paris. 'We all thought we would get to France in 1924. A mad dream but it kept us going.' She finished with the disaster and Father Hewer's crushing letters.

'Son of a bitch.' Florian sounded actually furious. 'You've got a great story there Rubes. Your first novel I think.' Much nodding. 'You're a natural story-teller. But just kill a few of the mongrels off in the fictionalised version please.'

The time flew. At 10.30 Lawton bundled Ruby into the car. The fog lay deep and heavy over the town. A pea-souper the locals called it. Thick, impenetrable and made driving very dangerous. But Lawton cautiously picked his way up the hill and around the winding road to Duck Reach. The house had no lights and no smoke from the chimney. It was unusual. Her father's car parked at the gate meant he had either retired early or had made his way over the river to the station to work late. But even the lights were off in his office.

'I'll walk you in. It's a bit dark.' Even the lights were out at the Birds and Lumleys. Not surprisingly as it had been a terrible day for both families. Lawton held Ruby's arm as they negotiated the front steps in the dark. The door remained unlocked, so entry was easy. Quickly she found the hall switch and a cool light filtered through the open door. Lawton stood wrapped in his coat, hat and scarf. He stepped over the brass plate into the foyer and pulled Ruby into his arms. The kiss demanded more than the previous one. She could feel the wetness of his lips and the closeness of his whole body pressing into hers. It made her gasp. It ignited that fire she felt previously, and she leaned back into him. She could lose her mind in the embrace, lose her sense of right, throw all she knew about morality out the window and just fall, and fall and fall. Passion…it made one mad.

'I'd better go before we wake your father.' Lawton stepped away. It felt like he pulled sticking plaster off tender skin.

'I wish you didn't have to.' Ruby whispered so quietly that she felt sure he hadn't heard.

'I will get to stay one day Ruby Pearl Hart.' He turned back to the car. 'I think I'll call you the jewel of the southern island.' Lawton smiled at her in a way that shook her to her core.

The car disappeared into the darkness. Ruby closed the door quietly fearing that the silent house would stir and ruin the moment. She turned to head to her bedroom when she noticed a note on the table. Her name in large letters on the folded part.

Her father had left a message regarding his whereabouts. *I'm going to Melbourne on the early steamer. Staying in town tonight so as to not wake you in the morning. Leaving the car for your use. Hope you will be okay. Will be away for 10 days. Stella is there if you need anything.* He had left ten pounds in the note.

No sense of his regret at leaving her alone. Not a well-wish, or concern for her safety, just the usual bland facts of his departure. Strange that he did not tell her during the day that he intended leaving or why he was going. Strange, incomprehensible and typical of her father.

Ruby felt the cold of the house without the fire. She crept to the bathroom to wash her face and gather warm garments to sleep in. The thought of Lawton brought back a fire that eliminated the brutality of the rapidly dropping temperature. She wondered if she would dream of him, or of the crescent moon, or the two mothers Capricorn saw in her trance.

The night fell to a greater silence. Under the pile of quilts and blankets Ruby drifted to sleep and if dreams came, she had no memory of them. If someone walked with her, there was no sense of them. If a storm was coming, then it would come.

CHAPTER 18

Ruby thought about Capricorn's strange psychic performance as she lay in bed the next morning. She would be lying if she said it didn't rattle her a little. Dawn light peeped over the horizon and showed a clear sky was coming. No storm today. Frost sat on every plant and fence post. The car windows were white with ice. And even under the covers she could hear the puddles beginning to crack in response to the weak rays of the new day's sun. A cold day needed a fire, and a cold body needed hot tea. As she knew she would be doing both, delaying putting her feet on the ground, postponed both forms of warmth.

The fire had been partially set with twigs and kindling. Perhaps this had been her father's effort. Smoky flickering sparks eventually burst into proper flames in the fireplace. The combustion stove had managed to maintain some coals ensuring it would quickly jump back to life with some air and fuel. The kettle boiled by the time she had washed and dressed. Tea, toast and honey fitted the bill. The rooms heated quickly and it seemed a shame to leave the cosy space to venture outside. Ruby settled herself at her typewriter and with her portfolio of stories beside her she made inroads into a story to share with Maxine about the girls at Craigie House. And a little start on her own story as suggested by Jules the previous night.

More tea, a stoked fire and silence were manna for a writer. The clacking of typewriter keys, the crackle of fire and the occasional scratch of her pencil in her notebook accompanied her frenzy of ideas. Despite the busyness one thought intruded on her creativity. In her folder she kept the two images Lawton had drawn of her. In both she appeared serene, introspective and fine featured. Nothing of the awkward giant her grandmother always described her as. Tall in her father's words. And she was. Taller than Maxine by at least six inches, taller than Capricorn by ten probably. She had grown to 5 feet 7 by the time she had turned 15. Not a dainty feather like Della, or short and stocky like Al but lean, strong, athletic. These weren't ugly words unless they were in the mouth of Edwina Hart. Lawton's images captured the strength of her jaw and the grace of her neck. His pencil line dipped to the hollow under her collar bones although in both settings where he drew her, she wore a shirt buttoned to the neck.

Ruby wondered about writing about the kiss. She had read Della's magazines and F. Scott Fitzgerald and her favourite Elmer Gantry. Even though the latter had been banned in Australia it made its way to Merrington via Della's family. These novels were too racy for the Australian literate so certainly were not appropriate for good Catholic girls, but they were read front to back and back again by all the readers in the dormitory. Love as the girls saw it was romantic and chaste, but the new reading material opened their eyes to desire. They were not ignorant of the facts of sex, the farm girls eliminated any doubts about what went where, but few had any real sense about falling in love. About the touching, the sensation of feeling a deep yearning that exceeded the wishfulness of handholding with a handsome boy.

Men seemed to write about the lust for a woman, and they went almost mad for desire. *But how would a woman write about it?* How would an inexperienced, newly kissed just becoming a woman write about it. Ruby felt both confused by the longing she felt in her body and yet could not name with any satisfaction. Perhaps writing on paper might clarify the conundrum. Her first sentences seemed trite and unsophisticated. A sexual encounter written by a corny hack who described something not even second hand. Third or fourth hand at best.

The effort of writing about a heated encounter was luckily interrupted by a knock at the door. Ruby put her sketches and weak efforts away before any visitor could see them.

'Hi Ruby. I hope you and your father don't mind a visitor.' Maxine had driven up to check on her to ensure she hadn't been too rattled by Capricorn. 'You really have to ignore Cap. She comes up with some crazy things sometimes. But she means well.'

Maxine sat in the chair by the fire. Ruby packed away her work. 'What are you writing?'

'A story about Shae. One about myself. And a bit of a…' She hesitated. 'A romance.'

Maxine laughed. 'You mean something saucy. I can tell by the colour of your face.'

'It's God awful. I've got nothing to go on.' They both laughed.

After more tea and some biscuits Maxine insisted that Ruby come down to stay with the gang while her father was away. 'Weird that he didn't tell you he was going. Never mind you can have my room and I'll bunk in with Madame d'Esperance.'

'Who?'

'Lady séance herself. Capricorn. Don't tell me you don't know who Madame d 'Esperance was?'

Ruby shrugged her shoulders. Maxine laughed. 'A famous psychic who toured the world manifesting spirits and messages from beyond.' She let her voice trail off in a most unconvincingly spooky manner.

The two women drove their own cars to the apartment. Ruby thought she'd need to get back to power station house a few times in the week her father spent in Melbourne.

'So you don't believe Capricorn has any gifts.' More a question than a statement.

'Oh I didn't say that. She is definitely fey. Got some mystic European voodoo going on.'

The house was quiet. Jules, Hollis and Capricorn were all in their respective bunks, cosied against the numbing frost. Maxine put Ruby's bag in her room and gathered up a few things to make room for the guest. 'Get the kettle on lovie. Everyone is going to need some strong tea to get them moving. Opening night of the play is in seven hours.'

Ruby found tea and the cups easily. The kettle had almost boiled when she heard the first inhabitants move from their rooms. Capricorn first, just in her knickers. 'Good morning, sorry to wake you.' Ruby averted her eyes from Cap's body. She was as tanned as an autumn leaf and sinewy, athletic in a miniature form.

'For God's sake you tiny ninny put some clothes on. No one is interested in those weeny tits you keep flashing around.' Jules pounced on Ruby and hugged her. 'She's a freaking menace that woman.'

Capricorn begrudgingly wrapped her diminutive form in a kimono and waited for Ruby to hand her tea. 'You don't mind do you *anjo*. She had a little look and liked what she see.'

'I hope you all don't mind me muscling in for a few days. My father's away and it's a bit dark and lonely on the hill.' Maxine and Hollis had joined the breakfast table.

'Only too happy to have you stay Rubes. You bring a little light to the place.' Hollis raised his eyebrows. 'I guess as the patriarch of the household I'll have to sleep on the floor outside your boudoir to fend off any marauder attempting to take the family virgin.' He put his hand around Ruby's shoulders. 'Although I think Lawton is much too fine a gentleman to do any serious marauding.'

Most of the day had to be spent at the theatre. Ruby went along with her notepads and sat in the wings writing, unless Maxine needed her to move things on the set or attend to a costume issue. She felt happy to be included in the wild preparations and heightened sense of excitement. Running lines with the more nervous members of the cast filled most of the day before the afternoon break. The theatre had an air of anticipation and exhilaration about it. Ruby loved watching the activity and the tremor of excitement as the moment moved ever closer to curtains up.

Pooky arrived with a bottle of *mehua hermoille*. 'Juice to quell the nerves.'

A loose translation from his native Finnish. Capricorn lit a plant concoction and waved it about to clear the bad *juju*. It led to a fit of coughing. The group hug and many *break a leg* wishes completed the ritual before the lights went up. Ruby took a seat deep in the wings so she could watch the entrances and exits, the sound and music maker and the frantic directors. Lawton sat in the lighting box with several others, flicking switches and moving spotlights. Only once in the whole evening did they lock eyes during the brief intermission. Everything took on a frantic mood. Maxine and Florian galloped around backstage pulling all the loose elements together. And it had been worth it.

The audience applauded ecstatically. They laughed at all the slightly salacious moments and collectively gasped on cue. *The Happy Club* went off without a hitch, or any noticeable ones.

'Was that woman in the green gown meant to be me?' Capricorn seemed most put out about her representation. 'She had no spirit. And no accent.'

'But she had your attitude Cap. Would fight the lid off a bottle.' And on reaching Margaret Street the celebration continued. Music, dancing and drink. Everyone talking over each other, shouting and overstating the most mundane things. Lawton and Ruby situated themselves on the floor, sitting on cushions with their backs against the sofa where Hollis had stretched out. Lawton wrapped his arms around Ruby's waist and nestled his face into her hair, occasionally kissing her cheek, whispering little nonsenses in her ear. They watched the shenanigans of their fellow Aphorism Club members and laughed when the pranks and mischief reached fever pitch.

The noise went on into the early morning. Lawton slept on the couch that Hollis vacated. Pooky and Florian curled up in front of the fire while Maxine shared with Capricorn and Ruby had the luxury of her own room. It became more obvious that Hollis and Jules shared a bed when the two kissed at the top of the stairs before entering their room. Ruby had drunk some of the Finnish firewater so at that point very little surprised her. Hollis would be of little use if marauders were ever to storm the house. And in her tipsy and exhausted state Ruby felt almost hopeful that Lawton might just breach the veneer of civility that her closed door offered.

Sunday began with the bells from the Church of Apostles calling all the faithful to Mass. Groans from heavy heads and queasy tummies joined the chorus of chimes filling the neighbourhood. Only Pooky seemed to have the constitution to survive the evening's excesses intact. Others in the household appeared in various shades of grey and levels of dishevelment that Ruby had never seen. Even though very circumspect about how much of the *elixir of life* she had consumed, the inexperienced drinker felt a little green herself.

'Ruby how did you manage the evening? Sleeping or dreaming?' Capricorn, despite having to be carried to her bed last night became the first to join Ruby in the kitchen.

'Dead a sleep. Didn't stir until I heard the bells.'

'Ah the fucking bells. They kill me every Sunday. The noise and the reminder that I'm a bad Catholic. You go to church anymore.'

'Not anymore. It's not God's fault. More his practitioners on earth.'

Capricorn nodded knowingly. 'Men in general make the earth unstable. Love them all but they got to stop thinking with their long plums.'

'Why are you speaking to the lovely Miss Ruby about the old boys' danglers?'

'Making a point.' Capricorn raised her eyebrows and Florian laughed.

'Pooks and I are going home. We are just up the road but I swear the bells are quieter there.'

And with that the day began.

The household eventually shook itself together. Lawton went to the gardens to fix some trellis at the tea rooms. Maxine tucked herself in a corner to make notes for her story. Hollis and Jules read. Capricorn turned cards, Tarot and solitaire and ate raw carrots. The crunching disturbing everyone.

'I think I'll head home for the afternoon. I'd like to see how Stella is and see if she needs anything. And I've left my typewriter up there and I want to keep writing while things are fresh in my head.'

'But you'll come back tonight. Don't stay up there in the cold.'

Ruby nodded. 'I'll be back before dark. I also need some work clothes for tomorrow.'

The Duck Reach house had become like a mausoleum. Freezing and tomb-quiet. Ruby collected kindling and some logs that had remained frost free and lit the fire. Small pieces under the combustion stove made for easy lighting of the hotplates to heat the kettle and boil some eggs. Eggs with toast and more hot tea made Ruby feel much better. The warmth of the fires brought the house back to a liveable temperature.

In front of the fire Ruby ate and gathered her writing material. She wondered about the quality of her work and thought about sending some to Jessie Burke to ascertain her assessment of her life story, such as it was, and several of the short stories and the article about Shae. Even her attempt at the love story might find its way into the envelope to send south.

Her thoughts were interrupted by a knock at the door. Ruby hoped in might be Lawton. Stella stood on the doorstep anxiously hugging herself. 'Why didn't you just come in Stella. The door is never locked.' Ruby stood back to welcome her neighbour in. 'How are you going? Getting any sleep.'

Stella stopped just inside the door and turned angrily on Ruby. 'I'd have slept better if I'd known where you were. Firstly some strange man drops you off one night and then the next you don't appear at all after going off with that woman.' Stella had wound herself right up by the time she spat the words *that woman* out of her mouth. Ruby's eyebrows rose in surprise. 'Your father asked me to keep an eye on you which becomes totally impossible if I don't know where you are. I mean anything could have happened to you.'

'Come and sit with me.' Despite initially being cross with Stella's implications, Ruby also realised that her neighbour was still in the grip of grief. 'The woman is Maxine. She's my boss and I stayed at her place last night because her play had its opening night. I offered to help.' Stella sat heavily in the chair closest to the fire. 'They are good people.'

Ruby added nothing about Lawton. 'It's pretty lonely up here at the best of times and the people I've met are creative types. You know writers and artists. I feel at home with them.'

'Creative types.' Stella's voice had an edge of sarcasm. 'Dangerous types more likely.'

Ruby tried to interrupt but Stella continued. 'You are just out of school Ruby. You know nothing of what people can be like. What motivates their behaviour.' A brief pause as she found her words. 'Men. Well they can…well sometimes they want…they do things…' Her voice trailed off. She seemed unable to make a coherent statement about her fears about men.

'Are you trying to say that men want to have sex?' Ruby always thought a bit of direct talk made more sense. A trait she picked up from Minnie. Stella blushed. And nodded.

'I'm young Stella but I'm not stupid. And I'm not at risk from these people. We are a writing club.' Ruby tried to find a way to make the group sound safe. 'Like a bunch of librarians really.' *Librarians who read tarot cards and speak to spirits, ones who sleep with men, and bootleg liquor, who want to save the world and one who kisses me in a way that makes me lose my mind.* These thoughts remained unspoken. Only reassuring words would help Stella relax.

'I still think you should stay here. I could come over once the girls are in bed if you're frightened.'

Stella's visit put any writing on the back burner, but it gave Ruby time to think. Women really seemed to believe that men were some kind of enemy and of course some were. The man who sexually abused Shae was the type of monster that Stella was warning her about. But of course, not all men were like that. Certainly not Lawton. Nor Hollis or Jules or Florian. And Pooky had only been very gentlemanly with her. If the truth be told she thought she might be more at risk from the sword wielding Capricorn.

Relationships seemed to be made complicated if you were unmarried, or young. Adults with a few runs on the board always thought they had to protect a girl until they could hand her over to a man who then supposedly had some responsibility to assume the role of guardian. But the visit to Craigie House, if nothing else, showed that not all husbands and fathers shielded their wives and daughters from danger. Sometimes the greatest danger lived in the house with them. Marriage provided no guarantee of safety. Ruby thought of Thora at Craigie House waiting for her trip to the asylum. If her husband hadn't killed the baby in the melee, would he have been charged with beating his wife with a metal pot. Probably not. How many women are subjected to violence from the men who allegedly loved them? How many girls were raped? Ruby wondered about how she would find out and what kind of story it would make, and would Maxine approve of her writing it.

The thoughts certainly put her notion of a love story on the to-do-one-day list. Instead she wrote to Burky telling her about her job, the ideas she had and that she would include some of the stories that had been completed.

CHAPTER 19

Douglas returned to Duck Reach. He made little of the reunion with his daughter until he'd spoken to Stella. Stella voiced concerns about the young woman who seemed to be away from the house more than she was in it. 'Ruby seems to have become friends with some writers. And stayed over at one of the journalist's houses.' Douglas immediately assumed the journalist was a man and began to go bright red. 'She's a woman. I met her one day up here. Very proper sort of person. Not much older than Ruby.'

Douglas relaxed his shoulders and let the indignation subside. 'She's got this job and that's keeping her busy. A few friends won't be a problem.' He started to scurry off to the power station when good manners turned him around. 'Thank you Stella. I appreciate your support.'

He did make a mental note to check that Ruby returned home after work. After all she had the car most days so there were no excuses. Then the thought immediately went out of his head as he buried himself in the work at hand. Alf Lumley hadn't been able to return to work after the death of his wife Bonnie. Douglas felt some sympathy for the man. He and the boy were spending their days since the funeral at Bonnie's parents farm in the midlands. Harry Bird had suggested that he felt it was unlikely that Alf would come back to work at all. 'He's broken to bits Mr. Hart. He hasn't got it in him to get on with life without Bon.' Douglas attempted some sympathetic words but only managed to say, 'Best thing is to get back to work. Distraction from the…' he paused to find a word. 'Loss.'

But Alf Lumley did not get over the loss. Two weeks after Bonnie died, he tendered his resignation saying he had decided to work on the farm and give Allie time with his extended family. It left a hole in the workforce that Douglas had to fill. It darkened his mood considerably. But all thoughts of Ruby went from his head. Finding an engineer, spreading the work amongst the workers he had left were more important considerations for a man who had the responsibility of keeping the lights on in an entire town.

The distraction gave Ruby greater freedom to come and go as she pleased. Douglas rarely left his office only returning to occasionally eat and bathe. It seemed to Ruby that he must have been sleeping at the station as his bed remained undisturbed most nights. Only on the weekend did he need their vehicle for his venturing out of town.

Burky wrote back and in response to Ruby's stories and explanation of her intended research she suggested the two women meet. Jessie Burke had been busy at the university both writing new courses and lecturing in her field. The place, while not teeming with women, had taken the registration of female candidates quite seriously. All degrees, including engineering and medicine, had at least one woman enrolled. *1928 has become a pivotal year for the advancement of women in academia* Burky wrote in her return letter. *Now it's your turn.*

Ruby shared the letter and her ideas with Maxine.

'Might lose you to the south then Miss Hart. What would you study?' Ruby referred to the list she created in her mind when she swam at the Melbourne Baths.

'Tinker, tailor, soldier, sailor.' Ruby smiled. 'Doctor, writer, anthropologist, archaeologist or a politician. I'm not sure I can make up my mind. And besides my father would never agree to me going.'

'But he won't rule you forever kiddo. You have got freedom ahead. You've just got to wait a bit.' Maxine put her arm around Ruby's shoulders and pulled her close. 'Keep the faith.'

More pressing for the two women were their stories. Maxine had suggested that Ruby track down the recently appointed female police officers at the Launceston Watchhouse. 'Also the special magistrate who has just taken up a position in the Children's Court. They might be willing to give a budding journalist some insight into crimes against women.'

The thought of conducting interviews appealed to Ruby. She loved to ask questions and wanted desperately to have some factual basis to support her gut feeling. In her experience given the opportunity people often wanted to talk if given the time.

This turned out to be the case. The first female officer in the Tasmanian police turned out to be quite the trail blazer with several women following in her footsteps. 'No job for a woman apparently.' The newly uniformed women laughed at the suggestion constantly lobbed at them by their male counterparts. 'We do policing differently. Use our brains.' Constable Rayla Short made the joke more than once when Ruby started questioning her about her role. 'And we mainly get the jobs with children and escorting women to prison.'

'And what about crimes against women?' Ruby wasted no time getting to the heart of the matter. The two officers sat quietly. Ruby waited, her pencil held against her notepad ready to write down their words.

'Can you not put our names to this?' Probationary Constable Fenella Brackston sounded cautious. Ruby nodded. 'Well it all depends on the crime doesn't it? We are asked to talk in terms of unjustifiable wife beating which seems to suggest that at some point it must be justifiable to take your fists to a woman.' Anger her prevalent tone. Frustration and sadness too. 'It is a silent epidemic where no-one speaks up about the treatment of women in their homes.'

Rayla added. 'We are prepared to take on the criminals who sell sly grog, the gamblers, the prostitutes and the razor gangs but what happens inside the home, or the bedroom is off limits.'

'Why?' Ruby's question sounded guileless.

'Shame. Fear. Shock. Take your pick. Women just can't make the complaint because they have no power. No money. Worry about their kids. Think the next beating might kill them.'

'But people must know.'

'Witnesses?' Rayla shook her head. 'Too uncomfortable to stick their nose into someone else's business. Easier to look away and hope to God no-one gets killed.'

The women were very matter of fact. Not much older than Ruby but somehow less hopeful.

'And children?' Ruby felt her heat rush to her face and a tear form. 'What about them?'

'There's plenty of laws now but again it's hard to get charges brought against anyone. Kids are unreliable and are accused of making stuff up.'

'Raped girls who get pregnant aren't making stuff up.' Ruby's angry tone matched the officers.

'Asked for it. Or lured a man into it.'

'Bull shit.' Ruby surprised herself with her outburst. The women laughed too.

'Yep it is a big stinking lie but it's how the courts think. It's how some of the most upstanding citizens think. Poor kids, particularly girls are the forgotten ones. Expendable.'

Even Fenella's eyes welled up at the thought of the children who couldn't be helped. 'Thirty percent of rape cases get a conviction. None of them that occurred in the home. None against girls and certainly none if the woman was a prostitute.'

Maxine's unwavering conviction that safety and hope had not trickled down to the poor was a shared belief. Women in this wonderous new century hadn't come very far after all. Unless you were rich. It became the story Ruby had to write and with Maxine's help, Burky's too, perhaps it could find its way into print.

Maxine waited impatiently for Ruby to return from the police station.

'Shae has gone missing. Left sometime last night. Staff at Craigie are worried because they think she may have gone into labour.'

Ruby held her breath. Fearful because the child was now in the most precarious situation. On the street, in labour and alone with the night falling quickly. 'What can we do?'

'The staff contacted the police so they will be on the look out for her. But where she would go is anyone's guess.'

'Her favourite place…' Ruby tried to remember what Shae said. 'I thought when she said it that it was strange.' Another pause. 'Something about the sea.'

'The wharf or somewhere on the river?' Maxine offered.

'No mermaids. It didn't make any sense to me then or now. What could she be referring to?'

Maxine grabbed her coat and dragged Ruby by the arm. 'We will think while we are on the road. I do better when I'm moving.'

The town still had its icy edge despite moving closer to spring but dark still fell early. Street lighting provided yellow pools between the shadows, but no young figure could be seen. Maxine had an idea.

'Prince's Square. It has the Val D'Osne Fountain. It has Roman goddesses in the middle. People call them mermaids. Maybe she's there.'

Under the southern lip of the fountain a little body lay. Shae curled into a moaning ball, frozen and dressed in a cotton frock and tattered cardigan. Her feet were bare. The front of her dress was wet and bloodied with the effort of labouring alone. The baby had been born and remained connected to her young mother. The effort of the labour, the shock of the blood loss left Shae unable to deliver the placenta. Her body shivered with cold. Ruby removed her coat and wrapped it around Shae and the infant.

'If we can get her to the car we can drive her to the hospital. It will take more time to find a phone and ring for an ambulance.' Maxine ever the pragmatist.

Shae weighed very little despite the pregnancy. The two women could lift her and the newborn easily between them. The tiny infant had died at birth or before. Her blue skin and curled limbs were cold to the touch. Not that either woman knew about the intricacies of childbirth but they both knew that the blood loss and cold meant Shae was in grave danger.

The hospital staff thought so too. Maxine and Ruby waited in the emergency room as Shae and the dead infant were whisked behind curtains. The matron from Craigie House arrived, bustling and business-like. 'Stupid girl. What was she thinking?'

That she was terrified about what was happening to her. Ruby's thoughts went unspoken, but Maxine's were not. 'She's a child. In pain and alone. The question really is what were you thinking? Why was Shae alone.'

The head nurse shushed us, mainly with a fierce look.

'She only had to tell us that the labour had started, and we would have looked after her.' The woman straightened her hat and pulled her coat around her defensively. 'Now it's a matter for the police. And if the baby is dead, she'll be held responsible.'

'Fucking hell.' The nurse shushed Maxine more vehemently and suggested we either sit or leave.

'You can't be in here swearing and arguing. This girl is fighting for her life.'

It reduced the hot-headed recriminations, and all our thoughts turned to the child who could die from these complications. And should she survive, the charges that would come and the incarceration that would follow. Even if the baby died of natural causes because Shae fled Craigie House she would be seen as culpable for the death. She had no way of winning. The best outcome, if she lived, would be a few days stay in a warm bed with medical attention and possibly a little care.

The two police officers arrived in time to hear the news that Shae had died from blood loss. 'She also had a fever. Possibly from lying in the cold and wet while delivering the child. Easy to get an infection if you're delivering in unsanitary conditions. None-the-less we have two dead children on our hands.' The nurse looked pained but sounded angry. 'Giving birth at 13 years of age. What the hell?'

What the hell indeed. Ruby couldn't define her emotions for a child she barely knew. Sadness for a life unlived. Rage for the unimaginable cruelty and pain endured by this little girl. Defeat in the face of a society that discarded her despite the potential she might have had if only she had been born into a family who loved her.

There were no answers. And fury was not part of any solution.

'All we can do is tell the story now Ruby. It's the only way she will have a voice.' Maxine's emotions moved to misery. She cried all the way back to the office. Ruby, usually prone to hiding and silence when life offered unbelievably harsh outcomes, found her courage.

'Shae's death is unlikely to be a one off. Craigie House will want to bury the story to exonerate themselves, but her story shouldn't be a dirty little secret. It should be a story that magistrates and politicians and all the do-gooders in the world take notice of.' She drew breath. 'We can't continue to know a thing and not do something about it. Either we fix it or we accept we are part of the problem.'

Maxine stopped the car abruptly at the end of Ruby's speech. 'Forget being a doctor or writer or a happily married lady Ruby Pearl Hart. You are made for politics. Maybe the first woman prime minister of Australia.'

In their collective misery and deep determination both laughed at the ludicrous suggestion. Men were not ready to relinquish that kind of power. Maxine thought for a moment. 'But Edith Cowan did it in Western Australia. It's not really impossible.'

But Ruby didn't want a political platform to change legislation and juggle the money doled out to the programs deemed deserving. She wanted to make a difference to the society around her. No more women like Thora being beaten to madness by her husband, no more children like Shae in unsafe homes and certainly no more babies born and dying in darkened parks in the chill of the night.

Ruby did not make the trek up the hill to Duck Reach that night. She stayed with the Aphorism Club in the home Hollis had made for the members. Douglas might be either furious or hardly notice her absence. She would wake early and drive home before he stirred from the bed he made at the power station or his own in their house. Stella would still be asleep as well and possibly would not note that she hadn't come home after work.

As usual the Margaret Street home spilled light and noise from every window. Florian and Pooky cooked, and Capricorn and Jules danced around like mad things. Lawton played guitar and encouraged the dancers to greater wildness. Hollis shouted a welcome to Maxine and Ruby but on seeing their distressed faces he rushed to them and held out his arms in a fatherly embrace. 'Dear hearts what an earth has happened?'

The party atmosphere sobered as Maxine told the story of the night. Lawton held Ruby to his chest and offered no words, just a comforting rub of her back. Capricorn brought a blanket for Ruby's shoulders. She had been out in the night without her coat as it had been bloodied by the dying girl and lifeless baby. It might never be cleaned.

But the love and care showered by the misfits, the creative souls and the extraordinary members of the club provided a balm to all the pain. Hot tea, a meaty stew and human hope were sometimes all that was needed to heal the heart.

'My jewel of the southern isle.' Lawton whispered before he kissed her. 'A ruby and a pearl. What could be more precious?'

CHAPTER 20

The first days of spring were tinged with a degree or two of increased warmth. The sun rose higher in the sky and the blue above promised that winter could finally be put behind them. Ruby and Maxine had a full schedule of spring garden parties and fundraisers to write about. New fashions for race meetings and afternoon teas had been imported and began to adorn the local shop windows. Light weight fabrics reflected the splendour of blooming gardens, and women from the better side of town, flocked in their masses to get the best dress for the season of showing off.

'Like the gardens they gather in someone has to be the showiest bloom.' Maxine found the whole party season somewhat ridiculous. 'These silvertails make me a tiny bit sick.'

'It reminds me of my grandmother and her hideous friends.' Ruby attempted to be amused. 'It makes me a whole lot sick.'

But the job required the two women to attend these soirees and look interested, taking notes and making the right sounds as yet another young, and not so young, society darling made her entrance. The events made for a powerful contrast to the stories Ruby wrote in her spare time.

The Aphorism Club started to meet outdoors on Sundays provided the weather behaved itself. Sometimes just across the road in the Brickfields Park, or beside the monkey cages in City Park and occasionally they made the trip to the Gorge rotunda to sip gin and eat cheese.

'Ruby your work is just superb. You've really grasped a style that transports the reader where you want them to go.' Hollis's praise felt too generous to Ruby's ears.

'It's coming along. I got some feedback from my friend Burky about the women's series I've written. She wants to publish the first instalments in the university newspaper.'

'Didn't you have a meeting with her?' Maxine was curious about how it went.

'We did last week. She came to Launceston to speak at the first meeting of the Australian Federation of University Women. Tasmania has been slow to embrace the movement but with her background in the suffrage crusade she roused the local academics up. Really gave them no choice but to agree with her.'

'Old bigot island doing its best again.' Hollis sounded exhausted but added little else to the conversation.

'She wants to use some of my work to promote an awareness campaign to lift social restrictions and increase women's legal rights. It's a long shot but if anything I put on paper can help make a difference I'm happy to do it.'

Jules asked, 'Will you put your name to it?' His tone sounded cautionary. 'It's just that some people get a little too upset when a stirrer comes to town. No one likes the status quo to be meddled with.'

Ruby wondered if Jules offered the information to halt her participation or to simply suggest that not all lofty ambitions were met with enthusiasm. Of course, some feathers might be ruffled but they have had plenty of time preening so maybe the time had come to tousle a few plumages. 'They are just stories about how society isn't as it seems when you live in your ivory tower.'

'Jules and Hollis are just suggesting that you might get a little push back from some sectors of society. Including the university.' Lawton held Ruby's hand as he spoke. He kissed the top of her head.

'Most likely only women will be reading it so there will be few roosters getting their coxcombs in a twist.' Maxine always had the last word.

Among the other readings of the day were poems and a short story about an unsolved murder that left everyone shuddering at the thought. Lawton sketched some images in response to each of the works. Beautiful images of rivers, plants and animals to accompany the ideas expressed by the writers. This time he sketched Ruby standing on the suspension bridge, her face identifiable but the body consisted of slinky waves that suggested her hips and breasts were barely covered. Wings or fabric billowed behind the figure.

She blushed deeply when he slid the drawing into her notepad. Beneath the image he's written the words like *Nike of Samothrace, Ruby Pearl goddess of the southern isle.*

'Give it a rest you two lovebirds.' Florian laughed as he threw a piece of cheese at Lawton.

Sundays were wonderful. Even when the weather momentarily turned back to the forgotten chill of winter. The group, frequently busy in the week with work, and drinking and carousing on Saturday always made Sunday the day for them all to be together, writing, discussing, fighting, eating and simply being. Ruby found herself looking forward to Sunday. It had become a day of freedom. Douglas had become a little more insistent that his daughter return to Duck Reach each afternoon when work had finished. But he had little care about the weekend. Ruby had explained that some Fridays she would stay with Maxine because they were attending a theatre show, or a ball or dinner, not as guests but as reporters. It made sense for Ruby to stay with her friend on those occasions. With her father distracted at the weekends she had free range to either stay in town or go home. He took little notice of her comings and goings.

On the walk back to Margaret Street for a late afternoon tea Ruby walked with Hollis. 'Why did you call this place bigot island?' Ruby's intense face when she caught hold of something that interested her made Hollis smile.

'Oh my dear Ruby. You have no idea.' He looked to laugh off her question, but he knew she could not be distracted. 'You must have some idea about me. And Jules.' Ruby nodded and looped her arm through his. 'If we made our relationship public. If someone saw us in each other's arms we would be arrested.

The Criminal Code gives a 21-year prison sentence for what they would call gross indecency.' Hollis's body tightened with the despair of such a thing.

'Why? Why would loving someone be a crime? It doesn't make any sense.' Ruby's disbelief matched Hollis's sadness. 'It makes so little sense that the law feels it has to make decisions about who we can love.'

'Dear Ruby you are a joy. I don't know if your innocence is a good or dangerous thing. But it is a delight.'

She tried to let go of the sense of unfairness. She tried to make the strange pieces of the world fit together but the more she tried the more impossible it seemed to be. While the others busied themselves with food and hot tea Ruby sat with Hollis in the garden.

'How did the Aphorism Club start?' A safer question that the previous one perhaps.

Hollis drew breath. 'Moths to a flame.' A pause. 'We all found each other wandering through a life that didn't particularly give any of us peace. Maxine saw an advertisement I placed in the paper renting out a room. I lived here alone and found it as lonely as hell. She applied and so did Capricorn. Two lovely young women both looking for a place to call home. Somewhere safe.' He offered more information about Maxine having just come out of a broken engagement. 'She called it off when he lost his and her wages on the gee-gees. Gambler. Drinker. And a bit of a rough neck. Probably fell in with a mob of guys doing the wrong thing.'

'Her family didn't take her in?'

'Her mother thought she had shamed the family by breaking her engagement. Would have preferred to see her with a monster than tarnish her reputation. Bloody ridiculous really.' His story about Capricorn more shocking. 'Beatriz and her sister migrated after the war. Sent to Sydney for a better life. But Adelina was raped and murdered by a gang in The Rocks. Poor old Cap never really recovered.' Ruby gasped at the horror of the story.

From here Hollis began his rescue mission. Two young women in need of the protection a home could offer. Warmth, food, shared lives…the basics for survival.

'And Pooky, Jules, Florian. And Lawton?'

'Broken in their own ways. Pooky just a lost citizen of the world. Jules rejected by his family because of his sexuality. Florian a flour-sack kid who made his way out of poverty by working hard. His teacher recognised his brilliance and got him a benefactor to help him continue at school.' Ruby had heard of the flour sack families. So poor that bags that held household food stuffs were repurposed as clothes or towels and nappies for babies.

'Lawton just a loner by nature. A brilliant artist but no real support to make his way in the field. He met Florian and Maxine at the theatre when he was drawing the characters on stage. It was a match made by the fates.'

Ruby contemplated her place in the moths to the flame analogy. Ruby red-face, a shunned child, too clever by half and perhaps an ambition beyond attainment. A strange little human whose family found her existence a nuisance.

'We are all a bit broken. Is that it?'

Hollis stopped for a moment while Capricorn delivered them tea and cake. She then sat with Ruby squeezing into an impossibly small space on the chair so that the two women were wedged together. Ruby removed her left arm and put it around Capricorn's shoulders. The tiny foreigner snuggled in like a child sipping her tea from a soup bowl.

Hollis smiled at Ruby's benevolent act. 'Do you know what kintsugi is Ruby?' She shrugged her shoulders having never heard the word. 'It is a Japanese word that means to repair broken ceramics. But not just fix them. The cracks are filled with lacquer and then dusted with gold or silver. The cracks become a beautiful addition to the item. The imperfections are not hidden but shown as a part of the history of the piece.'

Ruby nodded. She understood Hollis's reason for the art lesson. 'The repair transforms the item. It's not just fixed but it becomes something beautiful in its own right.' Ruby checked to see if she'd understood his meaning.

'There's another word. Wabi-sabi. It means beauty in imperfection. It recognises the transience of all things.'

'I will call you wabi-sabi Miss Ruby from here on.' Capricorn touched Ruby's face.

Petite larme and now *wabi-sabi*. A collection of nicknames for the raspberry splodge under her eye. But a name given with love is a fine thing. 'Happy with that but why are you called Capricorn?

She sat up, virtually on Ruby's knee. 'Sea goat wabi-sabi. Half goat and other half fish.'

She stood up and waggled her tiny bum in Ruby's face. The explanation made no sense but in Capricorn's mind all had been explained.

And with that the day of revelation ended. Lawton drove Ruby back to the power station. Her father's car was not parked in the usual spot. Even Stella's car was nowhere to be seen. As the daylight faded Lawton held Ruby close and kissed her in the way that made her lose all sense. His perfect face, his lean body, the strength and tenderness of him left Ruby senseless.

'We need some time alone Ruby. Time when we can have more than covert kisses and hand holding. Space where we are not snatching minutes or seconds where we are just touching and then have to part.' The thought of time alone with Lawton thrilled yet terrified Ruby. Would it mean that they would sleep together? Did it mean sexual intercourse? Her heart thumped in her chest with both longing and fear. Her body said yes, every time he looked at her, but her head said she was entering dangerous waters if she agreed.

Time alone. How that would ever come to pass Ruby wondered as Lawton drove away.

Her father remained absent for the rest of the night. At some point the car returned but he must have taken himself straight to the office. On the hall table he had left the keys, some money and a brief letter about his intention to have some time in Melbourne in November. There was no invitation for her to join him.

Ruby felt surprised that he'd taken the time to inform her of any plans he made. And she could seriously care less if he went to Melbourne or the moon.

At work the next morning there were two messages. A telegram and a letter. The letter from Burky confirmed that the first two essays had been published in the University Paper and had received acclaim. And some criticism from several history professors. *Old men my dear Ruby. Nothing to worry about.*

The telegram came from Sydney. 'You're a popular girl Miss Hart. All this correspondence.' The newspaper receptionist never missed an opportunity to state the obvious. Ruby simply smiled. The telegram briefly stated that Della de Guise, her dearest Merrington friend, would be arriving on the Loongana on Wednesday morning. *Can I stay with you.*

Maxine helped Ruby with a return telegram that confirmed that Della could definitely stay and that they would pick her up at the wharf on the arrival of the steamer. Ruby could barely contain her excitement. Thoughts of Lawton's suggestion, her father's plans, the response to her writing were all swept away by the impending visit of her beloved friend.

Like many joys they seem to be balanced with the less pleasant aspects of life and in this case, it came in the form of a man. He banged his fist on the polished walnut reception desk demanding the attention of Mrs. Bounds who could rarely be ruffled. 'May I be of some assistance sir.' Her distain for the man could be heard in the tone. She was nothing if not the first line of defence at the paper.

'Looking for those women who did bugger all for my girl when she was dying.' He oozed a stench associated with the unwashed and the heavy drinker. He had a meaty, flushed face that had not seen a hot flannel in a while. 'They said two uppity bitches took her to the hospital. My girl. Just a little kid.' He swayed even though he rested his arms on the bench that separated Mrs. Bounds from any visitor.

'I'm afraid you actually can't be in our offices in your condition sir. We can do nothing for intoxicated people. Particularly if we have no idea what they are talking about.' The tone could have frozen fish. 'I am asking you to leave. Please feel free to come back when you are not under the influence of alcohol.' Now she sounded arctic. Two male journalists joined Mrs. Bounds at the desk. They themselves had a weightiness delivered by excesses of food and wine but thankfully had youth on their side.

'Move on old mate. There's nothing for you here.' John Hooks stepped forward as if to move the drunk man on.

'I'm here till I get something for me loss. The hospital says that some women from the paper dumped my kid. Didn't do nothing to help her when she was having a baby.'

The penny dropped then for the staff gathered around Mrs. Bounds. This derelict shamble was Shae Harper's father. John Hooks had written the story about the discovery of the girl and her dead baby weeks ago. Seems that Mr. Harper had only just caught up on the news of the disaster and had decided to hunt down anyone who he thought he could shake down for a florin or two.

'The big nurse at Craigie House said it had nothing to do with them and that some woman had been interested in me girl's life. Made a big fuss about Shae's story. Should be made to pay.'

At that point Mr. Dryden arrived at the bottom of the stairs. 'On your way sir. We can't do anything to help you.' Harper lurched towards the editor. Hooks got in the way. 'You've been told to fuck off out of it, now move your arse.' He gave the man a reasonable shove in the direction of the door just as Maxine and Ruby returned from the post office.

'This them. You got to cough up a few bob. You look like you might be worth a few quid.' He put his hand out and dragged Maxine by the arm. She took a swing at him with her handbag and collected him fair on the chin. She was quite tiny but fierce enough to defend herself against a drunk. 'Ya bitch.'

Hooks put his foot in his back and propelled him out the front door. But not before he spat in Ruby's face. She recoiled in disgust but did not shrink from the odious man. She didn't have a handbag to swing but she had a few choice words. 'You might look to yourself sir if you're trying to find someone to blame. You might look to your own household to see who should take responsibility for that little girl's death.' She paused and dramatically wiped the spittle from her cheek. 'You'll never get a cent out of me or anyone else you monster. Go back to the swamp from which you have crawled.'

Hooks slammed the front door on the staggering drunk. Then the office burst into laughter. 'Miss Hart you look like a princess, speak like a queen and yet I'd be loath to take you on in any kind of stoush.' Mr Dryden smiled at the young protégé's chutzpa. The male journalists backed their boss with similar words of appreciation for both Maxine and Ruby. Even Mrs Bounds smiled for once.

'World's doing okay with girls like this in the ranks.' She offered nothing more than a few icy looks at the journalists who were standing far too close to her personal domain of the front counter.

'Dear God, what next?' Maxine sat heavily in her chair. 'Peace and quiet you think?'

CHAPTER 21

The minute Della stepped off the Loongana and half ran to Ruby the world seemed a better place. The spring day promised wonderful things. A long hot summer, Christmas, writing success and a dear friend to share it with.

'Petite larme how you have changed. You are so grown up.' Della hugged Ruby in a long embrace, so long that the recently arrived friend could not conceal part of the reason for her visit. She smiled at Ruby who had become somewhat confused. Della's long coat could hide the obvious to the eye but not to the touch. 'Yes. It's a bébé. I'm going to be a mother.'

Ruby felt unsure of how to respond. 'Is this a happy thing?'

Della laughed at her friend. 'Always a question Rubes. Always testing the water.'

And even an answer affirming the joy Della's eyes filled with tears. 'It's a long story mon amie. One for tonight.'

Ruby loaded her precious cargo into her father's car. Della had not travelled light so it could be assumed that the visit would become more than a brief reunion.

'And you drive. Is there nothing you cannot do?'

Avoiding the obvious, Ruby talked about her work, her new friends and Lawton. She could not help blushing when she mentioned his name. 'And I need your advice. I think we might love each other, and he wants something more than goodnight kisses.'

Della laughed. 'You are grown up in so many ways and yet still a child in others. He wants sex, am I right.'

'Yes.' Ruby hesitated to finish the thought, but this was Della. 'I think I do too.'

'So much to talk about dear Rubes.'

Ruby had mentioned to her father that her friend would be staying with them. It wasn't a request for permission merely a statement of fact. She had made up a bed in the third room and placed some flowers and floral cushions around to make it welcoming. Knowing how cold the nights could still get she also purchased a new quilt made of pink embossed satin. The room looked warm and charming. The closet had always been empty so there would be plenty of room for Della's clothes.

'So lovely Ruby. Thank you for this.' Della draped her arm around her friend's shoulder. 'Is your father here.'

As it turned out Douglas had left for Hobart to attend a meeting of engineers. He would be there for a week, which gave the two girls plenty of time to talk about the way life had gone in the past year. That first night together extended beyond midnight and only ended when the two could no longer stifle their yawning. But the discussion had to be had. The father of Della's baby had abandoned her as soon as he heard of his impending fatherhood. Gabriel Dupont, a Belgian refugee like Della's family, was beautiful. 'He is so handsome and I thought a good man but he just didn't want to leave the life of a party boy to settle down in a marriage.' Della showed no bitterness. 'We talked about it and he said the truth about his feelings. He loved me. But the me who was not going to be a mother.' She shrugged her shoulders.

'What about your mother and aunt? How did they take the news?'

'Well I'm here aren't I. They thought I should have a break. Be somewhere where I could pretend to be Mrs. Dupont.' She held up her left hand to show a gold wedding band. 'It's my grandmother's. A little circle of gold to cover the shame.'

Shame is such a burdensome word. Usually heaped upon women. Dupont can just wander off without a sense of disgrace but the girl he leaves must carry the dishonour. And what is there really to be ashamed of. Loving someone. Giving into the feelings that Ruby felt so indefatigably when she thought of Lawton. Having a baby? 'I mean what is there to be ashamed about having a baby without a husband? Most of the work is done by the mother anyway.' Ruby was almost talking to herself.

'And tell me about this Aphorism Club.' Della steered the conversation to Ruby's life.

'They are just a wonderful group of people who write, paint and direct plays. Everyone is clever and many just a tiny bit weird. I can't wait for you to meet them.'

'And Lawton?' She pressed.

'Beautiful. Gentle. Smart, kind and tender.' Ruby had to pause. 'He's alive in a way I can't explain. It's as if whenever he is in a place it has more light. More sound, more of everything.'

'Look out dear Rubes. Sounds very much like love.'

Ruby felt reluctant to leave Della in the house alone, but she had to work.

'I'm happy with a book, the fire and a pot of tea dear one. Go to work and we will talk about the future and your man all night if we must.' Ruby had little idea about pregnancy but uncovered, Della's body looked swollen enough to not convince anyone that she had just gained weight. And despite her glorious good looks, Della looked tired. Not from lack of sleep but from too much life. Perhaps quiet days at Duck Reach might be good for her.

The weekend came soon enough and after a long sleep-in on Saturday morning the two set off so that Ruby could introduce Della to the others. Maxine had been keeping everyone abreast of the newcomer including the pregnancy. It didn't matter to anyone that she was an unmarried mother to be, but they had been told to accept the charade of the marriage and the separation for whatever reason that was yet to be concocted.

Lunch had been set in its usual chaotic manner. The long table had been set with mismatched crockery and delicate wine glasses that each resident and friend had purloined from their pasts. They had all dressed for the occasion. Lawton wore a light cotton suit with a white shirt unbuttoned to just below his collarbones. Jules and Hollis wore matching smoking jackets, Florian sports pants and a polo shirt matched Pooky's similar outfit. Maxine in her wide sailor trousers looked elegant and very much the hostess of the lunch. Capricorn on the other hand went for her most eccentric look. A coloured headscarf, a silk house coat that did not conceal the sheer petticoat she wore under it. 'Trajede laviadeira. The scarf is from my home in Viana do Castelo.' She pronounced proudly.

'And what about putting on something other than your skivvies Cap?' Jules shook his head at her. But she could have cared less. Her interest focused solely on the newcomer.

'And a bebê I see. Most wonderful.'

'It's becoming a bit hard to disguise isn't it. I seem to be bursting out of everything I own at the moment.'

'You don't need to disguise anything for us lovely girl. Come. Sit here with me and we will talk.' Hollis could not be fazed by anything and his natural paternalism towards all his friends was genuine. Della fitted into the Aphorism Club without a hiccough. She, being the most beautiful of Hollis's kintsugi.

Lawton introduced himself and hugged Della. Then immediately kissed Ruby. He smiled at her as if she alone was in the room. His hands softly touched her waist as he directed her to the chair beside him.

'I made for you all lohikeitto. Soup of the fishes.' Pooky spoke with great pride about the food he brought to the communal table. Bread, cheese, butter and Capricorn's fire dogs rounded out the lunch.

'Be careful of the fire dogs. Very spicy. But hard to resist.' Florian warned Della, worrying that an expectant mother might not be able to handle the chilli infused meat.

The madness began. Everyone talking about their weeks at work, the writing done, the things seen. The main point of interest was the altercation at the paper with Mr. Harper and his accusations. Ruby could feel Lawton tense up beside her. His hand on her shoulder tightened.

He directed his question to Maxine. 'Are you both safe from this nutter? I mean has the paper put anything in place to keep him away from you. From you both.'

'He's a drunk grifter Lawton. I don't think we have anything to worry about. And with my vicious handbag action and Ruby's very terse marching orders I don't think he will be any worry to us. Possibly so drunk he doesn't even remember coming into the office.'

The general consensus around the table concurred with Maxine. Just a crazy old chiseller trying to squeeze the newspaper for money. Lawton's tension, however, did not lessen. It made Ruby wonder if there really could be something to worry about. But the discussion abandoned the incident and flowed on to the next play Florian and Maxine were writing.

'Not writers this time but ghost hunters. With a madam psychic thrown in.'

'That's me again. You are going to have to start paying me for the privilege of using my persona.' Capricorn loved being the centre of attention. 'Now I will do a reading for lovely Della. I tell her what kind of bebê she is having.'

'What kind? I'm not sure that's that hard is it Cap. Human. Possibly a boy or maybe a girl.' Hollis teased her. But she was not to be put off. She settled Della at the little card table and laid out the tarot and the tea cups. Her conclusions were that the new life would be a girl. She warned her of a storm and that love would be the conclusion.

'I got a storm too in my reading. I think it is inevitable living in the south that we might get a storm.' Ruby smiled at Della who remained unruffled by Capricorn's visions.

The two left the group in the late afternoon after too much of Pooky's soup and Cap's spicy sausages.

'I've thought it would be a girl too. All those feminine vibes at Merrington have rubbed off on me.' Della laughed at Capricorn's predictions. 'Now let's talk about Lawton.'

Della agreed with Ruby that he had a terribly handsome face. 'It's obvious that he is very much in love with you Rubes. But are you ready for the big step. How much do you know about sex dear one?'

Ruby knew enough of the biological elements of intercourse. She knew what her body did whenever he touched her. She certainly knew that her head could not get her body to obey it when he kissed her. 'Enough to know that I want to but I…' Ruby hesitated to add.

'To get pregnant like me.' Della finished the sentence. It was true Ruby wasn't at all sure about the motherhood thing. She always thought she might be like her Aunt Minnie and remain a spinster who simply managed her own affairs and lived alone. Lawton was a complication in that future plan. Somewhere in her mind she could envisage a life with him. A married couple, maybe a family and probably living in Minnie's place in Melbourne. Eventually she would inherit Elwood too, but she'd never live there. Sell it or burn it to the ground would be her preference.

'You can get the man to use a prophylactic and it will give you protection. The chemist will sell them to married women and men. I could get you some. This magic ring on my finger might work wonders convincing the pharmacist that I'm eligible to buy them.'

'He might also think the horse has bolted Della.' The two laughed their way to bed. The day had been wonderful. And the plan to meet in the rotunda had been made for the next day.

While Della slept, Ruby wrote. She wanted to add to her series on the roles of women. Particularly the expectation of mothers, motherhood and pregnancy out of wedlock. She couldn't let go of the imbalance between men and women on so many levels. She had covered crimes against women and children, the pay discrepancies, the inequity of the law and the disproportion of power in society. But she hadn't written about shame. It loomed large in her mind given that she had first-hand experience of being made to feel ashamed for things over which she had no control. Her own family humiliated her for her birthmark and made her feel she had discredited the Hart name because of it. Father Hewer lay the blame of the incident at the spring dance at the feet of the girls who simply defended one of their own. Shae's father blamed Maxine and her and seemed comfortable in his belief that they had to take the blame for the horror his child experienced. Even some women perpetuated the blame game. Mainly those women who hadn't had to face the ignominy of poverty, or shame for who they were or what happened to them. 'We are not always to blame.' Ruby verbalised the thoughts as Della continued to sleep. She wrote late into the night.

The Aphorism Club had its full complement of creators at the rotunda. The day spoke of the sunny weather to come. The sky had a light to it that said summer was near. And although the weather in Tasmania could be fickle, it could also have a hot summer where the days were long, and the sun did not set till at least 7 in the evening. Ruby imagined herself swimming in the deep, cold water of the Basin in the months to come. Della did not join the group for the afternoon. Her feet were swollen, and she felt the fatigue of carrying the weight of her baby in her back. Walking the cliff path would be far too taxing and Della didn't want to horn in on Ruby's gathering. 'There'll be enough time for me to get to know them. And I have no intention of writing anything.'

Ruby had become used to the rough path and dressed in her tennis shoes and light pants she could make the swinging bridge in less than an hour. She had become leaner and stronger in the time she had come to the island. No soft rides on the trams, no Sunday cakes with Mrs. Rowlands, no treats appropriated by Sister Reggie and despite being a driver, she had engaged in a lot of leg work getting around the town.

Lawton arrived first and had set up the table. He heard Ruby call his name and he ran across the lawn to sweep her up in his arms. 'Jewel of the southern isle you look as fresh as sunshine today.' His mouth met hers before she could respond. Deep and persistent he kissed her. His arms held her body to his unrelentingly. She felt breathless at the urgency and strength of his greeting. 'You two down there. Give it a rest. We'll all be arrested for indecency.' Hollis shouted and laughed.

Lawton stepped only a few inches away from Ruby who wasn't sure she could stand. But the moment sealed her intention. 'We need to talk about how we can have some time alone.'

He simply nodded. 'It's a date.'

The discussion focused on the play Maxine and Florian had started to write. The opening scene featured a séance where the psychic, Madame Mumbler, led a ridiculous series of readings for the assembled characters. Florian, Maxine and Hollis read the parts. Hollis making a most convincing clairvoyant. The group found it hilarious. All but Capricorn.

'You lot mock my gifts but I tell you I know the messages.' She looked like a spurned child. Ruby put her arm around her. 'I believe you Capricorn.' She planted a small kiss on the top of her head.

'That storm I said. That storm is still coming. You watch yourself wabi-sabi.'

When a quiet moment came Ruby spoke about her new idea. 'Shame. And blame. Seems to be a good topic that women might understand.' Her idea met with much nodding.

'Is this because of Della?' Maxine seemed have the sixth sense like Capricorn.

'Partly. Mostly. But also my own experiences, and Shae's. It just seems that our gender gets all the blame and none of the benefits. It's like a boat that has all its goods stacked on one side and then everyone wonders why it tips over.' Ruby felt genuine sadness.

'My dear Rubes its life. But it's not just women who have the burden of shame. Look at dear Jules and me. We are not just shamed but we are seen as criminals as well.'

'Bloody diculous.' Pooky added.

'Ridiculous.' Florian corrected.

'No pretty diculous if you're lucky.' Hollis hooted at his own joke.

Lawton was very quiet. 'But women are the victims of men, the law and other women too.' He was obviously thinking deeply. 'My mother...' He stopped. He started again. 'My father beat my mother like she was a stray dog. Nothing she did was right. No shirt was clean enough, no meal hot enough, no floor swept enough. I came to believe he just like hurting her.' The group remained silent. 'When he turned on me one day and he hit me with a fire poker she couldn't take it anymore. So she took the kettle off the trammel and hit him around the head with it. He was out cold. All we could do was run. But with nothing we couldn't run far.' He took an enormous breath in. His voice shook. 'She was charged with assault. A mad woman who savagely attacked her husband without provocation. The police wouldn't listen to me even though my wrist was broken. Even though she was covered in bruises and cuts, they only listened to him.'

'What happened to you mama Lawton?' Pooky leaned towards his friend as if he would need to catch him.

'She died before the case was brought to court.' His chest heaved.

'She sick old boy?' Pooky full of disbelief.

'In a way Pooks. Despair is a terrible illness. She jumped out of the prison window when no-one watched. And no one cared.'

Ruby gently reached for his hand. What words could comfort that story? How could that ever be made right? 'You must write your story Ruby Pearl. Write about the fate of women. You can use my story if it helps.'

It brought the meeting to a sombre close. Everyone's thoughts included Lawton and his long silence on his background. 'What happened to you?' Capricorn's question on all their minds.

'My Irish mamó came to the party. She'd lost her daughter but she'd be damned if her grandson would ever be touched by George Timblett again.' He smiled for the first time in the story telling. 'He went missing you know. I do think Granny got him.'

The day ended with a laugh and the long walk back to Duck Reach. The laughter, the sadness and the tragedy all unfolding in the few hours the club spent together. And perhaps, the promise of more joy than could be contained in one life.

'We will need to talk.' Lawton left her with that thought.

CHAPTER 22

Summer arrived early with hot days at the beginning of December. Only one altercation marred the approach of Christmas. Della's pregnancy became more obvious each week. Douglas barely noticed the girl in the house, let alone her condition. Both Ruby and her friend floated in and out, busy with one thing and another. Work, friends and writing took up most of the time. Della often spent her days in the library or with Hollis while Ruby worked but sometimes, she stayed at the Reach and pottered around the garden, and it was here Stella made her acquaintance. 'You're Ruby's friend from Melbourne.' A statement that needed only a nod. 'And French.' Almost an accusation.

'Non. From Belgium. But close enough. Lovely to meet you Stella. Ruby speaks very well of her neighbour.' But Stella was not to be persuaded by cheap compliments. She was on a mission.

'I see you are expecting a baby. It must be close.' And before Della could answer she added. 'Where is your husband?' The tone did not imply gentle curiosity, more feverish suspicion.

'There is no husband I'm afraid to say. He was to be a husband but he got very chilly feet.' Della smiled to ease the tension.

'Cold feet is the saying. And men do that when they have got what they wanted.' Stella made no bones about her attitude to Della's presence in the house. 'It's not right that you are corrupting a young girl like Ruby. She shouldn't be around someone…' A hesitation. 'Like you.'

'Like what Miss Stella. A person like me. Do you mean foreign? Or just pregnant?' Della could match anyone in a verbal skirmish. And she couldn't keep the distain from her voice.

Stella immediately spoke to Douglas, who as she had rightly suspected, had no idea about the visitor's condition nor her unmarried status. A ruckus ensued. Ruby, who genuinely liked Stella shouted in all directions that busy bodies should keep their noses out of her business. 'She just needs to leave Ruby. It's not a good look for you or the others who have to live here.' Douglas spoke adamantly.

'A good look. A pregnant woman is not a good look. What are you talking about? Have you got any idea about human beings at all?' Her fury didn't only blaze away at her father. Stella got a serve or two as well. Maxine immediately came to Della's defence and offered her the room at Hollis's. She could stay at the gate keeper's cottage with Lawton until things settled.

'I can't ask you to leave your bed for me Maxine. I'll find something.' Della wanted peace at all costs and if push came to shove, she most likely could look after herself. But the group wouldn't have it. Accommodations were shuffled about to everyone's satisfaction within days of the blow up. Ruby refused to return to her father's house and therefore further shuffling had to be created. Pooky stayed with Lawton. He loved the cottage over the gorge. Capricorn happily moved in with Florian which meant Della and Ruby could stay at Hollis's with Maxine and Jules. There didn't seem to be anything all of them wouldn't do for one, or two of their own.

Ruby barely spoke to her father or Stella. If Douglas noticed Ruby had left the house, he didn't say. She left the car but took her bike and a few belongings. She left in such a huff her typewriter and folio of work were left on her dressing table. 'I'll have to go back for them at some point. Burky loved the last essay on shame and is hoping I'll do a follow up before the new year.' The thought of facing her father left her feeling sick. But with a sense of right on her side she knew she could muster the courage.

The newspaper provided plenty of distraction as well. There were a dozen stories about Christmas preparations, decorated public spaces including the townhall. Streetlights and shop fronts were festooned with lanterns, paper chains and gaudy baubles to mark the coming of the festive season. Large trees and boughs of Christmas bush seemed to take up space in windows in the main street. Maxine and Ruby reported on the lavish Christmas feasts that were being planned by the city's elite families. Even the middle class stretched their budgets and imaginations for the big day. The house at Duck Reach remained unadorned.

Even Margaret Street got into the spirit when Hollis decided a Christmas tree needed to be sourced and placed in the front room where everyone could put their gifts for each other. He had assumed, rightly, that no-one was going anywhere else for the big day. Pooky decided he would take charge of the menu and no-one questioned how he might acquire the ingredients for the feast.

The social events numbered in the dozens, so Maxine and Ruby went their separate ways to report on the parties. Often two or three events were scheduled for the one night and there was no way they had the time to go to them all together. Without her father's car Ruby went to the occasions around the city. She could walk to most of them and then return to the office to type up the article, then walk home the few blocks to Margaret Street.

The stories were pretty much the same. The guests, the music, the food and the special moments like young debutants appearing in outfits more expensive than a homemaker's yearly budget. Despite herself, Ruby did love the dresses. Sparkling and figure hugging, shimmering and moving like water over the young bodies as they danced and flirted. It could be her life if she wanted it. The Harts of Elwood had the social gravitas that could open doors like these, and possibly ten times over. It was not, however, a world Ruby ever wanted. She wanted purpose and the power to decide the direction of her own life. And Lawton. The thought of him distracted her again. Every time she thought of him, she got lost in the image of his body and hers.

Distraction became a downfall. So caught up in the notion of him she failed to notice the fast-approaching footsteps as she turned to lock the office door.

With her back turned to the footpath the assailant had every opportunity to floor her with a single blow. The tyre iron hit her right ribs, cracking several. It knocked the wind out of her and the force of the thump sent her to the ground. The pain and shock stunned her but within a few seconds she realised the peril she was in. Shae Harper's father staggered under the force of the swipe he'd taken at Ruby. If he'd been less inebriated, he might have cracked her spine, but the plonk interfered with his aim. Even breathless and hurt Ruby knew she had to keep her eyes on him. The instinct to roll into a ball and protect herself would not stop him bringing the metal bar down on her head. She had to watch where he was and despite the first injury, either deflect the next strike or attack him before he could do more damage.

Ruby had long legs. Strong legs and strength some might find unflattering in a woman. But both her height and power might just be the things to save her. Harper came at her again, an unstable approach but threatening and dangerous if she couldn't fend him off. With enormous fortitude she rolled away from the steps giving her more room to move. Her action momentarily put the drunk off kilter. He attempted to right himself and brought the bar down near her hip, but he missed. Ruby took the opportunity to strike out at the bent over figure as he attempted to lift the bar again.

'Fuckin' gonna smash ya brains out bitch.'

Saliva drooled from his lips like a slathering dog; he looked like a wild animal. But boozed up madness and bravado made his actions slow and careless which gave Ruby time to kick out with her foot connecting with the side of his knee. It destabilised him and toppled him easily. Harper's fall made more of a crack than Ruby's ribs. On his back clutching his knee he became helpless. Bawling and yelling he kept swearing about the terror he'd inflict on Ruby. 'I'll kill you. You won't know it's coming.'

Ruby got to her knees and picked up the iron bar Harper had dropped. 'Not if I kill you first.'

It occurred to her that she could actually smash his face in. While his intoxication kept him on his back like a turtle, she could avenge Shae, rid the world of him and make him suffer while she did it. But she chose not to. Instead, she got to her feet and only by holding onto the railing could she begin to get her balance. The excruciating pain in her ribs and back had her staggering in the same way as Harper. Perhaps if she had been drunk the agony would not have made her so lightheaded.

'Had a bit to drink have we love?' As if by providence two policemen arrived behind her. He's out for the count.'

Fury and indignation forced Ruby to her full height. 'This man attacked me with a tyre iron. He's threatened me before. I'm a writer for The Examiner. Now could you actually help me.'

The two men were taken aback by the clarity of Ruby's summation of the situation. Gathering their senses one of them came to her side to hold her up. 'Better get you up to the hospital girly. You look pretty done in.'

'As for this bloke he's off to the lockup.'

Events happened without Ruby's involvement. A car arrived and when she opened her eyes, she had several medical staff gathered around her. 'You have family we can contact?' Someone asked her. Even in her state the last person she wanted to see was Douglas. She managed to give them Hollis's address. 'They are my family.' Quietly she slipped into a twilight where the broken ribs and bruises from the fall were untroubling. The morphine eased all worries, all concerns about what might happen next and most importantly any physical discomfort. The night went on without her.

In the hour before dawn Ruby woke. Sensation and awareness returned. Beside her, in a chair, Lawton slept with his head resting on the bed. Curled in another chair Maxine made the soft sounds of sleep. Beyond the curtain she could hear voices. Hollis, the police perhaps and another voice she knew but couldn't name until his face appeared between the white drapes. Her boss, Mr. Dryden had been summoned by Maxine. Ruby's initial account and Maxine's statement about Harper's earlier threats required corroboration of a man apparently. Dryden gave the police not only the account of what he knew he also made it very clear that the accounts given by his female journalists were beyond integrity. His last words stayed with Ruby as she floated to sleep. 'How dare you cast aspersions against Miss Hart. She is not only brilliant she is one of the most morally scrupulous young women I know. Your superintendent will be getting a call in the morning.'

Bruised and sore, but not defeated, Ruby lay in the newly made bed at Margaret Street after the hospital eventually agreed she should rest at home. Everyone in the group took turns to sit and talk, help her out of bed when she needed the bathroom, bring tea and food and in the case of Lawton, simply hold her hand and watch her sleep. Mr. Dryden had insisted she take at least a week away from work. Maxine finished the rotations of pre-Christmas stories and John Hooks wrote the story about the assault and the charges Gordon Harper faced. He had been remanded in custody until the trial. Hooks had written in the article that the assailant had several previous charges for drunkenness, theft and receiving stolen goods. Attacking female journalists apparently a first for the awful man. Lying in bed Ruby wondered how many times he might have beaten his wife and child. She thought that while Harper waited behind bars, she might find Shae's mother and ask her.

'You are not getting out of bed to go off interviewing dangerous people Rubes. You have broken ribs.' Della virtually held Ruby down in the bed. 'Did you happen to hit your head as well?'

Ruby laughed, but only briefly. Laughing hurt. Moving hurt, sometimes even breathing hurt. 'Just a few cracked ribs and a spectacular bruise on my bum. If I don't get up and move I'll go mad. The doctor said I could walk about but just no more street fighting.' Della helped her dress and navigate the stairs so that she could sit on the couch with the one notebook she'd managed to grab when she left Duck Reach after the fight about Della's pregnancy. 'I've got to get back to the house to get my typewriter and my folio. I've got things in there I'm working on. And I owe Burky a story.'

Della shook her head. 'I don't think you're going up there by yourself. Hollis is out at the moment but perhaps he might drive you up there when he's back.' It was a plan as good as any. Ruby had her bike, but cycling was absolutely implausible given her injuries. Just as Della poured the tea a rapid knock came at the door.

'Someone's forgotten their key.' Della went to let in whoever had arrived home.

'Where's Ruby?' Douglas and Stella were most unexpected visitors. 'We had to read about what happened to her in the paper.'

'It's been days and you're just finding out now?' Della sounded simultaneously angry and incredulous. 'Well since you've made such an effort you had better come in.'

Ruby sat more upright not wanting to give any indication that her body pained her. She had no interest in their concern or sympathy.

'I'm surprised you didn't bother to contact your father Ruby. Afterall this is a very serious matter.' Stella the obvious spokesperson for the pair. Douglas looked bewildered more than concerned. 'You should have been at home where you could be cared for properly.' Stella was getting up a head of steam. 'Instead we had to find out from the papers and then had to go to the police to find out where you were.'

Della stood mute but definitely amused by this strange interaction.

'I'm going to stop you there Stella. Yes a man attacked me. Yes I have a little injury. No I wouldn't have gone to Duck Reach because I'd have been alone. And I've been perfectly cared for here in this house.'

Stella attempted to go again but Douglas intervened. 'I'll remind you Ruby that you are still a minor. You might be twenty but I'm still making decisions regarding your life.' He pulled himself up out of his usual stooped posture. 'I am your father after all.'

Whilst not furious, Ruby's spark ignited. 'You are my father Douglas. You have rights in that role but you know nothing about me. You haven't ever known me. I've been raised by Minnie and Merrington and nurtured by these friends in this house. I'm not going back to the Reach.' She paused for breath to ease the pain that began throbbing in her side. She stood. Imposingly she stood over her visitors. 'I'm safe and I'm happy. Thank you for checking on me.'

Ruby meant this statement as a sign they should leave. Stella had other ideas. 'We can get the police to force you home you know.' Douglas looked as shocked as Ruby and Della at this development.

'There'll be no need for that.' Hollis had arrived home. Looking like a city banker in a suit instead of his usual satin smoking jacket he continued. 'As Ruby's solicitor I'd suggest you'll have quite a fight on your hands trying to force a young woman to do anything.' The two girls looked at each other as the revelation or blatant lie of Hollis's occupational pedigree came as a complete surprise. 'I think you can see that Ruby is content and safe here in my home. She has Della and a second young woman who is her colleague to protect her from harm.'

He sounded like a lawyer. His demeanour had little of the usual bearing the girls were used to.

'Well as long as you're happy Ruby and not badly injured I suppose you can stay here for a while. Probably just as well as I'm going to Melbourne again just before Christmas. I thought you might come too.' Ruby's wild head shaking indicated the unlikeliness of that. 'But I'll leave it at that for now. We can talk about things after the New Year.'

Stella wanted to bluster a bit more and Ruby thought it best to calm her down before she left. 'Thank you Stella for caring about me. I'm grateful that Douglas and I have such a good friend in you.' It defused but didn't fully placate her. Her suspicions were not eased by the arrival of Capricorn. As they stepped out onto the porch, escorted by Hollis, Capricorn arrived in all her glory. Green satin jacket and peacock blue pants, a startling, feathered cloche on her head made for a startling contrast between her and the visitors.

'Oh good the cleaner has arrived.' Hollis ushered Capricorn through the door with a slight push. He followed her quickly and shut the door on the disbelieving duo.

'I'm no fucking cleaner Hol. I'm the girl who brings the spirits and the good times. I'm here to cure wabi-sabi.'

'Be quiet Cap. Just clearing out Ruby's unwanted visitors.' Hollis was back to his old self. 'Well what fun that was. Sit down Ruby you look very pale.'

'A solicitor Hollis. Is it against the law to impersonate one?'

'Impersonate?' He said indignantly. 'No impersonation my love. Absolutely qualified and bone fide legal practitioner.' He smiled. 'Surprise!'

He was right on both accounts. Ruby was surprised and she felt light-headed. The visit caused her pain, and it didn't simply arise from her injuries. Her father would never have bothered to check on her or order her home. He rarely noticed her at all but obviously Stella had a real bee in her bonnet. She had gone from a wonderful companion to a controlling harridan since Bonnie's death. Grief makes people act in strange ways, but this seemed quite extreme.

Capricorn stood behind Ruby and placed her hands on her temples. Her cool little hands took some of the heat and fight out of Ruby's head. A tender massage of her scalp and shoulders took the pain out of her body.

'Family. Break your mind with their crazy shit.' She never missed the mark with her observations, and she couldn't have been more correct with this one.

Break your mind indeed.

CHAPTER 23

With her body healed enough Ruby returned to work within days of her father's visit. She had called him to ask if she could have the car while he was away in Melbourne. He agreed and let her know he'd leave money in her room so she could buy herself something for Christmas. *Not sure that's how it works*. Ruby thought about her father's inability to act like a parent. *No practice, I guess.*

At work Ruby focused on writing up a few of Maxine's stories and a short piece on the history of Christmas traditions. She also wrote up a list of reputable stores where meat and accoutrements for the big day might be purchased. *Only folks with money need attend*. Hardly the conclusion that would make it through editorial but the truth of it worried Ruby. Those who had the means would have a very merry Christmas. Those without most certainly would be scraping the bottom of the barrel for meat of any kind to put on the table.

'There's more folks than not on the bare bones of their arses this Christmas.' Another of Maxine' pithy observations.

'Not sure that by-line will get editorial approval either.' And while Ruby laughed at Maxine's choice of words an idea had percolated and could not be easily dislodged. 'I'm just going out to stretch my legs for a bit. Get that worried look off your face I'm not going far.'

No point in sharing the idea with Maxine, yet. She had to see if the idea had the legs to make a story. At the city watchhouse she asked to see Constable Rayla Short who appeared within minutes. 'You've been having a rough time of it Miss Hart. How are you feeling?'

'I'm fine Rayla. I'm a good healer. And a bruise or two isn't likely to stop me for long which is why I've come to ask for a favour.'

'Sure but I can't kill Harper no matter how much he might deserve it.' A bit of a gallows joke but the two laughed.

'Maybe that would be possibly easier than what I'm really here for.' Rayla motioned to Ruby to sit. 'I want to speak to Mrs. Harper, Shae's mother.' Rayla sat back and lowered her gaze. She knew what Ruby asked for was somewhat inappropriate, but she had also read some of Ruby's work and knew that this young woman would be hard to dissuade.

'I can tell you where they were living the last time the police had anything to do with them. But I am advising you not to do it. They are a wild bunch and even with Harper out of the way there's no guarantee you'll get any kind of welcome.' Rayla put her hand on Ruby's shoulder and looked into her face. 'I love the fact that you are trying to make a change for these women, but you are just one little girl with a pen and a notepad. You might just be pushing water uphill with a stick.'

Rayla wrote the address on a small card. Josephine Harper, and what was left of her family lived in Inveresk. *The swamp* as it had become known. The suburb had been built virtually on the mudflats of the Tamar River with several streets at river level, a few below. The North Esk River bordered the houses on the southern side, the Tamar River on the west. Ruby crossed the bridge on foot and walked the block to Dry Street. The tidal flats had their own stench. Wet mud, algae and something akin to human detritus. It didn't do any good to dwell on what she might be smelling. She placed her hanky over her mouth and nose and walked as quickly as her sore body allowed.

The houses were in poor condition and the Harper's cottage on Dry Street, perhaps the most ramshackle of them all. Broken timbers and chairs that had seen better days filled both sides of the small porch. The windows that weren't boarded up with timber had sad and grimy curtains grimly hanging against them. From inside Ruby heard noise that adequately informed her that life went on. She politely knocked a few times. Footsteps, heavy and reluctant approached the door. The woman who stood in front of Ruby had the most worn-out face of any person she had seen. Dark circles and pouched under eyes spoke of weariness stretching across decades. Her hair greasy and pulled back in a matted bun did nothing to enhance her look. And there was a smell too. As pungent as the river miasma, it seemed that Mrs. Harper may not have had a bath for a while.

'We don't want no religion here love. Take y'self off now.' Mrs. Harper had mistaken Ruby for a do-gooder trawling for souls to save.

'I'm sorry Mrs. Harper to come unannounced and I don't want to disturb you but I would really like to talk to you.' Ruby hurried to add. 'I'm not from the church or any other organisation. I'm from The Examiner.' Josephine Harper's eyes widened in fear. 'I'm Ruby Hart.'

The revelation set Josephine Harper into near hysterics. She said a number of things but through the tears and howling noises Ruby could make no sense of it. Two youngsters joined their mother at the door. 'What you want lady? We ain't got nothing.'

Luckily Ruby had stopped at the Chinese fruit market and bought a bag of apples and plums and with the tentative offer of the gift the Harpers became less defensive. Josephine stopped crying and the boys pounced on the food.

With some calm established Ruby started again. 'I'm not here to cause you any trouble Mrs. Harper. I'm really not. But I'm sure you know that I'm the woman that your husband attacked. I guess I'm the reason he's in jail.'

Josephine dropped her head. 'I'm sorry he did that to you. You're just a kid.'

'I'm older than Shae. I really loved meeting her and I'm sorry I couldn't do more for her.'

The older woman looked up. 'You the girl who took my baby to the 'ospital.'

Ruby just nodded. 'You want to come in?'

While Ruby felt reticent about entering the house she felt the invitation was sincere.

The inside of the house was no better than the outside. A dampness permeated every surface, but the family offered her the best seat nearest the stove. 'Mrs. Harper…' Ruby started.

'I'm Jo. Just call me Jo. And this is Bobby and George. Me two biggest boys.' Everyone nodded a more civilised greeting.

'Jo I want to write about what happened to Shae and perhaps what has happened to you. I'd like to know your story.'

Jo sat on a small stool. The boys left with the rest of the fruit to the tiny backyard. 'I ain't got much of a story lovie. It's not one for the movie films.' But what Jo Harper didn't know, was that her story was more important than any romance or song and dance film shown on the big theatre screens.

Ruby began gently. She asked about Jo's childhood. 'I was put in care as a baby. Father up and left, mam had seven kids and we had nothing much. Didn't get schooling and when I was about eleven I worked on the docks. Met Gordie down there. He was eighteen.' Jo had relaxed a little. Ruby wrote a few notes on her pad. 'It weren't great but he had a bit of a shack he'd built down on the river. It weren't great.' Ruby recognised that statement as an extraordinary understatement. She had to keep the shock off her face as she thought about this woman as a child living with Gordon Harper. 'We had twenty years together. Lots of babies. Some of 'em didn't live long.'

'You're thirty-one?' Ruby would have placed her at fifty or more. And to deflect from her disbelief she asked a question. 'You said it wasn't a great life. Was that because of Mr. Harper or just the troubles.'

A long silence ensued. Eventually a little fighting spirit emerged. 'He couldn't keep his hands to himself. Even when my belly was full of his babies. Got drunk, nasty and then punched and kicked like he thought he was in the ring.' She shook her head. 'He'd beat the kids too. Shae real bad. Only girl we had and he thought she'd be a waste of space.' A small sob.

'And then she became pregnant.' Ruby prompted her. Jo cried for real.

'Gordie's stinking brother got to her. Right here in me house. I tried to stop him but Gordie smacked me so hard he knocked a tooth out. He's just having a bit of fun.' She looked at Ruby, angry, hurt. 'A bit a fun with a kid who just got her monthlies. I wanted to kill the pair of those bastards.'

Jo Harper talked for an hour. Ruby forgot the discomfort of the smells and chaos of the surroundings. She just listened. She wrote a few notes but mainly she just listened to the harrowing story of Jo Harper's life. Mud, despair, filth and the depravity of Gordon Harper and men like him. She heard the desolation in her voice. The anguish when she spoke of the hopeless future for her living children. The beatings, the lack, the drunkenness and the darkness of her life made for a torturous story. *Where is the light Jo?* The question stayed with Ruby.

The walk back to work was slow.

'Where have you been? I thought something awful had happened.' Maxine's face showed her anxiety about Ruby going missing for a few hours.

'Sorry Maxine. I met Josephine Harper at her house. Wanted to know about her life. About Shae. About him.' While looking exhausted Ruby also seemed to have developed a greater strength in the time she'd been out of the office. 'The walk did me good. And I've got an idea for my new story.'

And it consumed her. Ruby wrote for hours. She called the piece *The Monster's Wife* and while she worried that the title sounded too melodramatic, she felt wedded to the reality. She didn't know what she expected to see and learn by turning up and talking to Jo Harper, but expectation and pre-conceived ideas are often proved wrong when one gets to the human face. Jo, at eleven, had her fate sealed by the connivences of the man who would become her husband. A man whose fists did most of the talking. Whose moral turpitude sank to depths that Ruby couldn't fathom.

After work she walked back to Margaret Street with Maxine. They talked a little about work, Christmas and what the new year might bring. 1929 seemed to stretch before Ruby with so much promise. A wonderful job, friends, Della's baby arriving, a year closer to independence and Lawton. A list of joys to be grateful for.

Before Christmas Day some shopping had to be done. Small gifts for everyone in the house and something for the feast had to be purchased. Ruby had already sent cards and small gifts to Mrs. Rowlands, Caleb and Elvie; letters to all the Merrington friends including Sister Reggie and big Rosie-P. With her new story she sent a card to Burky wishing her all the best for the season and the New Year. In it she expressed her hope to gain a place at university when her father's control of her life ceased.

'Summer solstice is upon us children. Time for a pre-Christmas knees-up.' Hollis loved a pagan celebration. He dragged them all out into the cold and lit an enormous bonfire on the shortest day in June. But for the longest summer day he planned an outdoor event to worship the sun with candles, dancing and Pooky's best firewater. 'Head-dresses for all. Jules is making them.'

'Moon bathing at midnight. Nude.' Capricorn's addition to the planning.

'Seriously Cap. I'm keeping my pants on.' Florian found her suggestion amusing and yet terrifying.

'I don't think I'll be getting my big belly out Capricorn. It's so big and white now it will be in competition with the moon itself.' Della laughed and arched her back to show the roundness of her pregnant body.

'Like the goddess Luna herself dear one. Perfect image for the season of life.' Hollis loved a dramatic turn of phrase.

'Moon bathing. Clothes on. Or mostly on. Depending on your preferences.' Maxine laughed along with the others.

Ruby had no intentions of removing her clothes, but the thought of Lawton stretched out under the moon brought a now familiar rush of heat to her body. He certainly sidetracked her, even the thought of him brought her undone.

Over the next few days Jules had made them all wild headwear. Conical shapes covered in bunches of herbs and flowers. He'd pinned fridges to the edges and used straw to elongate the points. To heighten the madness, he had cut calico masks and drawn flowers around the eye holes. For Hollis he had found a pair of stag antlers which had been sewn to an old bowler hat. It would look magnificent under the candlelight.

The Saturday afternoon saw everyone involved in setting up the yard. Candles had been placed on every stable surface. Several card tables appeared, and Jules covered them with vibrant cloth. Plates and glasses were placed on one, leaving room on the others for drinks and food. Hollis had purchased a new gramophone for the occasion. His record collection covered many musical genres, Jazz, dance, classical and the newly popular American blues. The variety ensured a noisy evening ahead.

Lawton arrived before five. He had to complete some planting at the Gorge gardens before he could get to the house. In white linen pants and a blue cotton shirt he looked beautiful, happy and ready for a celebration. He scooped Ruby up in his arms. Kissed her briefly and put her down to look at her. In a sleeveless shift dress and bare feet, she embodied the images Lawton kept drawing of her. The back of the dress plunged between her shoulder blades and the front dipped low enough to show a hint of her decolletage. The bruising and soreness remained, but strangely joy overrode pain.

Cold chicken, cheeses, bread, salad, olives and cold trout with spiced mayonnaise found places between the bottles of champagne and Finnish firewater. Lawton had brought beer and a bottle of gin. 'A gift from the manager for Christmas. Thought we might as well give it a whirl tonight.'

Blankets and cushions were strewn under the trees and as the light began to fade the candles added a wonderful mystery to Hollis's yard. The party could have been anywhere in the world with its mysterious guests and shadowy ambiance. The headdresses, the masks, the blasting music and the gyrating figures all mixed with a little alcohol not only brought the house to life but the neighbourhood as well. By midnight more than a little alcohol had been consumed, even Ruby had too much champagne and felt liberated, or legless. She and Lawton danced and kissed, and when exhausted fell into a pile of cushions in each other's arms. Della had fallen asleep under a blanket despite the noise. Inevitably Capricorn removed her clothes to stand naked under the moon, still in her conical hat and eye mask. Maxine, Florian and Pooky relentlessly danced like pagans abandoning their glasses to drink straight from the bottles. Jules and Hollis curled together with their backs resting against a low brick wall, watching the show, kissing and touching one another in a manner that spoke of their love, their commitment, the trust they felt.

Ruby wondered at the joy the Aphorism Club generated. She felt quite tipsy and very full having eaten more food in one evening than she had all week while she recovered. Lawton's hand rested on her bare back, his face buried into her neck, his eyes averted from the mad antics of his dearest friends. He had nearly fallen asleep when the festivity ended abruptly.

The neighbours, having had enough of the noise and wild goings on had called the police.

The beefy sergeant's voice cut through the sound of the music and the general yelling. 'Shut that music off.' It was the sort of command that one wouldn't ignore.

Capricorn sauntered to her dressing gown, impervious to the looks of disgust on the four officers' faces. Hollis extricated himself from Jules's arms and stood to calm the troubled waters. 'Gentlemen. Our apologies for the noise and merry making. It is the season for a little celebration.' The police were unmoved by his geniality. They were more interested in the appearance of indecency.

'I suppose you are aware of the Criminal Code of 1924.' The sergeant stepped up to Hollis.

'Section 122 I suspect you are referring to?' Hollis matched the officer's demeanour. 'Acts against the order of nature.' He turned and looked at the bewildered faces of his friends who had gathered behind him. 'Nothing unnatural here my dear friend. Just a little dancing under the moon. And too much conviviality.' He put his hand on the officer's shoulder. 'Would do you good to join us.'

And that was the step too far. In a single action the sergeant pulled out his baton and brought it down on Hollis's wrist. 'Get your hands off me you old faggot.' A second swipe caught him on the shoulder. Two officers who had been standing back immediately yanked Hollis forward and handcuffed him. He was deeply shocked and utterly speechless. Jules tried to move protectively but his drunkenness saw him fall to his knees but Pooky, under the influence of his own brew, flew into action. Ruby and Lawton heard the ruckus before seeing it. The sergeant lay on his back with Pooky straddled across his belly. He looked like he was riding a walrus. Maxine attempted to pull her friend off the stranded officer but also had to hold the diminutive Capricorn back from entering the fracas. With Hollis thrown to the ground, the other three uninvited guests dragged Pooky away and arrested him.

'Stop it. Stop now.' Della sounded quite authoritarian and momentarily everyone gave pause to the madness. The sergeant, who had eventually gained his feet swung his baton in her direction. 'So you'd hit a pregnant woman would you?' Her sheer belligerence tempered his behaviour. 'This is a private event. You can't just come in here and arrest people.'

It sounded like a reasonable argument. 'Assaulting an officer of the law is my reason to arrest. Be thankful I'm not taking you all in. Especially the odd bod with her clothes off. But I'll take the foreigner and the queer. It will do for a night's work.' He sounded breathless and simultaneously arrogant.

'Fear not my friends. I will make my own defence in this diabolical travesty.' Hollis shouted as the officers dragged him down the side path. And with that the party ended. The mood shattered, along with several glasses and plates, put an end to everyone's sense of fun.

'I'll go down to the watchhouse in the morning and see what is going to happen.' Lawton's calmness settled the shock and disbelief. He scooped Jules up. 'I'm putting him to bed. He won't be any use in the morning if we need him.'

'Go to bed too Della. You look exhausted. And while I know you are the boss of all of us do this one thing please. Think of your baby.' Ruby retrieved her practical side after the disbelief lessened. 'The rest of us can clean up and get everything inside.'

Della didn't argue. She felt drained and the thought of packing up and hauling everything inside did not sit well. The others, under Ruby's direction, folded blankets and washed plates and glasses. Pillows were returned to lounges from where they'd been taken, broken glass found its way to the bin and food that hadn't been consumed went into the icebox to keep for the following day. The candles were extinguished and by 2 am in the morning Capricorn and Maxine walked with Florian to his place.

'I'll sleep on the couch Ruby.' Lawton kissed her. 'It'll be alright you know.'

In her bed she heard Della snoring delicately and Jules with less refinement. But her thoughts lingered on Lawton laying downstairs. Overpowering thoughts that she felt inappropriate given two of her friends were sleeping in a jail cell. More than inappropriate when she thought of how Josephine Harper might be spending the night. But intense and all-consuming thoughts can't always be extinguished.

She stood at the top of the steps and simply said his name. 'Lawton.'

CHAPTER 24

Ruby had never felt the sensation of bare skin on bare skin. Lawton's body felt like satin as it moved against her. His hands touched every part of her. Moving lightly in places like her breasts, more demandingly over her back and arms. Gently as he placed his hand between her thighs. The sensation demanded all her attention. Nothing could enter her mind other than the exquisite pleasure of him. 'Are you sure Ruby? Are you sure you want this?' Lawton raised his torso above hers so that he could look into her eyes as if he sought absolute assurance that she wanted him to make love to her.

Breathless, unsure, desperate for the sensation to never end she whispered, 'Yes.'

How could it be possible for pain to feel so wonderful. The pressure of his thighs pressing hers apart, the penetration and the wild rhythm of his thrusting hurt and thrilled in equal measure. His collapse onto her and his mouth open and warm on hers brought the crescendo of his orgasm to finality. She could have laid there forever. 'I'm sorry Ruby I have to remove the sheath. It's a bit unromantic this bit.' Lawton ever the gentleman.

On his return to the bed, he brought a towel with him, and he held her warmly, her side against his belly. 'Are you alright Rubes? Pop the towel under you because the first time might cause you to bleed a little.'

She didn't answer immediately. Her mind filled with thoughts, questions and fear. 'Yes. But everything feels like it has changed. I've changed.'

'It's not a terrible change. It's just life. Two people love each other and this is part of that love.' Lawton sounded like a teacher explaining the birds and bees. Her silence worried him. 'Ruby?'

'I'm fine. I just have to think through everything. It's just me.' She paused. 'Do you love me Lawton?'

'So very much. You're all I think about. And I've thought about this night a thousand times. I thought it might be a little more romantic, perhaps not after so much nastiness. Nor so much gin. But here we are.' He laughed gently. 'Not all plans go the way we might imagine they will. Sleep now. Think less.' He yawned. 'We'll talk in the morning.'

Ruby had never really shared a bed. Even as a tiny girl Aunt Minnie always sent her back to her bed. At school sometimes in a big storm someone might sit on the bed if they were scared or had to spill a secret or to have deep and meaningful discussions, but no-one ever shared the space all night. It felt warm, then too warm; too crowded and then just perfect. Lawton breathed deeply, no snoring, just long slow breaths. She felt his body ease into sleep. His arm heavy across her bare belly delayed her sleep. *Changed and yet the same*. The girl with the raspberry birthmark was different now. Someone loved her. And here he was in her bed. And if people like Stella were to be believed she was now ruined. *Ruined for what?* The question remained just that. A question. At some point in the early morning, she too fell into a deep sleep. Love making, champagne and the minor brawl with the police eventually had to be let go. Tomorrow the problems would be solved.

When she eventually woke Lawton was not beside her. At the end of the bed Della stood with two cups of tea. Her smile reflected her suspicions of the night's events. 'Well petite larme a big night I think.' Her belly stretched the satin fabric of her nightgown. She looked so beautiful. Ruby on the other hand felt she must have looked quite the mess. She wriggled to a sitting position and reached for her robe in an effort to cover her body. With a little effort she tried to smooth her hair and lift her chin as if to imply there was nothing to see here. Della sat beside her in the bed. 'Are you happy Rubes? Did everything go to plan?' And not waiting for an answer she continued. 'Tell me you were sensible and insisted Lawton use a…'

Ruby stopped her. 'Yes. Yes. And yes he did.' She sipped the tea, grateful for the heat and the fluid as she felt parched. 'It was a strange thing Della. This sex thing. It hurt and I felt afraid but it was also the most extraordinary thing. It's like you lose your mind.'

Della laughed. 'You do lose your mind. We'd never do it if we were sane in the moment. And it's especially wonderful when you choose to do it, and with whom you do it. Altogether different if it's not your choice.'

The two women sat quietly for a few minutes, drinking tea, looking out at the morning sunshine and forgetting the life changing events and even momentarily forgetting they had friends in trouble. 'I've run a bath for you Rubes. It will make you feel a bit better. Lawton and Maxine have gone to the police station to see what can be done for Hollis and Pooky. Jules is bawling in the kitchen. Lawton decided he'd be of no assistance if he went with them.'

The bath did wonders. A piece of toast and more tea helped Ruby feel closer to normal. She sat with her arm around Jules who had the worst hangover and a dreadful sense of guilt. 'Poor Hollis. I was no use at all to him. I couldn't believe that copper hit him like that. Why did he do that?'

'Because he could.' Ruby hadn't meant to sound so cynical. 'Go and clean up Jules. Put on some clothes because we might be needed.' As he climbed the stairs like an obedient child Florian and Capricorn arrived. Very much the worse for wear. Coffee this time for the new arrivals. Ruby hugged her tiny friend. 'Was this the storm you predicted Cap? Are we done now? I think we've all had enough.'

Capricorn, miserable with a headache from too much firewater, still in the previous night's make-up looked forlorn. 'Dearest girl we are not even close to the storm that's coming. Last night was just a spring shower.' She took her cup and toast to the lounge. 'I can only eat laying down. Standing up is too hard this morning.'

The church bells reminded everyone that it was Sunday. And as if heralding a triumphant return to home base the front door opened. Pooky and Maxine appeared. Behind them Lawton virtually carried Hollis whose face had traces of blood from his nose and a swollen eye closed shut by bruising. Maxine immediately cleared the couch opposite the one Capricorn occupied. 'Can you chip some ice out of the icebox and wrap it in a towel. Some warm water and a cloth too.'

'What happened?' Florian's question quite redundant. 'Jesus wept.'

'They really did a number on him. I think his nose is broken.' Lawton strained to keep his tone passive but the anger in his eyes said it all.

'That fucking fat man.' Capricorn always helpful with her descriptions.

'Not just him. A few others came to the cell and knocked him around.' Pooky had gone beyond rage and wept openly at the events that unfolded. 'They put me in another cell so I couldn't help him. I could just hear it.' He nursed his own black eye.

Maxine tended to Hollis so gently. Wiped the blood from his face and placed the wrapped ice on his eye. 'Sorry old darling this will hurt a bit.'

'Flo you'd better go upstairs and let Jules know what's happened. It will be enough of a shock with a warning and worse without.' Maxine continued to stage direct the unfolding.

'Maxie you're a rough old nurse. But I love you darl.' Hollis spoke for the first time. Lawton helped him sit up a little. 'Well happy summer solstice my little band. How are the hangovers?' Hollis groaned a little as Maxine moved the ice to the bridge of his nose. 'This had better not mess up my beautiful face.'

Jules could be heard before he appeared. 'Hollis what have they done to you? My dearest.'

Lawton prevented him launching himself on top of his lover. 'He's in a bit of pain Jules go easy.'

'Will there be charges?' Ruby's pragmatic mind kicked in. 'We need to think about what we do next.'

'That's my girl. Should be a lawyer Ruby Pearl. You've got the mind for it. But it appears that the charge of indecency will not be laid. Drunkenness and aggressive behaviour towards the constabulary came with a warning. You are free to go Mr. Bright.' Hollis took a long pause. 'How kind of them.'

So much more needed to be said and done but for now everyone was safe. The delight of the night ended in violence for some, joy for others and terribly sick heads for the rest. Once Hollis was helped into the bath and put to bed everyone, but Ruby and Maxine curled up in spaces for afternoon siestas. Sleeping off the tiredness, the sadness and the pain.

'Maxine was Hollis beaten because he's homosexual? Is that really what happened?'

'Ruby sometimes I forget how young you are. Half the world ignores what is blatantly wrong and the other half fights what it sees as different. And the other quarter try to fix it.'

'There's something wrong with your fractions Max. But I get what you're saying. But I just can't understand why people are so afraid of anyone who looks different or believes something different or loves someone who others don't approve of.' Ruby pondered the madness of people. 'How could Hollis's and Jules's love for each other hurt those men. What does it take away from them if people of the same sex live together? Why isn't kindness enough?'

'Stop Rubes. You are going down the rabbit hole. People are lazy in their thinking. Someone decides something is wrong and we never question it. They just categorise people into two groups. Those like us, those not like us. The first group always seem to have the power.' Maxine yawned. She too needed a little nap.

'And they always seem to be men with money and power dividing us.' Ruby's last thought sent her to her room to write. Lawton had fallen asleep in the bed they had been in only hours ago. She felt tempted to lay beside him but wanted firstly to get her ideas down on paper. She went to the kitchen table instead. When she opened her notebook, she found another of Lawton's sketches. This time she was asleep, the simple strokes resembling the sheets under her bare breasts, her hair wild across the hint of a pillow and the raspberry birthmark shaped as a heart. Shocked, delighted, mesmerised by the beauty of the simple sketch Ruby stared at the image before she tucked it away. Then she wrote about injustice. Wrote more about kindness and its power and then wrote about the confounding and complicated nature of love making. This time the romance story she tried to write months ago came to life with authenticity and maturity. A proper love story.

The few pages left in the pad reminded her that she would have to go to Duck Reach. She needed to retrieve her folio and typewriter but with Christmas two days away it was most unlikely that she'd get up there. Her father most likely would be away until after the new year, so she had time. Both she and Maxine would do a full day's work on Monday, Christmas Eve and even though the paper wouldn't go out again until the 27th of December, stories had to be written, typeset and readied for printing. She felt it unlikely that the Aphorism Club would feel like celebrating Christmas, but the plans had been made, and life would go on. Gifts were wrapped and set under the tree that Hollis insisted on. *To hell with the half that don't like us. To hell with you all. And a merry bloody Christmas*. Ruby's last thoughts made her laugh. Perhaps one day she would be as bold as Capricorn and use her favourite word. *Merry fucking Christmas*. But she wasn't that bold yet.

CHAPTER 25

Despite it all Christmas was merry enough. With a few days in between the craziness of summer solstice and *the birth of our Lord Jesus Christ* as Florian insisted calling it, all the drunken heads healed, and the battered ones were on the mend. Hollis appeared to be returning to his normal self, but the spark hadn't rekindled. In quiet moments he seemed lost in thought, occasionally he would sit with his elbows on his knees and hold his head in his hands. 'Everything alright Hollis?' Ruby asked tentatively. She sat beside him and placed her hand on his back.

'As right as it can be dear one. Just a bit sore.' He made some attempt at a smile.

'Perhaps you are a little sadder than you are sore. Both can feel the same sometimes.'

'Your observational skills are a credit to you Ruby. Yes I'm disappointed with the world. It has let me down.' He sat back and looked at his young friend. 'And you look so very grown up these days. The perils of the Aphorism Club, we've aged you.'

Ruby blushed and looked away. 'It's a good thing to come to understand the world Hollis. I'm grateful for the home you've given me and the friendship everyone has shared.' She paused. 'But I think I'll have to go home eventually.

Or find a little flat somewhere with Della and allow Maxine and Capricorn to have their bedrooms back.'

Before he could offer advice, the Christmas crew arrived in a wave of noise and movement.

'Champagne, presents then the feast. That's the order for the day.' Capricorn had fully recovered and seemed prepared to go down the hangover road one more time. No one denied her. Drinks were poured and gifts handed out. Pooky and Florian spent time in the kitchen juggling baking dishes in and out of the oven. Music played and gifts were opened and genuine joy was expressed in the giving and receiving. Lawton left Ruby's gift until last. Inside, two lovely things took her breath away. A frame holding one of Lawton's drawings was one that he'd obviously worked on, as the face had touches of watercolour. The likeness so exact it could have been a photograph. He had captured the shape of her eyes and the small lines that appeared when she smiled. And more importantly he didn't hide the birthmark. He used a pale pink to show its shape, its movement under her eye and the lack of uniformity in its border. For the first time she could see that the mark had an element of beauty, a uniqueness that brought her face to life. So enamoured with looking at it she hadn't realised the room had quietened.

'It's so beautiful.' Della broke the silence. 'You are so beautiful petite larme.'

'There's also this.' Lawton held up a cuff bracelet. 'I'm afraid this time the rubies and pearls are just paste but one day they will be real.' He kissed her gently. 'Jewel of the southern isle.'

'Enough sentiment. Let's eat and drink and fall down.' Capricorn leapt up and danced a little wildly. 'And when I'm properly drunk I'll sing you all fado.'

'No Cap. Not that miserable Portuguese wailing. It's a day to be happy.'

'Then it's the music of my homeland. Pelimanni polkas and song.' Pooky did not want to be out done.

'Let's just start with some jazz. The rest of the suggestions might cause too much heartburn while we eat.' Maxine put a record on the gramophone and moved everyone to the kitchen table. The club had managed to gather a feast.

Vegetables roasted in fat, a huge leg of lamb, fish in a creamy onion sauce, fat spicy sausages, cheeses and fruit laid out on great platters.

'Before we eat a toast. To the chefs, to the friends, to the ones absent. To love and to new life that will grace our little club soon enough.' Hollis raised his glass to Della. 'May we be happy in the lives we have chosen and in the joy to come.'

With glasses filled they all raised them to Hollis. 'Cheers.'

'Saúde.'

'Kippis.'

'À votre santé.'

'To our very good health.'

The diverse gathering of cultures was not lost on anyone. Those who'd come here from wars, broken hearted and alone. Those who'd suffered through poverty and loss. Those who'd sought to be themselves in the face of bigotry and stupidity. And a girl with a raspberry birthmark who suddenly realised she had everything she had ever wanted. A family who loved her, freedom and hope. Ruby looked down at the faux rubies and pearls on her wrist. She loved them more for their poor quality, they were not being something they weren't, each piece of cut glass had its own story, a glimmer and a little colour all its own. And it had been given with love. Something more valuable than any gem brought up from under the earth or the sea.

The day passed with bellies filled. Late afternoon siestas were mandated by too much wine and overeating. Chairs, couches and blankets outside held the sleeping bodies in pairs and singles. Della stretched out on one of the couches, she felt too weary to take the stairs to her room. Maxine and Pooky took the other one laying end to end with their feet meeting in the middle. After a minute or two of playful kicking they curled up on their individual halves and started the slow descent to dozing. Capricorn took a blanket to the back yard and lay beside Ruby in the sunshine. The two lay on their sides chatting quietly before Lawton and Florian joined them. They had been cleaning up and putting food away with Jules and Hollis. Ruby turned away from Capricorn and lay belly to belly with Lawton. 'Darling girl how are you feeling.'

Ruby could have given him a dissertation covering the gamut of her feelings, but one word summed them up. 'Happy.'

In his embrace, in the perfect December sunshine, Ruby dreamt of her mother. Alma stood with her arms outstretched on one side of the bridge that spanned the river that rushed into the green basin in front of the Gorge gardens. Ruby couldn't tell if her mother was beckoning her or telling her to stay back. Her gestures seemed confused and yet, somewhat desperate. She woke with a start. Soft voices spoke around her. The group had all woken from their slumbers and had made their way to the garden. Ruby was the last to wake. Lawton sat beside her drinking a beer. The others commencing round two of the Christmas celebration. Even Della looked brighter and sipped on chilled lemon barley water. Only Capricorn noticed Ruby wake. She lay on her side staring at her. 'More bad dreams wabi-sabi?'

'Don't know if it was a bad dream or just a weird one. I think the woman stood on a bridge. She might have been my mother.' Ruby yawned and sat up.

'She's bringing you a message. The storm. It's still coming you know. I'll read your cards again.' Capricorn got up and rummaged in the enormous bag she insisted on taking everywhere.

'Not the bloody cards again Cap. Were all fortune told out.' Florian laughed as he picked the tiny mystic up and swung her about. 'But if there's money and fame in the future I'll have a listen.' He kissed her on top of her head.

So, she set to laying out her cards for each one in turn. No-one had a reading that predicted fame or fortune. But she insisted that change was afoot. For all of them. 'Ruby has a storm coming and it looks like we might all get swept up in it.'

'My apologies friends for dragging you into my tempest.' Ruby attempted to laugh off the dire prediction.

'Storms are not always bad things. Painful and sometimes you get a bit broken but they clean away the past.' Capricorn struggled for the words. 'It scrapes the pipes. You know like cleaning down the holes.'

'Good God Cap that sounds like a medical procedure. And I don't want anything scraping my pipes.' Hollis's salacious implications made them laugh.

Then more food, more Finnish firewater and a long night of music brought the day to an end.

'Pook is obviously not moving from the couch tonight so why don't you come back to the cottage with me. It will give us a chance to be alone.' Lawton smiled. 'To talk. If you want to.'

Ruby suspected that the suggestion to talk might have been a euphemism for other nocturnal activity. She nodded and went to her room to gather clean clothes, her notebook and toiletries. No-one noticed them slipping out. The air had cooled but the temperature remained mild. In the silence Ruby could hear people inside their homes closing down the day. Their footsteps were accompanied by the sounds of the river moving sluggishly between the banks. Only when they got to the Kings Bridge did Lawton speak. 'We really can just talk tonight Ruby if you're not sure, it's just that we get so little time on our own. Always seems we are sorting out something for someone and we don't really just talk to each other.'

The steps to the cottage were concealed behind a white gate. They were steep and uneven. Just like everything on the Gorge path they had been cleaved into the natural rock face. The little house appeared to emerge from the cliff and teeter over the path. Inside the rooms were orderly and cosy. At the front of the building the lounge and kitchen took in the view of the gorge and bridge. The two bedrooms came directly off this space. Lawton had one, and recently Pooky was in the other. The place had a sparseness but was very neat. His work clothes that had been recently washed were hanging on a wire strung between the two sides of the veranda. 'Would you like a cup of tea?'

Ruby settled herself at the table and took the cup from Lawton. He sat opposite. And with the greatest of ease, they began to talk. He spoke a little more of his childhood, the ugly bits and the wonderful love he received from his grandmother. He talked about his ambition and his determination to be a manager one day, possibly of the Gorge or City Park. 'But I don't want to sit at a desk all day. I still want to be able to get out into the dirt and the plants.' Then it was Ruby's turn. Her childhood had a different kind of ugly and she too had enormous affection for her rescuers. 'Not only Minnie but Caleb and

Elvie too. And then there was Merrington.' She took a sip of tea. 'If you think boarding schools are all a bit like a Dickens workhouse, you'd be wrong. I loved school and the people in it. Even big Rosie-P became our greatest ally.'

'What the hell is a big Rosie-P?' Lawton couldn't wrap his head around the existence of such a person.

'Sister Rose-Philippine. We thought she must have been ten foot tall and had a head the size of a rhinoceros.' The two laughed at the image. 'But she was just one of the very best. She had her faith and took the tenets of the church seriously but she also believed that her job was to ensure we could hold our own. Hold our own in a world that didn't want us to.' Ruby looked up at Lawton. 'Girls have to be able to determine what they want for themselves. And that takes courage.'

Lawton came around from his side of the table. He took Ruby's hands in his and pulled her to standing. 'Darling jewel of the south you can be anything you want to be. I just want to be able to be with you to watch it happen.' It sounded like a vow. It felt like a covenant between lovers. And the night finished with love making that was equal in its earnestness and yet more in synchronicity. Lawton, less tentative and Ruby more confident as they came to know each other's bodies. The effort exhausted the pair of them. Sleep came and the night ended.

Breakfast on the tiny cantilevered veranda started another wonderful day. The early summer sun had a bite to it. The air was still and beginning to warm up. She wondered what the sleepers at Margaret Street might be thinking when they noticed her absence. Ruby felt no concern. There was no judgement in the house.

'I must get up to the Reach to get my typewriter and folio. But I'll have to go back to Hollis's because I can't walk in these silly sandals. I'll be able to drive back if my father has left the keys to the car.'

'Lucky for you I've got my new motorbike running. Bought it from Shippy last month.' Ruby looked confused. 'Shippy is the boat builder down the river. Not his real name of course. I think its Bethel or something else quite biblical. But he did sell it to me for a good price. It's not that comfortable but we aren't covering a huge distance.'

Not comfortable turned out to be something of an understatement. The rear of the motorcycle had a short, padded seat over the rear tyre. Ruby had to hold onto Lawton's waist for grim life. She wedged her small bag between them for safety. As they took off over the Kings Bridge Ruby was grateful for her decision to wear trousers as the wind ruffled her clothes as Lawton gathered speed. If she'd been in a dress, it might have blown over her head. The noise drowned out every other sound. It roared up the hills and kicked up dust and rocks when they got close to the Reach. Ruby felt certain that if her father had been at the power station he would have heard them coming for miles. She worried what Stella might think if she were at home. It was most likely that in Douglas's absence Stella's husband would be managing the turbines.

Luckily the Birds car was absent from the front of their house. Douglas's Citroen stood in its usual spot which meant Ruby did not have to return on the back of Lawton's bike. She took her bag and indelicately removed herself from the seat. 'Head back to the gang. I'll be there soon once I look around the house and get my things.' She kissed him and he let his hand rest on her hip. He said something but the engines chugging made it impossible to hear.

As she climbed the steps to the front door she could hear the thrum of Lawton's bike in the distance. The door had been locked but the key had been put under the front planter. The house was dark and cool. The curtains had been closed since Douglas left for Melbourne. The keys to the car and an envelope lay on the hall table. Ruby blinked in disbelief at the one hundred pounds her father had left for her. It almost equalled her yearly pay from the newspaper and would be useful if she had to find a place for Della and herself. And the baby when it arrived. Her wages would hardly stretch to cover all the costs of living independently. But that problem would have to be solved another day.

With the money and keys Douglas had left yet another note. It seemed he could say very little to Ruby's face about any matter. The note covered several issues. The first, a Christmas greeting and his hope that she had a *reasonable* celebration. Ruby shook her head at the strange adjective. Secondly, he expressed his concerns about her living arrangements and his hope that she would return to the Reach particularly as, his third point, that he would be travelling to London after the new year. He had been offered the opportunity to meet with other hydro power experts from Europe which would benefit the expansion of the Tasmanian hydro grid. *As I'm away until the beginning of March perhaps you could return to our house, with your friend, at least until I return.* This suggestion solved at least one of Ruby's concerns. Della may not wish to be at the Reach given its distance from the town. Or as Ruby had learned from Stella, perhaps Della could be taught to drive. Nothing could be decided until she spoke to her friends, but it would be rather pointless to drag all her work to Margaret Street if she intended moving back into the house.

While she thought she did a little housework. She stripped back her bed to let the mattress air, opened all the curtains to fill the rooms with light. The combustion stove needed a clean out and some of the wood that had been cut needed to be stored inside to ensure it would be dry enough to get the heat going quickly. The icebox had no ice in it, so some would need to be ordered, and food purchased if she decided to come home. Not particularly arduous tasks. The garden, however, needed more attention. In the year since she arrived the annuals had bloomed and died and with some care they'd flower again over the rest of summer.

In the shed she found a pair of fairly new secateurs and a very blunt scythe. Ruby thought she would spend an hour attempting to cut back the worst of the dry grass and weeds so that on her return, should she decide to, the garden project wouldn't be too onerous. Walking around the side of the house she pulled up when Harry Bird blocked her progress. 'Sorry Ruby I didn't know who was in the house. Just saw the door open and heard your footsteps coming around. Thought it might be someone breaking in.'

'No just me Mr. Bird. No break-in. Using the keys.' Ruby wondered what he'd been told about her flight from the house. 'Just read my father's note about his travel plans. I'm going to move back in while he's away.'

'Stella told me there had been a ruckus. And that some bloke attacked you. She and Doug were really worried.' He sounded genuinely concerned. 'Don't like to think of a young kid like you being the victim of a drunk. You okay now?'

'It certainly shook me up a bit. And I had a few cracked ribs but my friends took really good care of me.' Ruby sounded a little more defiant.

'Look Ruby I know fathers and their children don't always see eye to eye. Jeez I belted my old man once when I was sixteen. Mind you he got the better punch in. Never did that again.' Harry laughed. And then got serious. 'But parents really do want to keep their children safe, particularly their daughters. And I know Stella gets up a head of steam and thinks she can boss everyone around but if you come back up we'll keep an eye out for you.' He took the blunt scythe from her. 'And you're more likely to hurt yourself with this old thing than cut any grass.'

Harry Bird offered no judgement about her flight to her friends. He just offered a genuinely caring hand to help. Stella might be a different story.

'And don't worry about Stella. She's all bark.'

CHAPTER 26

With Douglas away it made perfect sense to move back to Duck Reach. It meant being able to set up her writing in the front room which had sun in the morning and cool shadows in the heat of the afternoon. Della felt less certain about moving with her. The isolation didn't really appeal and the thought of Stella even less tempting. But she did want to be with Ruby, the others were a wonderful distraction but her dearest friend provided an unfaltering strength, particularly as she faced the final months of her pregnancy. 'If I'm totally truthful Rubes I'm frightened. The birth is one thing but being a mother is terrifying.' For the first time Della cried.

'It will be okay Della. I know nothing of motherhood myself but I'm sure we can work it out.' She held her close. 'I'm sure there's a book we can read about it.' The two laughed. 'Or we can call on Capricorn to provide some wisdom from beyond the veil.' More laughter. 'How hard can it be?' Ruby's question was not easily answered.

New Year provided the club with another reason for celebration. A little more toned down from the summer solstice debacle. But a night that finished with the promise of several sore heads, absurd resolutions for being better selves in 1929 and with Ruby and Lawton laying in his bed talking about the future. 'What is ahead for you Ruby Pearl? Other than spending more time in my bed.' Lawton curled his body around hers.

'I think I'm going to speak to Burky about university. In Hobart. I always thought I'd go back to Melbourne and study there but I love my life here. And I can't see a way of leaving you behind.'

Lawton sat up. 'I'm not going to be a reason that you hold back Ruby. Whatever the life you want I'll support you. I'll follow you to the moon if necessary.' He sat up and then straddled her hips. 'I love you. I just hope that's enough.' He bent down to kiss her but kept his eyes open. He stared into her eyes seeking confirmation that it would be enough.

'It's more than enough.'

The year began with long warm days. Launceston's climate had the reputation of having freezing winters and long wet spring seasons but only the locals knew that summer in the town could be hot. It didn't have the instability of Hobart with the Antarctic winds blowing from the south all year. Nor did it have the coastal sea breezes that kept the towns to the north and east temperate. Days were spent at work with fans blowing and windows opened to catch the slightest waft of air. Late afternoons and weekends brought the town to the First Basin to swim in the cold green waters that took the heat out of hot bodies. Even Della, who was known to have an aversion to deep water, floated about on her back with her belly to the sun. She wore light shorts and a billowing shirt as her swimmers no longer fitted. Ruby resorted to her racing bathers. The longer leg covered the tops of her thighs, but the fabric couldn't hide the muscular nature of her body. Fearlessly she swam across the expanse of the water while the timid and water averse sat on rocks dangling their feet.

'There be monsters out there wabi-sabi. Get back here.' Capricorn continually insisted that Ruby would be snapped up by some slimy leviathan that lurked in the depths. 'Your splashing around will call it up.' But Capricorn's warnings were unheard or ignored. Ruby's strong front crawl action saw her glide through the glassy, impenetrable green at speed. She recalled the freedom of learning to swim and then upskill her style while at Merrington. Water, when one could swim, offered a special kind of freedom.

Lawton swam beside her some days, but he couldn't match Ruby's speed or grace. He hadn't had lessons but managed a wide arm swinging action that kept him afloat and propelled him slowly across the surface. Ruby attempted to teach Pooky and Capricorn to swim, but both had little inclination to embrace the instruction. 'Better stay on land and put my feet in.' Pooky sat in his underwear with his ankles just submerged. 'Better the fishes eat just my feet and not the whole of me.' Ruby splashed him and his squealed like a child at the cold water hitting his body.

Maxine embraced a new style of swimming costume and had little, or no intention of getting it wet. 'I look fabulous and I want everyone to know. How could they see how wonderful I look if I'm under the water?'

And January and February passed in this way. Working, writing, swimming, eating and spending weekends with Lawton. The difficulties of December faded until Gordon Harper's trial. It had been slated for February 24th, and Ruby would be called to give her account of what occurred on the night. John Hooks, Mr. Dryden and Maxine were also expected to be questioned.

The court building was located around the corner from The Examiner offices. The witnesses walked together arriving early so the prosecution could speak to them. Ruby, as the victim would be on the stand first. 'Just tell the story of the events of the night and add nothing else.' The lawyer seemed to expect Ruby to embellish the events for some reason. 'And the same for the rest of you. Just what you saw and heard.' While he sounded angry, Ruby suspected his tone reflected his weariness more than his dislike of journalists.

On the stand Ruby gave a very creditable account of the events of the night Gordon Harper attacked her. Her clear answers left little to interpretation. The description of her injuries and effort to protect herself left little to the imagination. But the defence had other versions of the story it wished to insinuate into proceedings. 'You knew the accused's daughter I believe Miss Hart.'

'I met her at Craigie House but I didn't really know her.' She could see the prosecution shaking his head. She was already giving too much information.

'But you went on some rescue mission in the middle of the night when she was in labour. That sounds like you knew her.' He almost sneered.

Ruby dropped her head for a moment trying to think of how to respond. 'She was just a little girl who was in trouble and anyone would have wanted to help her.' She lifted her head a little more. 'Anyone who cared.' The police magistrate gave a little cough that got Ruby's attention. He said nothing but the look suggested she keep her insights to herself.

'I believe you had dealings with Mr. Harper on an early occasion when he, himself was assaulted. By you and several witnesses I believe. Is this true?'

Ruby looked at Harper. 'After Mr Harper yanked the arm of my colleague and then spat in my face he was removed from the newspaper office. For my part I simply wiped his rancid spit from my face and told him to get lost.' She paused. Several women in the public gallery gasped. 'I did say he should return to the swamp from which he'd crawled. Perhaps that was unkind. But hardly an assault.'

'Thank you Miss Hart.' She was summarily cut off from further description. John Hooks could be heard laughing. Even Maxine had to smother a smile.

The defence had a few more questions but he seemed to have lost the head of steam he started with. Perhaps confronted with the fresh and youthful face of the victim it seemed improbable that the outcome would see Harper acquitted.

Maxine, then John and finally Mr. Dryden were called to give their evidence. It all added up to a compelling case against Harper. The previous charges against him simply added the nail in the coffin.

'Mr. Harper undoubtedly you feel aggrieved regarding the loss of your child particularly under the circumstances in which she passed away but that in no way gives you leave to assault a young woman who was not much older than your said child. In no way did Miss Hart nor Miss Whitlock provide a motive for your actions. You have behaved in a most unsatisfactory and uncivil manner.' The police magistrate could not have been any clearer. The two years Gordon Harper would serve meant no-one would have to worry about his drunken violence. It did mean, however, that Josephine Harper and her children would have no income and God only knew what that might mean for them.

On exiting the court, and only fleetingly out of the corner of her eye, did Ruby see Jo and one of the boys scurrying away. She briefly thought about calling out her name but hesitated as the woman most likely would be embarrassed to be seen. Instead, Ruby decided to gather some things to help ease the family over the initial burden. Some of her father's money would be better served paying the Harper's rent and putting food on the table.

Over a celebratory glass of champagne Ruby outlined her plan. 'I'm going to get some food, clothes and maybe a few blankets for Jo Harper and her children. I've got some money that might keep them afloat for a few months.'

'She might be able to get a susso payment.' Jules knew a little about what supplements might be available from the government. 'The sustenance payments are pretty thin but some of the benevolent societies also give out food and before winter comes warm clothes for children.'

Ruby wondered how Jo might feel about charity. Not keen she imagined. But a gift from someone who cared might be more tolerable. Even a gift that came anonymously. Maxine and Della could see Ruby's mind working overtime. She got a particular look on her face when she worked out a problem.

By the end of the week Ruby had a fair collection of items that with help from the others she intended delivering to Jo. There were clothes for the boys and her youngest ones, and both Della and Maxine donated several outfits for their mother. At Woolworths Ruby purchased soaps, flannels and towels. Nothing like a good clean to make a person feel better. Hollis had a collection of clean woollen blankets that would be welcome in the winter and also generously shopped for food basics that would ensure the family didn't starve. On top of the large parcel Ruby tucked an envelope with a twenty-pound note. She wondered if she should give more but in reality, Jo might not have been able to manage a larger amount. And more might see her less savoury neighbours making her a target.

In the late evening Hollis drove the girls and the gift across the river. Dry Street didn't have a soul about, no lights, no music, no happy chatting to while the night away. The package wasn't so much heavy as it was awkward. On the very top Ruby left a bag of apples and plums having remembered how the boys feverishly polished off those she brought on the first visit. As quietly as they came, they stole away back to the city side of the river. Leaving behind the mud and despair and perhaps, this time, a little hope.

Other things, as they do, became a priority for the Aphorism Club. Maxine and Florian had completed the writing of their play. *Madam Mumble's Manifesto* had started auditioning for the key parts. The Aphorism Club had many readings as the script came to life. It was part farce with an alluring element of spiritualism and other worldliness. 'I want to play the ghosts. All of them.' Hollis loved the thought of being on stage.

'The ghosts are just voices. No appearances Hol. You'd never cope without the spotlight.' Jules hit the nail on the head. Capricorn insisted that the Madame Mumbles character be treated with respect and reverence. She wasn't, and Cap felt quite put out until the final scene was written. 'Old Mumbles is the real deal, just like you Cap.' Maxine placated the club's own resident tasseomancer. 'We totally believe in your gifts you darling soothsayer.'

Ruby never felt confident in Capricorn's predictive abilities but her constant warning about a storm coming frequently bothered her. *How many more storms could there be?*

Douglas had sent a letter which arrived in mid-February. His plans to return had a slightly firmer date. By late March or early April, he'd return to Tasmania. Harry Bird had everything ticking over at the power station and Douglas stated he had gained enormous insight into the industry. Typical of him, the details of the advancements in engineering filled most of the letter. At no point did he express any interest in what might be happening in Ruby's life. The longer he stayed away the better as far as she was concerned. It meant she had time to write in the evenings when she wasn't with Lawton and happily shared the house with Della on the weekends. Della stayed with Hollis during the week and the two of them had formed a strong bond. He loved it when people assumed she was his daughter. And with a father at her side no-one questioned Della's marital status. That little gold ring became her passport to freedom. The baby, she thought, had a due date in April, or possibly earlier. 'Not a precise thing I'm afraid Rubes. I guess I wasn't paying enough attention to that.' In

Ruby's mind that meant that there could be several weeks before the baby came. Who knew what would happen then. Ruby assumed that by then Douglas would be back so she and Della might find a small place for themselves. Even with the dire predictions of an economic downturn in the coming year Ruby convinced herself that she could support Della, the baby and herself. Naivety can be a blessing as much as a curse.

Maxine and Ruby wrote stories about autumn fashion, more fundraisers and occasionally Mr. Dryden would allow them to do features on working women and the major social reformers of the day. Ruby had written dozens of articles about the women she admired. The early suffrage campaigners, and the latest crop of amazing women who fought for their gender around the world. Much of the work inspired long letters between Ruby and Burky. Some of it made it into the women's section of The Examiner but only when highly censored by the editor. 'Can't have sedition and feminist rabble-rousing young Ruby.' To which she always asked, 'Why?'

Ruby felt particularly drawn to the lives of Matiel Mogannam, a lawyer who was fighting for women's rights to education in Palestine and Marie Stopes a British activist who believed a woman should have access to birth control. On top of Ruby's list of women's stories was the Canadian Five. Five women fighting to change the legal definition of person to include women. 'A legal definition of person that just means men.' Her outrage reddened her face and made her teeth hurt from clenching. 'What are we then if we are not a person?'

Hollis rubbed her back to ease her anger. 'The law is well behind the times dear one. Sadly a woman might be seen as a possession.' Ruby turned on him. 'I don't think that lovie. I think women should run the world. We men have buggered it up numerous times. And quite frankly I don't want to run the world.' He smiled at her.

'And you certainly don't want a woman as a possession. Or you'd better not.' Jules flippantly entered the exchange.

Even with the light-hearted end to the conversation Ruby agonised about the limp stories she published. The fire in her language had definitely been extinguished by the editorial team. But in her work for the university paper she made salient and clear connections between the fight for women's rights and social justice movements. Although poverty wasn't just an issue for women, women bore the brunt of the outcomes. When they couldn't clothe and feed their children it wasn't society that got the blame; it was the mother. A lack of freedom, exclusions from professions, and an absence of legal rights were at the intersection where social justice met feminism.

Her last piece titled *Feminism: The Fight for Social Fairness* brought her the kind of notice she'd never imagined possible. The University of Tasmania had asked her to come and visit the campus and speak to the female academics and students about all the work they'd published from her. 'I mean what could I even begin to tell these women. They are so much more educated than I am.' Ruby had cold feet, but it was her boss who insisted she go.

'Ruby you have a voice. And a damn good one. It's women like you, young and keen who have a chance to change the world. Go and see what happens. I've even bought you and Max train tickets.' Mr. Dryden held the tickets aloft. 'Now get out of here and give me five minutes peace.'

CHAPTER 27

Ruby felt she had to sort everything out before she could leave. She spoke to Harry and Stella saying the newspaper was sending her and Maxine to Hobart for work. It wasn't exactly a lie but a stretch of the truth. They were grateful that she shared her plans with them. Stella even gave her a small hug and wished her safe travels. Della in particular with the imprecise due date concerned Ruby. 'The baby will come when its time is here. Whether you are here or not Rubes. Now get on the train and stop worrying.' Della would continue to stay with Hollis and Capricorn made solemn promises to be her shadow.

'Nothing can happen while I'm on guard duty wabi-sabi. I can even deliver the child if it comes to it. I've seen it happen and I know where it comes out.' Capricorn's convictions did little to settle Ruby's anxiety.

'We all know where it comes out Cap. Not sure that will be much use if we all have to play midwife.' Jules always had a little joke at his friend's expense.

Saying goodbye to Lawton became equally difficult. 'It's only five days Ruby. I'm going to be here at the train station when you return and I'll miss you every minute.' The kiss goodbye lasted a few seconds longer than it should according to Maxine.

'For God's sake you two she's only going to Hobart and will be back before you know it. Surely you can be apart for four nights.' She pulled Ruby playfully away from Lawton. 'Or can't you?' She teased Ruby.

The train pulled away and started the slow slog out of Launceston. The railway stretched to the east of the town and made its way south through the farms and hills to Western Junction. Here passengers would change to the bigger train that would have them disembarking at the Queen's Domain in Hobart. 'Well we have six hours to fill in Ruby. Should we eat our sandwiches now or wait?' Maxine had packed a mini feast for them. Chicken sandwiches, lamingtons and two bottles of Cascade ginger beer had been packed into a small wicker carrier. The tea trolley would roll by several times for travellers to purchase hot drinks or more sweet treats. They were unlikely to starve.

The time gave Maxine and Ruby time to talk. Work, writing and the new play got the ball rolling. Ruby's past and her strange relationship with her father next. 'But what about your family Max? Do you see them at all?'

Maxine swivelled around in her seat and brought her knees up to rest in the space between them. 'I'm what one might call a disappointment to my family. My mother really wanted a married daughter who could just be happy living in a middle-class suburb with middle-class values. Instead she got a disaffected loudmouth who didn't want to be married to a narcissistic gambler.'

'What was he like?'

Maxine paused. 'Undoubtedly he was beautiful. Looked stunning. Like he was made for the movies. And initially he was a great lover.'

'Initially?'

'Well yes. He then got distracted by being in debt to some very unpleasant types. He kept borrowing money after he'd spent all mine and these men were quite threatening. So in the love-making department he lost interest. Things didn't seem to work so well in the downstairs department.' Maxine could see Ruby's confusion.

'I'm sure Lawton is always in working order but some men can't always get it up.' She whispered the last bit.

'I thought it was sort of automatic. You look like you're interested and then its…' Ruby struggle for a suitable phrase. 'Elevated.' The two fell about laughing at the ridiculousness of the word.

'It's all so complicated isn't it. The stuff between men and women.' Maxine nodded at Ruby's observation. 'Do you want another boyfriend Max?'

'Not really. Not now. You know I've slept with Pooky a few times.' Maxine smiled at Ruby's shocked face. 'He's always elevated.' They couldn't look at each other without laughing for the next hour.

The last hours were spent reading, writing and eating. The tea trolley did good business with them both downing several cups along the way. In the approach to Hobart Ruby became fascinated with the changing landscape. On the banks of the Derwent the huge Electrolytic Zinc Company had started producing tons of copper sulphate and zinc. It spewed sulphur fumes and smoke into the air. Ruby wondered at the impact of the pollution on the people working in and living around the plant.

The train pulled itself up the last of the winding hills before slowly pulling into the wharves where Burky had arranged to meet them.

With the introductions made a taxi took Ruby and Maxine to Hadley's Orient Hotel. Burky had organised a shared room for them. 'The university is paying so I've ensured it's a nice room and a table has been booked in the dining room. I'd assumed you would be hungry after your trip.' Burky then left them promising to send someone to collect them the next day for a tour of the city and a visit to the university.

'I'm so proud of you Ruby. You've done very well.'

Dinner, bath, a little chatting and then sleep.

A young man waited in the foyer for them at 9.15. 'Miss Hart. Miss Whitlock. Nice to meet you. I'm Richard Barton. Professor Burke sent me.'

With greetings completed they set off for a tour around the town. The Domain, the governor's home, the city shopping precinct, the Sandy Bay yacht club and the hills above the city. 'Can we go up the mountain? It looks amazing.' Ruby loved the thought of being able to stand on top of Mount Wellington and look down on the city. It dominated the western vista.

'On the agenda for later in the week. But you'll need your woollies. It's bloody cold up there.'

At the university Burky ushered them into her office. 'Rich I'll need you back at four to take the ladies back to Hadleys.' He nodded politely and left.

Burky was not one for small talk and once Ruby and Maxine were settled and tea poured, she got to the business of the visit. 'Tomorrow Ruby I've invited a group of students and several faculty staff to meet you. They are all interested in the essays you have written for academic publication. I thought it would be good for you to talk about your inspiration for the work.'

She explained that not all those who would come to listen would be social reformers such as herself. 'Some of the older staff and even a few young men are still very chauvinistic about women in the hallowed halls of academia.'

Maxine rolled her eyes and made her best disgruntled face. Burky nodded her approval at the response. 'We are rolling a ball uphill in a tornado Maxine trying to change some attitudes. Nothing that common sense or a big gun can't change.'

After Burky outlined the progress being made in some ways she walked the visitors around the grounds. Each faculty area had its own classrooms, laboratories and staff common rooms. Students wandered in the gardens or gathered in the study spaces, all appearing engaged in deep discussions or reading. 'Would you like to be a part of this Ruby?'

In her head Ruby had already imagined being part of this world. The thought of all the potential knowledge that could be gleaned from the lectures, the study and the reading excited her. She couldn't answer with words, but her face said it all. 'If only.' She eventually got out.

'And have you been keeping away from too many dragons?' Burky's noun for men.

'Mostly. There's just one I've not been able to resist.'

'There's always one.'

The following day Richard picked them up again. In the central lecture hall chairs had been set in an informal circle. A second row had been added in case more than the twenty invitees turned up. And more did. When Ruby sat beside

Jessie Burke the circles had increased by several rows. Ruby started to panic at the number of faces staring at her as she and Maxine sat more or less at the arc of the inner circle. Some faces were enthused and more than a few were hostile.

Burky started. 'As many of you know I am Professor Burke. Some of you I've passed and more than several I've failed.' She waited for polite laughter. 'But you are I believe all familiar with the work of my guest Ruby Hart. She is a talented writer and I say without fear of contradiction an intellectual who I hope today will be encouraged to join us as a student in the near future.' She nodded at Ruby. 'I've asked Ruby to talk about what has motivated her to write with such commitment to the cause of women's rights and perhaps to answer a few questions.'

Very much out of her comfort zone Ruby moved to the front of her chair. She clasped her hands together and lifted her chin. Small actions to calm her nerves but once she started the words began to come. She spoke of her childhood and the influence of Minerva. 'Aunt Minnie provided me with the building blocks that young women need. Courage, desire for a better world, the need to include all persons and take responsibility for your own life's path.' Talking about Minnie gave flight to her ideas. She spoke of the women who inspired her. The Olympic swimmers Mina Wylie and Fanny Durack and their struggles to even find a place to train motivated her to learn to swim. Then she described the girls and teachers at Merrington, who taught Ruby about resilience. 'Yes and even some of the nuns which I know is surprising to some of you.' Ruby found her voice and kept her listeners silent for nearly an hour.

'For women it has been a series of things to overcome. Paths that must be hewn with very few tools for the job. And all the while hearing the words a girl can't do that. Or a girl shouldn't do that.' She took a breath. 'In my own life I've been fortunate enough to find strong women who have helped me find my voice.' And before she was about to thank Burky and Maxine a male voice interrupted.

'Your own voice is it? Sounds like all the claptrap we have heard from all these self-opinionated women before you.' With that, the dissenters commenced chipping away at the points Ruby made.

'You're not even qualified to speak. What gives you the right to speak about anything?'

'Women want to take over do they? Let's see how they get on trying to run the country. Or keep us out of a war?'

'Who's going to raise your children eh? Expect a man to stay at home and do a woman's work?'

'Do you think the feminists are going to fix that thing on your face?'

The crowd erupted. Voices from everywhere attacking the last speaker. Louder voices shouting them down. Chairs were scraped and a few were knocked over. Maxine reached for Ruby's arm as if to pull her away from the fracas. But she did not run. Burky took her cue and sat still and unruffled by the noise. Eventually the commotion settled. The shouters were rather taken aback by the unwavering stillness of the guests. Ruby stood. Her height always lent weight to her strength. 'My face is the least of my worries. In fact it is not a worry at all. It is merely an accident of birth. A vascular anomaly is a more accurate description. I do hope the young man who shouted that last insult isn't studying medicine.' The tension eased as the front row laughed. 'Let me finish with this. A woman's status as a person in her own right takes nothing away from a man. Lifting the poor from the slums in which we have enslaved them will take nothing away from the middle class. Providing equal rights for all our citizens, women and men, foreigners who choose to make their homes here and our own native people is not about taking away. It is about giving us all a better future. Fairness is not a means to destroy a society it is about how we build one.'

Maxine led the applause, jumped to her feet and looked in bewildered admiration for her young friend. Burky joined her. The front row of students and many of the faculty in the second row stood. Several of the male students who'd come to disrupt even had to begrudgingly applaud the woman who had so eloquently put the chauvinists in their place.

The hall emptied after a few well-wishers came to shake Ruby's hand and nod appreciatively at Professor Burke. They laughed out loud when just the three of them stood alone in the hall.

'Oh my God Rubes. You were amazing. When you stood up I thought you might be about to run that snotty boy down.' Maxine hugged her. 'Damn this is going in a play.'

'You are more magnificent that I thought you might ever be my dear Miss Hart. I think in a few years I will happily hand over the reins of this job to you.' Burky led them back to her office. 'I think a little brandy is called for.'

Richard returned the girls to the hotel. 'I'll pick you up for the mountain trip at 10. Professor Burke says you have the whole day to yourselves and I'm to look after you.'

After a surprisingly deep sleep and a huge breakfast Richard arrived exactly when he said he would. Burky had insisted on providing her two visitors with thick coats, two woollen hats and two sets of gloves. Neither had brought any winter clothing given the late autumn in the north had remained warm. Their lightweight jumpers would not suffice on the mountain.

The car handled the steep ascent, with Richard managing the many twists and turns as the road zig-zagged its way up. The temperature began to drop quickly, and Ruby and Maxine were grateful for the blankets Burky also had the driver put on the back seat. 'We will stop at Ferntree on the way back down. It's nice to have lunch there. We will stop at The Springs before we try to get to the Pinnacle Road.' Richard was full of information about the mountain. 'The local indigenous tribe call it kunanyi and its 4170 feet above sea level.'

At The Springs they filled bottles supplied again by their thoughtful host with ice-cold pure water. It tasted so clean and earthy. The coldness of it making them cough a little. Further up the mountain the road became too difficult to navigate in the car and Richard suggested that his passengers could walk a bit further up if they wanted to.

Dressed in borrowed winter garments Ruby and Maxine stepped out into the biting wind. Even through the wool they could feel the southern pole's influence. The day was perfectly clear and the view down to the city and the sea was unimpeded by fog or cloud. 'The air feels different up here. Or is it just the cold?' Maxine's question almost immediately whipped away by another blast of wind.

'It's like being a bird.' Ruby put her arms out wide as she stepped up onto a huge dolerite boulder. Maxine held the bottom of her coat, fearful that she'd fall. 'I'd like to fly.'

'More likely fall on your head. Get down. Please.' Maxine seemed to have an aversion to height in the same way she did deep water.

Richard patiently waited for the two, chilled to the bone, women to return. He then immediately drove to the Ferntree Hotel, located at about the halfway point. A big fire had been lit in the double facing hearth where they stood for a few minutes trying to defrost their limbs. They ate lunch at a table looking out over the gardens where wallabies and echidnas hopped and shuffled under the tree ferns.

'I want to grow those ferns in my garden. Dicksonia Antarctica.'

'Wow Ruby I didn't know you were such a botanist.' Maxine sounded genuinely impressed.

'I'm not. Lawton keeps educating me on the botanical names of plants. He thinks my plant knowledge is severely lacking.'

'And what if you come to Hobart to attend university? How will Lawton's botanical education continue?'

Maxine didn't expect Ruby to answer but she knew it would be a stumbling block for the young couple if she moved and he stayed. Maxine also worried that Ruby might choose to return to Melbourne as the university there had more prestige. She was after all a Melbourne girl.

Back at Hadley's the two farewelled Richard after arranging the following day's activities. Another half day at the university to sit in on Burky's lectures. And then a visit to The Mercury newspaper offices to meet some fellow journalists. Maxine knew several of them as they had started their writing lives in the north. The following day they'd be back on the train heading home.

The day passed quickly. Being busy and meeting new people meant time flew by. Ruby felt she didn't really get to know the city at all in the brief visit. But it was enough to ignite a little longing for a life of study.

Maxine slept most of the way home. Ruby wrote and contemplated the future. Her father remained the problem, at least until she turned twenty-one.

By the end of the year, she would be emancipated from her father's decisions. Finally, an adult but not a person with many legal rights. She would, however, inherit Minnie's property and have a roof over her head should she return to Melbourne.

At the station Lawton stood in the rain. He held an umbrella over his head. Pooky stood beside him with another. Thoughts of moving away faded as she saw the happiness on his face when he spotted her. Gathering their cases and bags both made their way to the door of the train.

'Jewel of the southern isle.' Lawton yelled his ridiculous greeting. Ruby fell into his arms and the embrace secured her to the spot. It felt like the place she wanted to be. Here with him. Or simply anywhere with him.

Pooky held the umbrella over Maxine and the four of them half ran to Hollis's waiting car.

'To Margaret Street please driver.' Maxine instructed Lawton. 'Where did this weather come from. We haven't had rain for months.' Then she turned and whispered to Ruby. 'Elevation anyone?' They laughed like school girls hearing their first bawdy joke.

Margaret Street was lit up and noisy. Food, firewater and a hundred stories. Della had not produced a baby and thankfully no-one had to act as midwife. In a quiet moment Della spoke to Ruby. 'Your father's home. He came here with a bee in his bonnet about something.'

Ruby wondered why he would bother to come here. She had left Stella fully informed about the plans to be in Hobart. But that worry dissipated when again she felt Lawton at her side. Her friends around her, the music playing and outside the rain pouring down. What could go wrong?

CHAPTER 28

One should never ask that question.

Douglas's early arrival by a week meant that Ruby's trip to Hobart coincided with his homecoming. Ruby couldn't imagine that he'd really care less about her not being there to greet him with open arms. She wondered what had riled him up enough to bring him to Margaret Street. It was a mystery. Perhaps he felt upset about the car not being in its spot, but he never drove anywhere during the week. Harry had already organised with him to pick him up from the dock when he arrived. Ruby even had firewood and kindling inside and plenty of food in the kitchen. And she was really only away five days. His taciturn nature must simply have been the issue. No social skills and his aloof demeanour most likely to blame.

Hollis ate breakfast with Ruby on Sunday morning before she drove to the Reach. He chatted away about Maxine's narrative about Ruby's triumphant take down of the unpleasant *pipsqueak popinjay*. Ruby laughed at Hollis's fabulous turn of phrase. He went on to say that Florian had almost cast the play and that he thought Flo should definitely put him in a frock and hat and make him Madame Mumble. 'I'm a natural for the role. Living with Cap for so long I am almost a psychic.' With Lawton at work and Della having a long sleep in, Ruby drove herself home. The rain had set in. The sky remained an uninspiring grey and there was no let up in the downpour. April had started with a rapid swing away from the mild days of March.

Ruby got dripping wet in the short distance from the car to the front porch. She shook most of the water off before stepping inside. 'Douglas? Father?' She called his name not really expecting him to be there. She imagined he would have been straight over to his office to ensure Harry had got everything right in his absence. But he wasn't. He sat in the front room, his face as thunderous as the sky above them.

'I can't believe this Ruby. I simply can't understand what has happened to you.' Douglas seemed incapable of expressing a cogent idea. 'You have gone too far. I honestly don't know what to do.'

Ruby's mind raced to make sense of what apparently terrible thing she had done. She thought of the nights she'd spent with Lawton but surely he couldn't have known about that. Unless someone had been spying and gossiping. Immediately she thought of Stella. Ruby simply shrugged her shoulders and continued her bewildered look.

'This.' Douglas swept his arm over the now empty table. The table where Ruby had left her typewriter and her folio. The drawings of her done by Lawton, one framed, the many others tucked into her notebooks. Her love story. The essays and her thoughts about life were all gone. The table stood bare.

'I saw those drawings and I read the material you…' He could barely spit the words out. 'Wrote. This corruption you call writing.' His face turned as red as Ruby's birthmark. *That's ironic*, she thought. 'What the hell have you been doing?' He continued.

Strangely Ruby felt quite calm. Once a performance of this nature would have her agonising in self-doubt, writhing with humiliation, all her private thoughts laid bare. Douglas started again. 'You have shamed yourself. And me. What the hell do you think people will make of a girl writing this rubbish?'

The word shame started to bite but not in the way it once did. She didn't cower under the weight of the word, this time all she felt was anger. It rose from her feet like a wave of heat, like lava that had nowhere else to go but out.

'Shame you say. How dare you.' It wasn't loud but her voice sounded like steel scraping on flint. 'Shame. For being clever. For wanting to write and explore ideas. For falling in love. For being made to feel beautiful. For acting with integrity.' She took a step towards her father. 'Shame. For being a woman. For saying no I won't settle for being less than a man. Is that what you've got yourself all tied up about.'

Douglas felt overwhelmed by the flood of words and invective. The questions were too logical and coherent for simple disgust to stand as an answer.

'The pictures…of you…' He couldn't finish.

'Because I look beautiful in them. Because a man actually saw me as beautiful. Is that the problem?'

'Because you look like a whore.' Douglas looked so shocked at the word that came out of his own mouth. He staggered backwards as if the force of it knocked him off his feet.

Ruby wanted to fight him. She wanted her strong fists to hit his horrible, miserable face. She wanted to kick him and trample him into the floor on which he stood. But she didn't. Ruby used stillness and silence to dominate the room. Her eyes never left her father's face. It took minutes for her to speak again.

'Well how typical. How typical to diminish a woman to a whore when you can't dominate her. Of course take it to the lowest point in order to crush her. Well I have bad news Father. I can't be undone by a word no matter whose mouth it comes out of.' Then she shouted to get over the sound of another torrent of rain. 'Where's my work?'

'Gone. I've taken it away to my office and that bloody typewriter too. You won't write anything else again if I have anything to do with it. I've locked it away so no-one else has to see it.'

The theft of her work and Lawton's precious drawings were the only body blow he landed. Years of work and all her ideas wrapped up in his rage and then taken, possibly destroyed. Shock turned her stomach. Hatred for this mean little man seared through her veins, his disinterest, his abandonment, his arrogance could only have one outcome.

'Fuck you.' But the words were drowned out in the continuing deluge. It was as if the heavens themselves were preventing the words reaching her father's ears. She went to her room; he bolted for the sanctity of his office in the power station.

Too hurt to cry Ruby packed all her things in the trunk she arrived with. She scoured the house for any sign she'd ever been there. Not even a whisper that she'd ever existed in his life at all. Surely that would finally give him some peace. His greatest shame evaporated, gone and no longer his concern. And then she wept. It was grief. Not for the loss of her father but for the skin she now had to shed. Like a snake she had to shake off the life that ended on this day. Tomorrow she would be new.

Dragging her case in the pouring rain felt like a dramatic final scene but she would be damned if she would take anything from him. The gravel road made for slow progress, the rain nearly consuming her, but she had no intention of giving in. *I'll drown first.* Childish but the thought forced her on. At the end of Corin Road she put her trunk on the ground and sat on it. The rain steadied to a more agreeable pattering. She could be no wetter, nor more unhappy.

Get up Ruby no one's going to do this for you. Minnie's words came clear and loud in her head, and heart. It made her stand and heft the trunk back into position. But through the rain came a car. Hollis at the wheel. He had hardly stopped when he and Jules leapt out. 'I had a bad feeling about this. Della was worried too. Cap kept shouting about the storm.' Then Ruby's crying started for real. They bundled her and the trunk into the car. Jules sat in the back and hugged her. Hollis sped down the hill to home. The household spilled out onto the path to pull her inside. Bedraggled and waterlogged the fussing began. Towels, tea and dry clothes and a seat near the newly lit fire. Through a few left-over sobs Ruby explained the explosive argument with her father. 'He has taken all my work. Saw Lawton's sketches and called me a whore.'

'That bastard.' Hollis had been more a father to her in the short time she'd known him than Douglas had ever been. His anger made her feel safe. Feel right to be so bereft. Della sat close, her arms holding her as close as her tummy allowed.

'Lawton is still working but he'll be here soon. Pooky and Maxine will be here for dinner. It will be okay. It really will.' Jules wanted it to be so. He hated to see Ruby so sad. He worried that she was broken and perhaps they couldn't put her back together. She looked so young, wounded and worst of all, bereft of hope.

Ruby sat in the hot bath that had been run for her. She washed her hair and let the warmth take the chill out of her body. She became aware that someone sat beside her. Capricorn looked at Ruby from a little stool beside the bath. 'Is this the storm Cap? Is it over now?'

Capricorn reached her hand out and stroked Ruby's wet hair. 'Not quite dear one. Not quite.'

Monday the rain eased. Maxine and Ruby started the day in their boss's office. Maxine again told the story of Ruby's speech. 'She was magnificent. A little scary but fabulous.' Mr. Dryden smiled at the thought of his young journalist taking down some privileged prat. He had only a few concerns about how worn-down Ruby looked. Pale, exhausted, sad. But the events unfolding had to take priority.

'We've got work to do ladies. The weather is predicted to get much worse than this. There's some worry that we going to see a flood. We have a duty to ensure we have the means to get a warning out if the banks of the rivers are breached and if people must evacuate.' He looked worried. 'Been a while since we've had a flood. This could be a big one.'

On Tuesday the rain intensified. It seemed impossible that rain could get heavier, but it did. Across the north of the state the skies simply remained black and poured water down as if the oceans were now the heavens. The streets and shops were empty except for a few desperate folks who'd seemed to have overlooked the weather. Mr. Dryden decided late on Tuesday to send all but a few printers home. He ceased printing the paper until they knew if the worst of the prediction might come about. Two documents had been typeset. One had already gone out as a single page warning about the impending inundation should the rain continue. The second, which had been held over, were instructions for evacuation should that be needed. The low-lying suburbs on the north side of the rivers were at risk. The towns of Longford, Avoca, Fingal, Lilydale, Ringarooma and Derby were also in danger should the waterways around them rise above their banks. Although it was hoped that the newly constructed Briseis Dam in Derby would hold back the worst of any flood.

Wednesday and Thursday ensured the rivers would overflow. The rain just continued. Lawton's manager sent him a message to cease all work as the South Esk already began to rage down the gorge. The narrowness of the cliffs both sides of the basin made it too dangerous for anyone to be near the gardens or the path. Margaret Street became the safe haven. Everyone bunkered down with blankets and food. But there was no party atmosphere. Something very dangerous seemed close. Ruby worried about Jo Harper and her children but there was little chance of getting to them as all three rivers began to swell. Communications failed on Thursday night. Luckily the power remained on even though it sounded like Duck Reach was under threat as the water diverted to the penstock had broken over the pipes.

Maxine and Ruby drove slowly to the newspaper office on the Friday. The gutters were spouting with rainwater, and roads were already ankle deep. 'Why are you two here? It's too dangerous to be out.' Their boss despite his concern was glad to have the company. John Hooks arrived too. The evacuation instructions had been sent out as a supplement. But it was almost impossible to get it to the low-lying suburbs who were most likely to go under. *When the post office bell tolls you must immediately evacuate and get to higher ground. Cross either bridge and make your way to the Albert Hall.* Simple, yet emphatic instructions. Terrifying too.

'Bad news from Derby last night before the telegraph lines washed away. The Briseis Dam collapsed. Seventy feet of water plus the flood has over-whelmed the Cascade River. It's taken out the town of Derby. The tin mines are flooded and people are missing. Sounds like we are for it too.'

John couldn't have been more correct. What had been started could not be stopped.

'The lot of you get home. I'm locking up. We can't do any more until the peak and then hope to God it stops raining.' And then the power went.

Ruby looked worried about what it might mean for Duck Reach. 'They've probably just turned off the turbines. Too much water coming in so they stop them to protect the station.'

Sodden and worried Maxine and Ruby returned to Margaret Street. The roads closest to the confluence of the rivers were already under water. It was possible that if the water got any higher the bottom end of the street where Hollis's home stood could flood.

'Not to worry children. We are nowhere near the flood area here. We are much higher than those poor buggers in Invermay.' Hollis had lit candles and ramped up the fire in the stove and the hearth. Things seemed safe but Ruby still had the nagging doubt about her father's welfare. And the Harper family. Jo might not have seen the evacuation notice and possibly couldn't read it even if she did. But perhaps she'd know what it meant when, or if the post office bells started ringing.

The Aphorism Club settled itself into wait. Wait for the rain to stop, for the water to ebb away and for sunshine to finally emerge. But each was a hope too far. At midnight Della woke Ruby and Lawton. 'Sorry kids but the bub has decided that she should come into the world on the worst night possible.'

Della's waters had broken, and the labour pains had been consistent since the late afternoon. Given the disaster outside she said nothing in the hope that she might be wrong. 'Better wake up Cap and Maxine. I think we might need all the women on board for this one.'

No-one had been deeply asleep. The rain and the fear had everyone on edge.

And then in the distance the bells tolled. Faintly through the rain, across the city the sound alerted the town that the water that gushed from the north and the south could not be contained. Evacuation was the only possible action. Della roared over the top of the mayhem outside.

'We men can do no good here. The girls have got the birth thing under control so I'm going to see if I can help with the evacuation. Must be something useful I can do.' Hollis, for all his flamboyance and excesses was a man who knew that one had to help others. The club was evidence of his deeply held philosophy.

Lawton joined him. Pooky and Florian too. 'Jules stay and look after the girls will you. Someone needs to be the gatekeeper.' Hollis kissed his cheek. 'Love you dearest.'

In the clattering rain they drove to the bridge at Tamar Street. At this point the road was passable, and it was possible that they could join hundreds of others who had turned up to serve their fellow citizens. Many of them would never have thought to enter the suburbs, never have thought of those who lived in poverty, maybe they even joked about it being the swamp and all its inferences. But there they were, men and women, entering the flooding streets to help people get out of the area before the force of the water became too great to achieve a rescue. Police officers and army recruits had been marshalled to direct the rescuers to areas that were just flooding. Those further back from the river might just have a chance to gather a few belongings and make their way over the bridges to safety. If they stayed, there were no guarantees they'd survive the night.

Within hours the rescuers had helped thousands of people make their way through the swirling waters. In the end three thousand had made their way, in the dark and the rising rivers to find safety. The Albert Hall filled with the bewildered evacuees. Some simply had the clothes in which they fled. Some had floated a few treasures on planks of wood and doors that had been hastily ripped from hinges.

Before the waters claimed the suburbs Lawton had tried to get to Dry Street. He knew Ruby would be panicked about the Harpers. But it was under before he could get close enough. Hollis had driven into the water as deep as he dared. Pooky sat atop the car with his lantern directing people to the direction of the bridge. Florian had gone on foot to help a woman who was attempting to carry two chairs, a bag and two small children. He wanted to throw the chairs, but the woman seemed to be determined to keep them. He carried them, the bag and one of the children to shelter. He went back to help haul Lawton from the river that seemed to be dragging him towards the swirling Tamar. They passed fathers carrying children aloft. Two police officers carried an elderly woman who clung to her bag of knitting as if it were her lifeline. Women, men and children, dogs and cats and household goods were struggling against the rising tide.

Beside them floated rubble, and animals that did not have the strength to out swim the inundation. The rain had exhausted itself. It had done its worst but still the water rose. The rivers dragged boulders and trees with them. If people survived the water, they still could be taken by the debris. The wave of humans clambered to safe spaces.

They could do no more in the car. The suburbs were under. A boat would be needed to get any survivors who were still left in the dark.

At Margaret Street the water had risen deeply at the river end but had just covered the gutters at Hollis's. The men were wet, muddy and exhausted. Inside the sound of labour had ended, the sound of a new life began. Between them all the women of the Aphorism Club, with the help of a reluctant midwife in Jules, Della's baby girl came into the world. All was well. And while she came into being without a father, one who didn't want a child, she would never want for love and care. She now had more aunties and uncles than would ever be needed.

This little girl had a voice. And by God she was using it. Her wailing at her introduction to the world in the middle of a tempest could only be eased by finding her mother's breast. There she rested. Della wrung out by the exertion of the labour looked beautiful. Possibly more so than ever.

'Is the storm over yet Cap?' Ruby felt sure it had to be.

'Nearly wabi-sabi. Nearly.'

AND
TOMORROW

CHAPTER 29

After every catastrophe there is a tomorrow. There's an aftermath that is usually accompanied by exhaustion and relief. There's a reckoning that must be faced and somewhere in that, action has to be taken to move life on, to ensure there are more tomorrows. But Launceston and the small towns of the north were in a state of shock, disarray and the homes in which they had made their lives had become a jumble of sodden timber and splintered furniture. In all, across the north seven thousand people had been displaced, some temporarily and others permanently as their houses had simply been washed away. Sadly, people were missing, and several bodies had already been recovered from the water.

Della and Estelle, the new baby, had been taken to the hospital for a few days of care. Although she had sailed through the birth the midwife on duty had deep suspicions about the competence of the birth attendees when they arrived with the new mother. Jules, flustered and little uncomfortable, and Capricorn, who had chosen another fetching outfit, were regarded as something of a threat to the austerity and sterility of the maternity wards.

Maxine and Ruby walked to the newspaper office picking their way through the rubbish that had washed into the city streets. The gutters still ran with ferocity, cascading over paths and pooling on low lying dips in the road.

After a few hours of sleep Lawton, Hollis, Pooky and Florian went back to the bridge. They were hoping to help with the dinghies that might be rowed on the now flooded streets to find any stranded residents. Some who'd missed the warnings survived by climbing onto the roofs of their houses. It had been a cold night for them. But at least someone had come back for them. Someone cared enough to check.

With no power or gas in the town, feeding and housing the homeless became a priority. And The Examiner intended on making its contribution.

'We've got stories to write and I want you all out gathering as much information as you can. We can get the presses up and running using tractor engines. We will get the paper out. We owe people that much.' Mr. Dryden knew information was a citizen's right. 'The more they know about what is happening the more they can plan.'

Ruby really wanted to go up to the Reach. She knew the power station had been damaged but she did wonder if her father, the Birds and the other engineers had survived. Firstly, she and Maxine were sent to the Albert Hall. 'Firsthand stories about how people got out of the flood and get a feel for how they are going to move forward to get the masses fed and housed.'

With several streets impassable by car or on foot, Ruby and Maxine took a circuitous route to the City Park. They were greeted by a sea of humans. Both the rescued and the rescuers shared the same air of shock. Charity groups and an army of volunteers had provided, almost miraculously, food stations where bread and hot drinks were handed out in whatever receptacles could hold fluid.

A boy drank tea from a saucepan, others from bowls and chipped cups. Some shared from a tin billy and despite the crush of misery no person pushed or shoved. Turn taking and showing patience, a degree of civility remained part of the city's soul. Ruby walked towards a group of women draped in blankets. 'Hello I'm Ruby Hart from The Examiner would you mind answering a few questions.' They obliged and what struck Ruby was not how harrowing the night had been, not the enormity of their losses but their gratitude for the kindness shown to them as they waded out of the mud. 'It was a bugger of a night for sure love. But here we are. All of us out and our kids too.' The woman smiled. 'And a hot cuppa. Can't complain can you.'

Her resilience, and that of her neighbours struck Ruby as extraordinary. Powerful. Hope had not been drowned in the disaster. 'But what about your homes? Your things?'

'Well if they're still standing we'll just get in and clean 'em out. And if everything's washed away well then they're washed away.' The woman gave a toothless grin. 'Didn't have much worth keeping any ways.'

And Maxine was told the same stories. There appeared to be little anger, just a resolute and steadfast belief that all would be well.

Inside the Albert Hall Ruby found Jo Harper's boys, Bobby and George. They remembered her as the fruit lady. 'Is your mum here with you?' Ruby noticed that the boys were wearing some of the clothes that had been left for them.

'She made us go without her. She had to get the little kids up and ready but we never seen them after that. A copper got us out of the water near the bridge and told us to come here.' Bobby gave a small shudder. 'We don't know what happened to her.'

A sick feeling in her stomach started but she didn't want to worry the young boys. 'I'm sure she's going to be here somewhere. My friends have taken a boat out and they will find her if she didn't get out last night.' The boys looked frightened. 'I've heard there's a whole lot of people sitting up on their roofs. With their chickens and dogs.' She hoped the image might cheer up the forlorn pair.

'We ain't got a dog but we got some chickens.' George looked a little more hopeful.

'You know outside you can get some bread and a hot drink. Why don't you see if you can get something to eat.'

Ruby went back outside. The air in the hall had been tainted with the mud and what she thought most likely human excrement. The air outside while fresher still had the taint of decay and sewerage. She walked as close to the edge of the flood waters as she could. People in boats rowed back and forth, from muddy banks to flooded streets. Sometimes triumphant with a resident who had survived the night, many times empty, occasionally a dog or cat shivering in the bow. One small dinghy had two sheep, another two bicycles.

As she watched she saw Lawton and another man rowing towards the bridge. The boat seemed empty but as they got closer several other men walked out to help them bring the vessel to a safe mooring. Lawton's face steely with the effort and with the terrible cargo contained within. The police and ambulance officers who went to aid the rowers dropped their heads. Sorrow became a heavy weight. Two small children, possibly aged four and five, sat dripping wet, howling with fear beside the wrapped body of a woman. In the sodden sheet in which the rescuers covered her, the shape of an infant, cold and still, lay on top of Jo Harper. Ruby could tell it was her, she had on one of the dresses Della had donated. A worn slipper hung off one foot. It was one of the pair she wore when Ruby first met her.

Lawton helped carry the bodies. Salvation Army officers took the surviving children. Ruby could hardly say the words. 'The two oldest boys are in the line for bread. Bobby and George Harper.' The charity workers left to seek them.

For all the triumphant stories and unyielding faith there would always be a tragedy, a story that ended the unwavering belief in a benevolent God. And Josephine Harper's death with her youngest child was that tragedy. She sent her boys to safety but in trying to keep her three littlest alive she left it too late.

'The kids were on the top of a shed. Jo must have hoisted them up there but then couldn't quite raise herself with the baby in her arms.' Lawton stood close to Ruby. 'She must have been hit by something in the water. She was caught by a fence post right beside the shed.'

So four small Harper children would now be virtually orphaned. With their father in jail they would go into care, hopefully together, but most likely not. And Jo's story, not like the movies, didn't have a happy ending.

Ruby, numb from the shock, moved through the crowd like a ghost. There were so many stories here, but her mind had settled on telling the one about Josephine Harper. Not just a story about the once in a hundred-year deluge, but the one about a woman who gave her life to save her children. *A most unlikely heroine.* The title had already taken form.

Her father came to mind when she thought about the story she would write. Most likely he had kept her writing in his office that now certainly, if reports could be believed, had washed away. She had to get to the Reach. She hoped he'd survived. Despite it all, he was still her father.

Standing outside the engineers' cottages Stella, Harry and their two girls looked across the river where the power station once stood. The wreckage of the buildings and broken lines, the smashed turbines spoke of the intensity of the water that poured down upon it. The office building had been fully washed away; the suspension bridge and the cable tramway had been ripped from their anchor points. The Birds had packed up their car and were ready to leave as Ruby arrived.

'He got out Ruby. Your father and the others. Once the flumes were overrun, they turned off the turbines and climbed up the north face.' Harry Bird put his hand on her shoulder. 'He most likely has taken refuge in the park somewhere.' Ruby remained unmoved. Harry persisted. 'The Waddamana lines will be restored soon and we'll have power in a day or two. All this can be rebuilt.'

Harry seemed to have mistaken Ruby's silence for her concern regarding the restoration of electricity to the city.

'Thanks Harry. Stella. Where are you going?'

'To my sister in Devonport. We think the roads are open.' Stella steered the girls to the car. 'All the best Ruby.'

The water still roared as it forced its way through the gorge. White water and crashing debris- filled waves swept everything before it. Somewhere in there the words Ruby had written, the ideas and the drawings were being pulverised by the sheer force of nature. Paper pulped and the words sliding off every page joined the struggle of water and rubble. She imagined the keys and type slugs pounding out letters as the typewriter disintegrated, trying desperately to make one last strike against the paper. She mourned their loss for a moment, and only for a moment, because she had seen what this storm could really do. It took life.

Over the noise a realisation came to Ruby. Those words were not just alive because they were on paper. They were in her, alive in her mind. The loss of the work did not silence her or diminish her voice. The work could always be rewritten. Perhaps better than it was before now she had weathered the storm. Lawton could draw more pictures of who she had become. Their relationship was not held in the sketches but in their memories of each other, perhaps even in the shared hope for the future.

Capricorn had predicted a storm. It had come in the form of a deluge which had saturated the city. It had torn the world apart and it would be no easy task to rebuild it all. It came as pain and in the dashing of naivety. It came as an unseen force, something ethereal perhaps, to wash away self-doubt, insecurity and the lingering effects of feeling unloved. The storm abraded Ruby, scrubbed that snakeskin off her new self, left her shiny and strong. What would come could not be known, not even Capricorn's special skills could make that clear. No tarot or tea leaves could outline the future. Only a belief in her freedom to choose how she would move forward might determine what might come next.

She left Duck Reach quite certain there'd be no return. At some point she would have to see her father. Perhaps she could even move closer to understanding him. *Forgiveness may take more time.*

The Aphorism Club had gathered and waited for Ruby's return. And as ever they surrounded her with love.

'Where have you been?' Lawton held her close. 'I was afraid.' Tears formed in his eyes. He was weary from the physical labour of the rescues, tired from the strain of the tempest, exhausted with worry for her.

'I just had to say goodbye.' She stood back and looked at him. He didn't really understand that it was herself that she farewelled. The old self, the girl with the raspberry birthmark who wanted to hide away. 'And hello.' To whom she'd become.

Capricorn joined the huddle. 'Storm over wabi-sabi. Easy way ahead.'

CHAPTER 30

And life fell back into its rhythm. The power turned on, the water ebbed, the streets were swept clean. People found homes, work resumed, and the storm became a memory.

Only the future had to be decided. Ruby had never felt the burden of choice before. Much of her early life had simply been determined for her, firstly by the accident of birth. A life seemingly privileged and yet marked by the misfortunes of careless adults and cruel fate. Opportunity unfolded primarily through the good fortune of her intellect and optimism. But choice seemed a foreign beast for young women such as herself.

Now, having watched the world upend itself through the wild power of nature Ruby found the quiet that followed disconcerting. It gave her too much time to think about what she had the opportunity to do. She had grown up quickly during the time in Tasmania. As Hollis said, the Aphorism Club had aged her. No longer a rangy, self-conscious child who felt her birthmark defined her. Ruby was a woman, with all the complications that came with it.

Lawton loved her. And she him. In the nights she was alone she thought of nothing else than his warm, lean body that lay against her in sleep, and moved with her when they made love. She felt the anticipation of it when she thought of him. The joy of his physical existence was equalled by his passion for life. His art, his defence of the down-trodden, the power of his intelligence and his empathy for his friends' suffering were all things Ruby loved about him. In his eyes she saw a version of herself that made her proud, worthy and so much more than a girl with a raspberry birthmark. *Ruby Pearl Hart, the jewel of the southern island.* He whispered it to her as they lay in his bed, entwined in each other's arms and tangled in the twisted sheets. He shouted it as he rode away on his motorbike and as he greeted her on the Gorge path.

It could be a truly lovely life being with Lawton. Marrying him, working at The Examiner. Perhaps she could even be a mother one day. But this life was not the only choice. Jessie Burke had secured Ruby a place at the University of Tasmania. She would be one of two women offered places besides twenty-two male counterparts in the Philosophy course. Ruby realised the vast opportunity offered by the chance to study at this level. Afterall it was only two years ago that this had been her only dream. More study, an immersion in learning that could fulfil her life's ambition and fill it with so much meaning. It meant moving to Hobart, starting over, with or without Lawton. It was not a choice to be easily dismissed.

And then there was Melbourne. Douglas Hart had returned to his family home and his mother in Elwood. He had no stomach, nor the spirit, to rebuild the power station after its devastating destruction in the flood. *It needed a younger man's energy.* This was his final decision. Ruby, now further disengaged from her father, wondered if his invitation to return to the mainland with him was given as a heartfelt suggestion, or one made from duty. Douglas could, at his discretion allow her to return to Melbourne and live in Minnie's house despite the fact that his daughter had not reached the age of twenty-one. In his mind, before the flood, she had become wild and lacking moral regulation due to her fraternisation with the bohemians and freethinkers of the creative set in the town. Douglas could not bear to think too deeply about the non-conformist views of his only child. Not to mention the biliousness that came upon him when he read Ruby's work. He was glad that the pages of her novel had been consumed by the deluge. He shuddered at the thought of a young woman writing such things and could only imagine the debasement that had been foisted upon her by that group she called the Aphorism Club. But kept his thoughts to himself as he did not want another confrontation like the one before the storm.

In truth he didn't want to think too much of Ruby and the last few years at all. If he gave it too much time, he'd recognise the guilt he felt in his treatment of his only child and his failure as a father. And not because he felt ashamed of her but of himself. His failure to see her gifts, her intellect and creativity. The child, his child, reflected the traits he saw in her mother Alma. And definitely in his Aunt Minerva. Now the chance had been lost to be a part of her future. As he stood by the ruined turbines, the twisted metal and the chaotic water that still forced its way down the narrow gorge he came to terms with the retreat to Melbourne. A small life would have to do. And a life without knowing Ruby.

Not so for Ruby. Choice lay heavily upon her mind and her heart. Everyone had an opinion. Al, who had married months after finishing school thought a life of security with a husband was what every woman wanted. Sister Reggie encouraged Ruby to take up the university course. *It's what you worked so hard for.* Elvie and Caleb desperately wanted their Rubes to come back to Melbourne where they could return to their surrogate parenting of her. Only Della offered no opinion. Only she seemed to understand that the future had to lie in Ruby's own hands.

Fly, fall, fly again dear petite larme. This is what we've waited for. To choose. 'My choices are more contained now I have a child. My Estelle. I must choose for her too as well as for myself.' Ruby wondered if Della and Estelle could move to Hobart with her if she chose that or to move to Minnie's house in Melbourne. Ruby's future did not have to mean choosing a life without her friend. And she had come to adore the baby, so chubby and perfect.

And why not choose to have it all. To study, to love, to move to wherever she felt called and with whomever she wanted.

This was the lesson of her life thus far. The world would open at her determination, with her fortitude and grit. And all the bruised knees, broken hearts, disappointments, hard won wisdom, foolhardiness and lost words were merely a small part of the life ahead for the newest member of the Aphorism Club. She was the one with the voice who spoke for those who feared to ask for what they deserved. She was a lover, a friend, *the jewel of the southern island.*

The girl with the raspberry birthmark was no more.

ACKNOWLEDGEMENTS

A writer can't write without the patient support of family…and I'm very lucky with mine. They are an excellent cheer squad and have an innate understanding of when a cup of tea should be produced, or silence must ensue or when it's dangerous to enter the room!

It's a real privilege to spend time with writers and authors who generously share their time, enthusiasm and insight so I am grateful to the 'night writers of the Eurobodalla.' All creative and wonderful story tellers who have made a difference to my writing.

And I must acknowledge my home town, Launceston, itself. It is a wonderful place, full of stories, natural beauty and great characters. I've always loved the Gorge, Duck Reach and the First Basin where I spent many childhood summers. The place has stayed with me my whole life.

Finally I must thank my grandmother whose name was Ruby Pearl and I've borrowed it for my central character. Although she is long gone I do hope that in some mysterious way she might know that she is being remembered here.